Francis Davis Millet

The Expedition to the Philippines

Volume 1

Francis Davis Millet

The Expedition to the Philippines
Volume 1

ISBN/EAN: 9783337329662

Printed in Europe, USA, Canada, Australia, Japan

Cover: Foto ©Andreas Hilbeck / pixelio.de

More available books at **www.hansebooks.com**

THE EXPEDITION
TO
THE PHILIPPINES

By

F. D. MILLET

SPECIAL CORRESPONDENT OF "HARPER'S WEEKLY"
AND OF THE "LONDON TIMES"

AUTHOR OF

"A CAPILLARY CRIME, AND OTHER TALES"
"THE DANUBE FROM THE BLACK FOREST
TO THE BLACK SEA" ETC.

ILLUSTRATED

NEW YORK AND LONDON
HARPER &. BROTHERS PUBLISHERS
1899

Copyright, 1899, by HARPER & BROTHERS.

All rights reserved.

CONTENTS

CONTENTS

CONTENTS

ILLUSTRATIONS

ILLUSTRATIONS

ILLUSTRATIONS

Expedition to the Philippines

CHAPTER I

COMPARATIVELY few persons had more than a very hazy idea as to the geographical position of the Philippines until the exhilarating news of Dewey's victory brought out the atlases. Manila was a familiar enough name. It suggested a short, thick cheroot over which there was a continual discussion as to which end it was proper to light, and was intimately connected with coils of bright yellow rope seen in every cordage shop. But the geographical position of this busy capital and of the group of islands of which it is the metropolis was about as vague in most minds as the situation of the last discovered irrigation area in Mars. The literature concerning the islands was phenomenally scarce, at least the literature in English. Only one book with any claim to thoroughness had been published in this language for many years, and this was not readily obtained because it had not found an extensive circulation. The reading public in the United States had more or less knowledge of the Hawaiian islands and of both Micronesia and Polynesia, first through the labors of the missionaries and more recently through the writings of Melville, Stevenson, Stoddard and others who have found a grateful stimulus to the imagination in these tropical islands. The Philippines, however, remained outside the kodak zone.

The mystery surrounding this reported paradise was naturally, a very strong element of atraction for adventurous spirits, and when the expedition of occupation and conquest was decided upon by the authorities at Washington, there was a scramble all over the country for an opportunity to join in the crusade. What was to come to pass in the West Indies could be foretold with comparative accuracy, but who could prophesy what adventures would befall an expedition to the antipodes where Spain, although crippled by the loss of her fleet, would probably make a heroic effort to preserve this lucrative colony? There was an irresistible fascination in this long voyage across the Pacific to the palm-draped islands where naked savages still live in primitive barbarism; to those pleasant lands of constant summer where the fabulous wealth of minerals and rare products of the soil have so long tempted enterprising traders to venture their lives on the chance of profitable barter or possible booty. The glamour of ancient Spanish power still lingered in this distant archipelago and there still remained, scarcely touched by the levelling forces of modern civilization or transformed by the lapse of time, the picturesque life of the tropical East as described by the sturdy explorers of Queen Elizabeth's days and which has furnished material for libraries of fiction to unsettle the minds of generations of schoolboys with dreams of Malay pirates and all the melodrama of adventurous life on the high seas. It was certainly no mean experience to take part in the first foreign expedition of the great Republic, to witness the very beginning of the inevitable expansion following an unbroken period of consistent isolation. It was to be a history-making event, the first act in the great international drama to be played on the broad stage where the great powers of the world are in active competition for supremacy. Who with a drop of red blood in his veins could fail to be tempted by this prospect?

We were ordered to be on board the *Newport* at the Pacific

Mail wharf in San Francisco not later than nine o'clock on June 29, and although I had made a hurried trip across the Atlantic and the continent in twelve days, I was as "journey proud" as a schoolboy that morning, impatient to see the troops, the ship, and to establish myself on board. Although General Merritt, whom I met at breakfast, assured me the sailing hour was fixed at ten, I could not linger about the hotel but was off long before nine with no eye for the boasted glories of the great town, scarcely noticing the morning throng of hurrying citizens. The sailing of five transports which, with the *Newport,* composed the third expedition, had been the occasion of a great popular demonstration two days before, and the edge of the public enthusiasm was therefore somewhat dulled. Still, the departure of the Governor-General of the Philippines with his personal staff, his corps and his departmental staff, was the climax of a series of dramatic incidents, and as such called together at the water-front a goodly number of spectators. Near the entrance of the wharf I saw my first soldiers, part of the Third Regular Heavy Artillery, looking as brown and hardy as if they had already been through a campaign. They had not yet adopted the tan-colored linen uniform which afterwards gave them a startling resemblance to the butternut-clad Confederates, but wore the dark-blue flannel shirt, faded to a variety of unpleasant colors, dark trousers and the campaign slouch hats moulded by use into characteristic individual shapes, alike in color and in general proportions but as different in outline as the features of the wearer shaded by the broad brim. Fringed around the street corners, sitting in rows on the curbstone, jostling and crowding at the saloon doors, they were as high-spirited, sturdy a lot of men as ever carried rifles and looked fit to conquer the world. Under the long dock-shed a shrieking locomotive rambled back and forth between piles of miscellaneous commissary stores and mountains of cases fresh from Chinese ports.

The promenade-deck of the steamer was covered with civilians with a fair sprinkling of officers in trim, dark uniforms, bearing various strange insignia on their collars which would require careful explanation to interpret and considerable study to memorize, and the main deck rail was lined with the rank and file who had already received assignments of quarters on board. Up and down the steep gangplank flowed a constant stream of women and children with patriotic decorations, messenger boys carrying bouquets and parcels, and a mixture of civilians and officers all looking hurried and anxious. Emotional women, already tearful in anticipation of the imminent parting with friends or relatives, gathered in sympathetic groups at the edge of the wharf, keeping up a spasmodic interchange of greetings with those on board, mostly consisting of a repetition of the one phrase: "Be sure and take care of yourself!" Stevedores, with the choicest vocabularies of quaint oaths, wrestled with piles of officers' baggage and belated consignments of stores.

Purposeless sentinels paced up and down with important solemnity, looking well the part they were supposed to play but having nothing and nobody to guard. It was evident from the voluble orders which were given on all sides with increasing energy as the time passed, that General Merritt was sure to be prompt to the moment and the men were soon marched in from the street and anxious non-commissioned officers scoured the neighborhood to corral the stragglers. Not a man would have missed the boat for a fortune, and one by one they came hurrying in, greeted by the jeers of their comrades already on board, until at last the only soldier on the wharf was a vigilant sergeant on the lookout for the very last private of all who finally did turn up, hot and flurried and shamefaced, and who sneaked aboard in temporary disgrace. The women tossed rolled-up flags and bunches of flowers into the outstretched hands far above them and volleys of brass buttons for souvenirs were returned in exchange.

It was a carnival of laughter and chaff and tears. Now the men began to climb the rigging and swarm up the topmasts even to the insecure seat on the narrow area of the truck, and worked off their exuberant energy in yells and shouts, rising and falling in volume and then bursting forth in a grand cheer in unison as a small party of officers, headed by General Merritt, easily recognized by everybody, came up the gangplank precisely on the stroke of ten. In a moment or two the first throb of the engine was felt and the *Newport* slowly moved away in that indescribable confusion of shouts, cheers, whistles and screeches which only an American crowd can produce. As the steamer rounded away from the wharf, a swarm of tugs and yachts gay with flags and bright costumes and each with a battery of kodaks, dashed after her to catch a parting word or to secure a final snapshot. The thousands of people blackening the wharf ends all along the water front, gave a long continued cheer; steam whistles and military bands competed noisily on every side and the dull roar of cannon came echoing up from the lower bay. The fastest of our escort was soon distanced and we were fairly away on our long voyage.

It was a brilliant, sparkling summer day and the long, glassy swell of the Pacific, meeting the shallows at the bar, looked pleasant and harmless as we approached. The first plunge of the bows and the general disturbance of equilibrium were a new sensation to most of those on board, for comparatively few had ever made a sea voyage, and many, indeed, had never seen salt water until they came to San Francisco. A few moments of this disturbing motion was enough to send a goodly proportion of the men below and to distract their thoughts from the recent farewells to the active considerations of personal discomfort. The initiation to regular sea life was sudden but prolonged, for almost before the bar was crossed and while the smoke of the saluting cannon was still drifting across the bay, a thin mist, like the haze of Indian summer, imperceptibly stole out of the West, softened the outlines of the grand headlands of the Golden Horn and veiled from our sight the rugged masses of the rocky islands near the line of our course. The temperature dropped rapidly, a breeze sprang up from the Northwest, freshening rapidly with vicious gusts, and soon developed into the strength of a gale. We pitched and tossed awhile, and, before we lost sight of land, the captain was obliged, for the safety of the ship, to alter her course and to put her head to the gale, under just enough steam to keep steerageway. For seventeen long hours we wallowed and tumbled and drifted to the southward, scarcely making enough westing to swear by. The pomp of military display had begun to vanish with the first tossings at the bar, but when the storm really struck us in earnest, there was no more semblance of discipline on the ship, among the soldiers of course, than on a crowded passenger boat on a rough excursion to the fishing grounds. The general hilarity caused by the woful plight of those who earliest felt the result of the motion rapidly degenerated to chaff of no agreeable strain, and at last even the voice of the Irish humorist was silent. He first raised a laugh as he came aboard and saw the anchor over the bow by asking:

"Who in the devil is a goin' to swing that big pick?" and he mercilessly ridiculed the "green-faced landlubbers" as they staggered away to their bunks, confident that his trip from Queenstown had seasoned him beyond fear of the common malady. His voice, at first sonorous and cheery and flavored with characteristic Hibernian humoristic quality, soon lost its charm, however, became forced and raucous, and was finally only audible in a feeble attempt to repeat the stale distortion: "Water, water everywhere and not a drop of whisky to drink." Then he, too, curled himself up in the lee of the bulwarks thoroughly drenched and totally collapsed. Sentinels had been posted at different parts of the promenade deck, partly for grandeur perhaps, and partly to regulate the movements of the men and to keep a small area free for the use of General Merritt and his staff. The necessity for these sentinels ceased, of course, when the decks were empty, but the officer whose duty it was to order the men below was probably too much occupied with his personal sensations to think of the men on guard. One by one the stalwart fellows grew paler and paler, and then, limp and dejected, without so much as calling for the corporal of the guard, staggered to their bunks, dragging their rifles after them in a most unmilitary style. One wiry youth on the weather side kept his post long after the others had retreated and, unable to pace the slippery deck, leaned against the engine room bulkhead and kept up a show of performing his duty, although he was too miserable to dodge the frequent showers of spray. The officer of the day took this moment to make his rounds and, approaching the sentinel, asked:

"Where is your post?"

"Here at this corner, sir!"

"How many of you are on guard?"

"Twenty-one, I believe, sir."

"Where are the others?"

"I'm the only one left, sir."

And this brief conversation was too much for him. Scarcely had he made answer before he staggered away without so much as "by your leave," and the officer of the day had the deck to himself and was free to meditate on the possibility of the Army Regulations providing for the duties of an officer in irregular conditions met with on an ocean transport.

Rank had no special privileges on this occasion, and in a few minutes the "Social Hall" belied its name, for only a small proportion of officers, General Merritt among the number, remained to uphold the dignity of their commissions. Perhaps it is as well to leave to the imagination the scenes on the *Newport* during the raging of the storm, certainly it would be unwise to chronicle the expletives which this record surprise of the Pacific wrenched from the pallid lips of those whose pleasant anticipations of a trip across summer seas had thus been rudely shattered.

Those of us who were proof against the prostrating illness had an excellent opportunity of making one another's acquaintance and of settling ourselves for the voyage.

The *Newport* is a steamer of 2200 tons measurement, with a horse power of approximately the same figure, and a maximum speed of fourteen knots. She was built for the run to the West Indies and consequently is well adapted in most ways for service in the tropics. In less than a week after she was chartered by the government as a transport, she was thoroughly overhauled, fitted with proper appliances for the accommodation of troops and well loaded with ordnance, ammunition and miscellaneous stores, including three months' provisions for the number of men she was supposed to carry. She has electric lights, an ice machine which would produce about 300 pounds a day, a distilling apparatus for drinking water and cold storage rooms of large capacity. The promenade deck is occupied by the Social Hall, a large number of staterooms, the cabins of the ship's officers and the wheelhouse. On the main deck are more staterooms, bath rooms, the dining-saloon, the galleys and the usual adjuncts. The cooking for the troops and the serving out of the rations were all done on the forward part of this deck. Temporary staircases had been built in the forward hatch and in two small hatches astern leading from the promenade deck to the cargo deck where the troops were quartered. The engine-room bulkhead alone broke this great area, and broad passages on either side of this obstruction gave plenty of air and afforded easy circulation. Ten fore and aft rows of three-tier wooden bunks extended from the engine space to bow and stern with a passageway between every pair, and each bunk was provided with a woven wire spring and a straw mattress. The lighting left something to be desired, but the ventilation was as good as could be and the temperature was usually a degree or two lower than in the saloon. The first sight of the great crowded lower deck, with every corner filled either by a soldier or by some of his impedimenta, and with bunk after bunk vanishing into the dim perspective, gave me a sense of oppression, and it was not easy to recover from the feeling that it must be hot and stuffy and generally disagreeable in this burrow of human beings. But frequent visits soon broke up this illusion, and I came to regard it as quite as comfortable as any place on the ship, certainly better ventilated than the steerage on the trans-Atlantic ships and with far more luxurious sleeping accommodations. Having been in the ranks myself, and also in the steerage, come to that, I had little sympathy with those novices who so knowingly condemned their quarters as "the worst ever provided for Christians," and the record of the voyage, which was remarkable for the excellent health of the men, proved that there was not much wrong with the transport. There were some great defects in the accommodations, notably the absence of mess-room and the inadequate capacity of the galleys and cramped space for the distribution of rations. It often took two or three hours to serve a meal, and when the men finally got their rations they had no place in which to sit in comfort and were obliged to perch and balance wherever they could, so that eating was often a ludicrous approach to jugglery.

General Merritt, with characteristic regard for the comfort of his men, had given instructions to allow them the free use of the decks, reserving for himself and officers only a small space between two deckhouses. This freedom more than compensated for the discomforts, and as there were no restrictions to circulation, day or night, and none of the ordinary troopship rules about remaining in quarters were enforced, the promenade deck and the tops of all the deckhouses were populous by day and were covered by night with prostrate forms. Without counting the ship's company, the total number on board the *Newport*, including the officers, did not exceed six hundred, for there were only the Astor Battery, in round numbers one hundred strong, and batteries H and K of the Third Regular Heavy Artillery, practically counting two hundred each. Although the ship carried more than would be allowed by the British regulation, which limits the number of troops on a transport to the number of hammocks which can be slung between decks, she was far less crowded than most of the troopships which crossed the Pacific. Still it was difficult to see where another man could be stowed away on board.

In the saloon and the officers' mess there were, besides the clerical force, the following officers and civilians: Major-General Wesley Merritt and his aids Major Lewis H. Strother, Major Harry C. Hale, and Captain T. Bentley Mott. The members of the Department Staff, Brigadier-General J. B. Babcock, Chief of Staff and Adjutant-General, Major S. D. Sturgis, Assistant Adjutant-General, Lieutenant-Colonel C. A. Whittier, Inspector-General, Lieutenant-Colonel Enoch H. Crowder, Judge Advocate, Lieutenant-Colonel James W. Pope, Chief Quartermaster, Lieutenant-Colonel David L. Brainard, Chief Commissary of Subsistence, Lieutenant-Colonel Henry Lippincott, Deputy Surgeon-General and Chief Surgeon, Major Charles McClure, Paymaster U. S. Army, Chief Paymaster, Major R. B. C. Bement, Engineer Officer, Major Richard E. E. Thompson, Chief Signal Officer, Major W. A. Simpson, Chief of Artillery, Major W. A. Wadsworth, Assistant to Chief Quartermaster, Major Charles E. Woodruff, Attending Surgeon,

WESLEY MERRITT

Captain J. M. Cabell, Assistant Surgeon U. S. A. (retired),
Assistant to Chief Surgeon, Major Charles H. Whipple,
Paymaster U. S. Army, Major Charles E. Kilbourne, Paymaster U. S. Army and Lieutenant-Colonel Charles L. Potter of the Corps Staff, Chief Engineer Officer. The officers
commanding the troops on board were: Captain James
O'Hara, Captain Charles W. Hobbs, Lieutenant M. G. Kray-
enbuhl, Lieutenant Lloyd England, and Lieutenant P. M.
Kessler, all of the Third Regular United States Heavy Ar-
tillery, and Captain Peyton C. March, Lieutenant C. C. Wil-
liams and Lieutenant B. M. Koehler of the Astor Battery.
Father Doherty, Volunteer Chaplain to the Expedition; Dr.
G. M. Daywalt, Contract Surgeon; Mr. Murat Halstead,
Mr. G. W. Peters, illustrator; Mr. Jerome of the Pacific
Mail Company, and myself, made up the contingent of those
not entitled to wear the uniform.

One other uniformed personage must be included in this
roster, not because he held a government commission, but because he was a conspicuous figure on the decks. This was a
Captain of the Salvation Army. He was not a cheerful individual, but was always in evidence. When the men were
miserable, his red-trimmed cap seemed to have an extra dejected droop and when there was any fun going, he stood
apart and gazed sadly at the mirthmakers. Just how he expected to continue his authority in this crowd of worldly inclined adventurers, one could scarcely imagine, and I fancy
he made little progress in his enlistments.

It was a good forty-eight hours before the Pacific which
belied its name with vicious persistency, had settled down to
anything like a reasonable condition of quiet. As the sea
gradually subsided, the sick crawled out of the hatchways
like half-drowned badgers, scattered over the decks and began to feel again that life was worth living and when, on the
morning of the third day, the ocean unfolded its great violet
expanse under the softest of summer skies, giving full prom-

ise of lasting sunshine, the effervescent spirits of the men
bubbled up with fresh vigor, and cheeriness and hilarity began to rule again. Under the harmonizing influence of
hardships and suffering common to all, the men rapidly fra-
ternized, and regulars and volunteers began to live in peace
together. Although the Third Artillery was a regular organization, there was only a moderate leaven of old soldiers
in its ranks, for the two batteries had been recruited up from
their peace quota of sixty odd men to their full war footing
of two hundred. The recruits were all picked men, exceptionally fine specimens of robust manhood, and most of
them of superior intelligence. The Astor Battery, or the
Asteroids as they were called popularly, were at first, perhaps, a little out of gear with their shipmates, chiefly on
account of the reputation they had acquired in San Francisco, where the press had chosen to resent their proper display of strict discipline and took pains to interpret it as an
indication of assumption of social superiority. The roll of
the battery numbered a goodly proportion of men who had
seen active service in other countries and a notable list of
college graduates, mostly athletes of some reputation.

When the Pacific ocean goes in for the business of charming those who trust themselves on her ever-heaving bosom,
she is irresistible. The gender of this great natural division
of the waters of the earth, I am aware, is commonly held to
be masculine, but after my experience with the temperament
of this ocean, I can never think of it except in the feminine
gender, and to speak of it as "he" is to contradict all the sentiment which my brief intimacy has initiated and developed.
In her friendly moods she is caressing and gentle beyond
description; her songs are sweeter than a lullaby and her
smiles are doubly fascinating because they reflect all the
soft and tender charms of the high-arched sky, intensifying
the choice and delicate tones which vibrate in the wonderful
atmosphere. By her subtle graces she bewitches the traveller

into perfect confidence that her face will never darken with a frown, and, enchanted by her soothing influences, he lives for the day only, for the joy of life steals into his heart and holds full sway there.

Thus, after her temper had passed, did she charm and bewitch us all with her glorious, unbroken shimmering expanse, inviting us onward to a distant, mysterious horizon where the summer clouds gathered in ranks and seemed to hide the expected land. The recent woes were forgotten, the future looked bright and hopeful, and, amid all the paraphernalia of war, the gentle spirit of peace pervaded the ship. Songs were heard on every side and from the roofs of the deckhouses, where kindred spirits had pre-empted an airy habitation among the spars and life-rafts, the tinkle of the mandolin and the strum of the banjo came floating downward far into the night—a night so beautiful that it were a sin to sleep—and the contented hum of voices never ceased.

The Fourth of July came while we were in the keen flush of enjoyment of the soft air and the soothing, gentle motion of the water. We welcomed this anniversary as all good patriots do and felt that it had a peculiar significance to us, representing as we did the might and dignity of the great Republic on the great waste of the Pacific and carrying there for the first time in history the Stars and Stripes on a military expedition. This thought and the desirability of providing some suitable decoration for the celebration of the day set us to look up the flags. We found to our dismay that we were shorter of bunting than of anything else and not a flag could be turned out except those belonging to the ship, which, of course, we borrowed promptly. In matter of fact, we actually did not fly the national emblem but perforce reserved it to lend that patriotic air to our place of assembly which is so stimulating to the Independence day orator. Later at Manila, this dearth of flags was even more to be regretted for the natives, who display the insurgents' flag in great profusion, could not comprehend our apparent indifference to the symbol of freedom which was conspicuous by its very rarity.

The committee that took charge of the celebration wisely decided that it was best to get over all the formal ceremonies as early as possible in the day and therefore we assembled under the awning between the deckhouses at half past eleven in the forenoon where brief exercises were conducted for the benefit of all on board, this being as public a place as there was on the ship and so situated that probably half of the men could see and hear. It was a strange and peculiarly impressive spectacle. Around the little knot of officers the rank and file stood in a compact mass reaching to the rail on either side where others perched in a solid line. The openings in the awning above were filled with heads and everyone was intent on hearing every word that was said. Never shall I forget the keen, earnest look of the men as they listened to the familiar words of the Declaration of Independence nor can I ever lose the echo of that swelling chorus of sturdy, masculine voices which rang out with such inspiriting vigor. In the saloon, which was made as gay as possible with the limited number of flags at our command, the luncheon assumed as much of the character of a banquet as could be contrived from the combined resources of the ship's larder, the commissary stores, and private supplies of wet and dry luxuries. It differed from any other similar celebration I ever attended, inasmuch as the decorations were the Stars and Stripes and the Union Jack in combination, and the sentiments of loyal respect for Great Britain and of confidence in the stability of the friendly relations existing between the two countries were expressed by several of those who responded to the toasts and applauded with genuine good-will by the entire company. The programme of the day was as follows:

Exercises on the Deck.

1. Prayer—Chaplain Doherty.
2. "Star-Spangled Banner"—Astor Battery Glee Club.
3. Declaration of Independence—Major C. H. Whipple.
4. "America"—Astor Battery Glee Club.
5. Oration—Chaplain Doherty.
6. "Red, White and Blue"—Astor Battery Glee Club.

Exercises at Luncheon—Toasts and Responses.

1. Our Country and Our President—Major-General Wesley Merritt.
2. Nations Friendly to Us and the Queen of England—F. D. Millet.
3. Our General Commanding the Army of the Philippines—Colonel McClure.
4. A Modern Crusade—General Babcock.
5. The Day We Celebrate—Mr. Murat Halstead.
6. The Girls We Left Behind Us—General Whittier.
7. The Army and the Navy—Colonel Crowder.
8. Our Good Ship *Newport* and Her Gallant Captain and Crew—Captain Saunders.

Unfortunately Mr. Halstead was seized by an illness which prevented him from taking part in the celebration and which, to our great regret, obliged him to part company with us at Honolulu so we had but a brief enjoyment of his society.

Our ship was now making about 325 miles a day and we did not feel quite settled on board—first, because we were looking forward to a call at Honolulu, and second, because we did not know how we should proceed after we left that port. The news of the arrival of Camara's fleet at Port Said reached us just before we left San Francisco and the anticipation of a trip to the Philippines at the speed of one of the monitors which we thought might be necessary as a convoy, was scarcely agreeable. It was on the books also that orders might reach us at Honolulu by the mail boat from Vancouver to await further developments before continuing our journey. Thus, as we neared the Hawaiian Islands we began to speculate more and more on what the immediate future might have in store for us and our impatience increased as we were able to count the hours before we should see land.

In the midst of this ferment of spirit, while we were at luncheon, the monotonous vibration of the ship suddenly ceased and the sound of the water against the ship's side, hitherto inaudible on account of the confusion of noises caused by the machinery, came in the open ports like the lapping of the wavelets on a quiet beach. The captain and the engineer left the table, trying their best to look unconcerned, and we gazed at one another and said a few things. The report soon came that the spindle of the condenser was fractured and that we should have to wait until a spare one could be put in place. The men were very hilarious over their new clothes which had been served out to them as the weather grew warmer and indeed they looked as if they had raided a ready-made-clothing store and had not been particular about trying on the garments, and now that the ship was quiet we realized how intimately we were living together, for a hearty laugh could be heard from bow to stern. Some one discovered sharks swimming about the ship and an ingenious private soon produced an improvised hook with a large piece of Uncle Sam's beef attached which he dropped into the water with the remark: "The bait'll kill him with indigestion if I don't catch him with the hook." In a minute, however, he had his victim and a score of eager assistants had the wriggling, flapping monster up to the level of the rail with a run.

The excitement was intense, the fishermen pulled so hard they broke the rope and with a tremendous splash the shark disappeared. Three times this game was repeated with the same result, each catch and each successive catastrophe raising a din of cheers and groans from the spectators that made the ship tremble. Thus the afternoon wore away as we gently rolled on the glassy sea without a turn of the screw.

In the early evening, six or seven hours after the breakdown, we were off again and we slept that night in expectation of landing before dark the next day. But the loss of time was not to be made good so easily and no sign of land rewarded our eager search until just at sunset on the 6th, at the moment when the horizon was tinged with ruddy purple and the ocean was sparkling with iridescent lights, we saw the bold mass of the island of Molokai away to the southwest as a translucent screen on the tropical haze. As the stars came out and Venus, shining with extraordinary brilliancy, showed us the road to the enchanted islands, rigid mountain forms began to appear in the distance and, before midnight, the breath of the land, almost too heavy with perfume, sweetened the stale atmosphere of the crowded ship and we dreamed of nodding palms and glittering sands and turquoise waters.

Some time in the night the ship stopped, but as soon as it was dawn she again started and rapidly approached the harbor of Honolulu. The beautiful line of towering hills covered with verdure, the tossing waters of the bay, breaking in a line of white foam on the shallow bar, the distant city scattered wide among the trees, and the tangle of masts and funnels of the shipping, spread out before us in a grand panorama as we neared the shore. We picked up a pilot and soon were anchored in the crowd of transports, colliers and craft of all varieties which filled the little harbor. The huge, grim monitor *Monadnock* with her attendant collier scarcely less bald and forbidding than herself, lay with scarcely a sign of life aboard, suggesting that something more startling than a rumor of a distant conflict might be needed to wake this sleepy leviathan from her lethargy, but the five other transports of our expedition which had sailed from San Francisco on June 27 under command of General MacArthur, the *Indiana, Ohio, Valencia, Morgan City* and *City of Para,* were as busy as ants' nests with their swarming multitudes, each of them devouring coal from clustering lighters.

The traveller is sure to feel a mild sense of disappointment on landing at Honolulu, for the commercial activity of the past few years has given the town a cosmopolitan aspect which destroys the distinctive character of the place, a transformation which excites the fear that the peculiar charm of the islands will soon vanish entirely under the levelling influence of modern progress. When a glaring sign, "The Silent Barber," meets the eye in a row of shops as near as can be like a block in San Francisco, it opens up a vista of all sorts of unlovely improvements. We did not see Honolulu in her normal state of drowsy quiet, for we landed at a time when the town was in a fever of patriotic emotion and when, moreover, annexation was in the air and there was a feeling of unrest and uncertainty among the people which could scarcely be disguised. The streets, too, were filled with the soldiers of our expedition, most of them wearing the fragrant wreaths with which the hospitable islanders decorate themselves and their friends on festal occasions, and many with silk badges bearing the words "Aloha nui to Our Boys in Blue." The bustle of the streets was quite abnormal, of course, and the general holiday air had an exotic flavor about it which was gratifying, inasmuch as it catered to our patriotism, but it was impossible not to feel that we were missing the real charm of the place. Nothing, however, can disturb to a serious degree the unique fascination of nature in this favored spot and the enchanting landscape, the luxuriant beauty of the tropical growth and the marvellous colors of sea and land absorbed our attention and made us forget war and politics and all the attendant train of evils.

It is impossible to gain much knowledge of a people on a brief visit like ours and particularly in such unusual circumstances, but neither a special training as a physiognomist nor a long residence among the islanders is necessary to induce the impression that they are gentle and lovable creatures with fewer irritating faults than most natives who have suffered from contact with civilization. We did not have much time to pursue the interesting study of the type, for there were formal visits to be made, presentations to the dignitaries of the Republic and various other little ceremonies which occupied much of the precious daylight, but still gave us an opportunity of seeing a considerable part of the town and the suburbs as far as the residences of the Princess Kaiulani and of Minister Sewall at Waikiki.

Everything was thrown open to the soldiers who wandered about in friendly intimacy with the natives, lay in the shade of the trees in the pleasant gardens of the bungalows or gathered in the palace grounds where the hospitable citizens gave to each detachment a gala dinner, a mixture of New England and Hawaiian edibles where doughnuts and pineapples, pies and alligator pears, gingerbread and bananas disappeared by the ton and the sagging tables were soon lightened of their burden by the attack of hundreds of stalwart and hearty soldiers. Mrs. Dole, the wife of the President, supported by several women friends, held an open air reception under the trees after the dinner and an excellent band entertained the great crowd with instrumental music and songs. The writing room of the palace was open to every man in uniform and stationery and postage stamps were provided without charge, a refinement of hospitality which was gratefully appreciated by the men. Some idea may be had of the use which was made of this privilege by the fact that the postage stamp bill for the first and second expeditions was more than five hundred dollars. Altogether soldiering seemed to be not such a bad game after all and the visit to Honolulu was remarkable for many things, not the least of which was the remarkable behavior of the soldiers who were orderly and quiet to a degree by no means anticipated by the police authorities nor even by their commanding officers. The Marshal of the islands told me as we were leaving that he had not been obliged to arrest a single individual wearing the uniform of the United States nor had he learned of a single disturbance worthy of report. First of all the majority of the men were self-respecting and understood what a disgraceful breach of hospitality it would have been for them to disturb the peace, secondly, the riotously inclined element was kept in check by the more soberminded who felt that they were all on show, so to speak, and were therefore bound to make a good record.

I heard a sergeant giving his orders to a large squad about to go ashore from the *Newport*. "Look a here, you fellows," he said, "you've got to put on your brown suits and leggins and have everything in the best order, for you're going ashore for the day. And I want you to understand if any dunderheaded galoot goes and gets a jag on we'll run him aboard and lock him up before he knows where he's at."

There was no one in that squad who earned that sonorous and dishonorable title. Several of us who accompanied General Merritt ashore took rooms at the hotel, glad enough to exchange the small boxes of staterooms with the swarms of mosquitoes for the clean and airy rooms among the palms and to break the monotony of the steamer's fare by a brief dalliance with the fresh and appetizing menu of the Pacific Club. Those who were not over-wearied by the succession of novel experiences of the day, attended a *poi* feast at the house of an artist friend where we sat on the floor until all our joints gave painful warning of dislocation and ate *poi* with our fingers in the most approved fashion. Soon, under the spell of the hour, the place and the delightful company, we heartily and sincerely wished annexation and the Republic further away, chiefly, it must be confessed, out of sympathy with the charming Princess Kaiulani who with several other Hawaiian beauties made even the eating of *poi* seem a graceful and ladylike operation.* The first cool breath of morning was in the air before we called a finish of the dance, and as we strolled home through the perfumed freshness of early dawn, the tinkle of a distant guitar came to us on the gentle breeze and the faint sounds of merriment which accented rather than disturbed the grateful peace of the night.

At sunrise General Merritt was up and off to the dock to learn when the coaling of the *Newport* would be completed and we shortly had the news, at the same time welcome and disappointing, that we were expected to be on board at eleven in the morning. A farewell glance at the beauties of Waikiki, we rushed down to the coal begrimed wharf and joined the wreath-bedecked throng on the deck of the *New-port*. Officers and men were fairly smothered in garlands of flowers and great baskets of fragrant wreaths almost vitiated the air of the saloon with their strong perfume. Mars made prisoner by Venus and Flora had little of the fierce aspect of a warrior about him, but had a jovial and festive air and appeared to take kindly to this pleasant custom of new friends which gave a typical Hawaiian flavor to the farewell to this tropical Capua.

------

*Since writing this I have read a newspaper paragraph announcing the death, on March 6th, of the Princess Kaiulani. Having first known her when she was a very young girl, our meeting at Honolulu was an unexpected revival of our acquaintance, which gave me the greatest pleasure, for she was a young woman of rare qualities of mind and of great personal charm. She was, naturally, much depressed over the foreign usurpation of the rights of the islanders and was quite hopeless about the future of the Hawaiian race.

CHAPTER II

At midday the steamer pulled away from the wharf when hundreds of citizens, of whom a notable proportion were women, waved adieu with shouts of *"Aloha!" "Aloha!"* and, escorted by a steamer with the Hawaiian band rapidly steamed to the southward where the other transports of our expedition lay waiting for the *Newport*. When we came near it was found that one of them had broken down so that the fleet, which was under orders to proceed together, could not sail for several hours. There was a diligent interchange of signals, and for an hour or more we were all in a state of anxiety as to our movements.

The situation was this: The mail viâ Vancouver had brought the news that Camara's fleet had begun to pass through the Suez Canal, and, if his ships sailed directly for the Philippines, as was doubtless the plan, it was a question whether we could reach Manila bay without being intercepted by one of the Spanish fast cruisers. The *Newport* with the commander-in-chief, his staff and five hundred soldiers on board, with nearly a million and a half dollars in cash and a valuable cargo of ammunition and ordnance was a rich and tempting prize and one which the enemy would doubtless make a desperate attempt to secure. If we followed the route of the second expedition under command of General Greene, which left Honolulu a few days before we arrived, we should probably pick up the monitor *Monterey* either at Guam or not far beyond that island, and have her as a convoy. On the other hand, if we adopted this plan of advance we should have to regulate the speed of our fleet to the rate of the monitor which was currently reported to be only five or six knots an hour and would arrive at Manila ten days or more later than we would if we ran at our full speed. Admiral Dewey had orders from Washington to meet us, in case of emergency, with a gunboat or a cruiser, somewhere on a direct line between Cape Engaño, the northeasterly headland of the island of Luzon, and a point on the Pacific six hundred miles due east, so that the choice lay between taking the risk of possible capture and the slow but comparatively safe plan of securing the convoy of the monitor. The alternative routes plotted roughly in a diagram which we studied with care showed considerable saving in distance in taking a direct course by way of the Farallon de Pajaros, the most northerly island of the Ladrones, and we, who had no responsibility, emphatically argued in favor of this route.

General Merritt, recognizing the fact that war meant taking risks, and conscious of the necessity of his presence at Manila, was not long in deciding on independent grounds that it was best to leave the fleet to make its way on the regularroute viâ Guam and to hasten on to Manila himself as fast as the *Newport* could carry him. He consequently directed Captain Saunders to lay the ship's course as straight as possible for the six-hundred-mile point. There was a sporting element in this trip which appealed strongly to all of us and this decision was welcomed with the greatest satisfaction by all on the ship. So off we steamed to our infinite relief and to the undoubted envy of those on the other transports and soon had them hull down.

The whole afternoon we sailed along the shores of the beautiful island of Oahu which presented a constantly varying, ever fascinating succession of bold headlands and pleasant valleys. Frequent slight showers cooled the air and the moist atmosphere gave added richness to the color of the vegetation which covered the hillsides with a carpet of brilliant and precious tints. As evening drew on and the violet sea grew more sombre in tone, contrasting with the orange hues of the western sky, a stately rank of clouds, like the turrets and crenellations of a distant walled city, gathered at the horizon and then the stars came out with amazing brilliancy, and Venus reflected in a silver line on the gently rippling water, beckoned us on toward the mysterious distance. A gentle trade wind sprang up directly astern and the evening air was deliciously soothing without the suspicion of a chill. Fatigued with the excitement and emotion of the visit to Honolulu, and content that at last the real journey was begun in earnest, the noisiest and most turbulently hilarious of the men ceased to chatter and soon nothing was heard on the ship except the throb of the engines and the swish of the water along the sides.

We now settled down to regular life on shipboard and one day succeeded another all too rapidly, for the weather was delightful, the sea smooth and perfect harmony prevailed in the saloon and between decks. The men began to be exercised in setting-up drill daily, inspection was held at intervals and the manual of arms practised frequently. There was no space large enough for even these elementary items of military education to be pursued without considerable difficulty and not very much time was devoted to this training.

Those of us who had any knowledge of Spanish began to form classes and all over the ship, in the shade of the awnings and in quiet corners, groups of men were busy half the day acquiring the rudiments of the language and committing to memory useful phrases the most popular of which were those relating to the surrender of an enemy. Captain O'Hara of the Third Artillery had spent some years at West Point instructing the cadets in modern languages, and there were one or two other officers who were proficient in Spanish, therefore the classes in the saloon made effective progress and the students soon became fairly confident, and stock questions and replies were exchanged with fluency and with a robust if not altogether musical accent. If there existed in our mess any musical talent, it never came out on the trip and we depended for entertainment of this sort mainly on the efforts of the Astor Battery, who gave one or two variety performances and started several distortions of popular songs which were immensely popular and never ceased to amuse. There is almost always to be found in every military organization some one with a talent for rhyming on the events of the day, and in the Astor Battery there was a topical poet who made a running chronicle of the incidents of their trip across the continent, setting the verses to the music of a well known song and celebrated Dewey's victory in a few couplets which were shouted out to the tune of "The Prodigal Son" until everybody knew them by heart. I quote from the first a couple of stanzas to show what elements of popularity this musical history of the battery possessed:

" At every country station that we came to,
  There awaited a reporter for an interview,
  He would ask your name and the date of your birth,
  Could you give any reason for your presence on earth?
  Are both your parents wealthy and how do you feel?
  Are you a college graduate and do you ride a wheel?
  You say you're fond of soldiering and he'd ask the reason why—"

And then was the time to turn him down with this reply:

" Chorus: — Zum ! We're natural-born soldiers ;
           Zum ! We're natural-born soldiers ;
           Zum ! We're natural-born soldiers ;
           That ain't no lie.

" Do you eat loose tomatoes with a knife or a fork?
  You could stand there and starve to death and listen to him talk.
  He'd talk about the gun-mules and never let you pass,
  Till you gave him some pointers on the ammunition ass.
  A reporter came up to me, a crazy galoot,
  And wanted to know if the battery could shoot ;
  I tipped him a wink as I jumped on the cars,
  Said I to him, ' My friend, we're a bunch of shooting stars !'

" Chorus : — Zum ! We're natural-born soldiers, etc."

A single verse from the next most popular song will suffice to show the character of that production:

> " They avenged our boys who were killed on the Maine,
>   They did, they did !
> The Spaniard won't try dirty tricks again ;
>   He won't ! he won't !
> When Dewey sailed into Manila bay,
> A short time ago, on the first of May,
> The Spaniards found it was ' moving day,'
> Sing ' Dewey, the king of the seas ' ! "

It is perhaps worthy of remark that after the action on the 13th of August, when the battery lost ten per cent. of its number, the song, "We're Natural-born Soldiers," was sung no more.

Life in the officers' mess was most unconventional and agreeable. The pajama brigade began the day with a bath under the saltwater shower apparatus on the upper deck and took off the keen edge of the appetite with fruit and coffee and then dressed for the regular breakfast at seven. Luncheon at one and dinner at six brought us together again and we usually spent the evening on the deck under the awning. We always went to bed early, because at the first peep of dawn we were sure to be awakened by the chatter of the men who slept on deck or by the shouts of those who came up from below to fill their lungs with morning ozone. Judging from the resonance of their voices, this stimulating element of the atmosphere had an immediate effect on the vocal organs. This disturbance was sometimes annoying and very often failed to appeal to our sense of humor. General Merritt, who occupied the smoking room which had been converted into a very comfortable apartment, was in the vortex of the confusion and lost a great deal of sleep in consequence, but he was too kind-hearted to interfere with the freedom of the men and therefore no vigorous steps were taken to suppress this annoyance.

In a day or two after we left Honolulu, the men settled down into their regular places and went through the same performances at the same time. I knew to a moment when Rooney would emerge from the hatchway, and could tell to a certainty who would begin the chaff with the good-natured old soldier. I could almost set my watch by the morning visit of the sleek and rotund "Texas," the shark fisherman, who stowed himself away by night in a hammock skilfully hung in the empty space between the piles of stores and the awning on the after part of the ship. The man in K battery with his seventeen hundred and thirty-five different designs in tattoo; the genius who could whistle two parts at once without puckering his lips; the private who had commanded a regiment of volunteers—I got to know them all intimately by the sound of their voices, days before I learned to recognize them by sight.

Under my window there always assembled a little knot of regulars who talked over every conceivable subject from the metaphysics of Nietsche to the construction of an iron-clad. Their method was to start a topic, get every man to express an opinion or to ask a few questions and then to tear all the theories to shreds and end up the argument by a general disruption of courteous relations. It always went along on the same lines—argument just for the pleasure of expressing contrary opinions. It was indeed amazing what a variety of abstract subjects they dug out and how warmly they would dispute over any statement that was brought forward, no matter how accurate it might be. After the flutter of a hot argument quiet would prevail and they would settle down to read or to one of the numerous occupations of a soldier's leisure. The books they read were as surprising as some of the topics they selected for discussion. Observing one young fellow for several days earnestly reading a dull-looking volume I asked him to show it me. It was "The Yorke-Wendte Discussion on the Primacy of the Pope, Church, and State." At a certain hour in the forenoon all the bedding and clothing were brought up to be aired and the ship looked for the time like the back yards of a row of tenement houses. This operation resulted in an endless amount of confusion for the articles often got hopelessly mixed but was part of an excellent system, and with the scrupulous cleanliness of the quarters contributed largely, no doubt, to the good health of the men.

We really did not need any entertainment in the saloon, for existence was pleasure enough, but the active and enterprising chief paymaster, Colonel McClure, persuaded us that we were pining for diversion, and therefore, by common consent, he set aside certain evenings for this purpose and selected his entertainers. General Merritt gave us a talk, "An Incident in the Life of Captain Joseph Ashe, whose Motto was: 'Six Feet of Earth or a Yellow Sash' "; Colonel Brainard, the Sergeant Brainard of the Greely expedition, told of the hardships of that adventurous voyage; Major Thompson started afresh the perennial discussion about the Custer massacre by relating his evxperiences with the force which reached the field immediately after the disaster; Dr. Woodruff took the conceit out of us by unfolding the horrors of degeneracy; Chaplain Doherty gave a brief review of the chief elements of the Christian, Mohammedan and Buddhist religions and I attempted to revive a dead interest in a past conflict by reviewing some prominent incidents in the Russo-Turkish campaign of 1877-78. There was material enough for our impresario to draw on for a long time, but, almost before we knew it, the backbone of our voyage was broken and we were approaching the Ladrones at the northern end of the group almost exactly due west from Honolulu, near latitude twenty degrees north and distant 3095 miles. It was the 19th of July by the sailors' reckoning but the 20th by all landsmen's calculations. On Tuesday the 12th at half past two in the afternoon, we crossed the meridian 180 degrees west of Greenwich and were told that the next day would be Thursday the 14th of the month. In matter of fact, although the subject was much discussed by the debating society on the deck near my room, none of us would have missed the day, they were all so agreeably monotonous.

The vicinity of land apparently caused a disturbance in the air currents, for the day in question opened dull and rainy. We had been visited almost daily by frequent showers, and nearly always there was a veil of rain drifting across the water in the distance, but the same tender, lofty blue sky favored us every day and at sunset we had the same rank of gilded towers and battlements all along the horizon. The thermometer meanwhile had varied between eighty degrees and eighty-four degrees in the day, dropping to seventy-six degrees or seventy-eight degrees at night.

On the 19th came a distinct change. It rained hard at intervals until about noon and the air was heavy and saturated with moisture. Then it cleared up a little and we could see a considerable distance. We were all eager to sight the land which had an additional interest for us because the island Farallon de Pajaros which we were approaching is an active volcano. In the latter part of the afternoon, far away to the southward there hovered in the mist the great conical mass of the volcano on the island of Asuncion, and then we saw, directly in our path, the smaller but more symmetrical cone of the Farallon de Pajaros, its base distorted by mirage but its slightly truncated summit clear and distinct and wreathed with smoke which floated away to the north and mingled with the cumulus clouds which were assembling for their sunset parade.

We did not get abreast of the island until after dark and then could see the crater fires reflected in a ruddy glow on the towering column of steam which puffed out at intervals, shooting up to the height of several hundred feet before it was caught by the casual breeze. The flanks of the mountain rose straight from the ocean, the perfect balance of the cone being broken only by a small low promontory jutting out to the southward, apparently an extinct crater of lesser size or a mass of lava. There was nothing cheery about the glow from the crater fires, nothing inviting in the rigid, straight lines of the mountain side which suggested, although we could not distinguish it in the darkness, a scorched and arid surface with no softening cloak of vegetation. It was a dismal and forbidding spectacle, this great dark mass crowned with a dull red light towering out of the water, isolated, dreary and solemnly impressive. We breathed more freely when we were out of the neighborhood of this uncanny peak which oppressed us with its grim majesty and caused us to brood over the uncertainties of the future and to conjecture on the reception we should meet in that land of devastating typhoons, shattering earthquakes and destructive fire-mountains of which this solitary cone was the active outpost.

Speculation grew apace as we neared the six-hundred mile point, and many and quaint were the theories advanced as to what it might be best to do if we should chance to be overhauled by a Spanish cruiser. The favorite plan often proposed by one officer was to haul down our flag when we were called upon to surrender, and to run alongside so near that our boarding party could jump aboard and capture the hostile vessel, at the same time hoisting our colors again. Another and more feasible plan was to ram the enemy in spite of her fire, an operation which, if it could be accomplished, would probably sink both ships; but sinking was better than being shot without the chance of a fight or being set ashore on a desert island. These and many other similar plans of campaign were brought forward in good faith and were sometimes discussed with a seriousness approaching the ludicrous. It was, after all, more or less of a risky business, going ahead, quite defenceless as we were, into waters which might be and which, indeed, we expected to be occupied by the enemy's fleet but, although we did talk a great deal about

GEORGE DEWEY

the situation, it did not worry us at all in comparison with the thought that the business of capturing the town of Manila might be accomplished by General Greene and his expedition before we reached there. Meeting a Spanish cruiser might be a disaster but a tame and peaceful termination to our long voyage seemed very much like a disgrace.

After we passed the Ladrones, the weather grew rapidly warmer and the mercury ranged within a degree or two of ninety, day and night. The atmosphere, too, became distinctly moister and the trade wind which had followed us all the way from Honolulu, died out altogether. We passed the six-hundred mile point at one o'clock in the morning of the 22d, and now everybody on board was more or less alert, expecting to see the smoke of a steamer, anticipating, of course, that Admiral Dewey would send out to meet us. The sea was quiet and the heat rather oppressive because the humidity was high, and clouds settled upon the water at times so we could see but a short distance ahead of us. Nothing more substantial than cloudforms and showers of rain broke the horizon until about five o'clock on the afternoon of the 23d, when suddenly, under a stratum of low clouds, we caught sight of low bluffs and rocks with breaking water off to the southwest, a dozen miles or so away. This was our first glimpse of Luzon and, two hours later, we were off Cape Engaño, four or five miles to the north of it. The high mountains which rise near the coast in this part of Luzon were completely screened by the clouds, and we could only distinguish the small headland and jutting rocks. As darkness came on we showed no lights and lay our course between Luzon and the Babuyanes, passing so near to Camiguin and Fuga that we could distinguish in the darkness the general conformation of the land. Not a glimpse of light, not a fishing-boat, not a single sign of life were seen, and we ran on silently the whole night.

Morning broke, dull and showery, and disclosed the great

headland of Cape Bojeador, the northwest point of Luzon in the province of North Ilocos. Now we could see that the whole country was covered with dense forests, extending even to the high mountain tops, which were shrouded with heavy clouds. Not a village was in sight nor even a clearing. It was a wild and desolate region, yet in its variegated mantle of rich verdure, flecked with spots of sunlight and accented by the dark lines of ravines which broke the billowy roundness of the foothills, it was refreshing to our weary eyes, and enticed us with its morning coolness. Suddenly, through the drifting mist ahead of us, the masts and funnel of a large steamer appeared standing across our course. We watched her with interest bordering on anxiety until the hull came in sight and then we saw she was a commercial vessel. Whether she saw us or not, she showed no signal and did not alter her course but stood away to the northeast and disappeared in a few minutes. As if further proof was needed that the situation at Manila had been unaltered by the movement of Camara's fleet, a large four-masted vessel came in sight about noon and followed the first one, paying no attention to us. At intervals through the whole day the clouds settled so low that we lost sight of the land entirely, frequent showers of warm rain, sometimes accompanied by tremendous peals of thunder, burst upon us with so terrific a deluge that the awnings were no shelter, and we huddled together in the saloon and perspired and fretted at this tearful welcome of the Philippines. The day dragged on slowly—the last day at sea always seems twice as long as the others—and, although we were relieved from all thought of the Spanish fleet, we were consumed with the fever heat of impatience to be at our destination and to learn what had happened in the month since we had had any news. Peace might have been declared, Santiago might have fallen, Cervera's fleet might have escaped, and so on through a long list of possibilities, the discussion of which did not tend to kill time but rather to increase our anxiety for news. There was nothing to divert us on deck, for a gray curtain of mist surrounded us and only broke occasionally to disclose a rounded headland and a sodden, dripping landscape. The sun struggled out once or twice, but gave up the attempt to disperse the dense masses of vapor and without the usual sunset colors in the west, darkness came on, and we still surged on through the mist without the guidance of shore lights but with the comfort of our own illumination.

Early in the morning, the 25th, we ran past the mouth of Subig bay, shortly bore around a little to the east, and soon after breakfast saw the lofty island of Corregidor, easily recognizable from its position between two passages of unequal width, directly in front of us. The rugged shores to the north across the Boca Chica showed no signs of habitation, and a dense jungle covered every spot except the black and jagged rocks at the water's edge, even to the great shoulders of the mountain range which thrust its summits into the rain clouds. To the south and east, the long line of a sandy beach with a rigid level of palm trees beyond, swept away in a gentle curve until lost on the perspective and, behind and beyond, distant, low foot-hills rose against the faintly seen masses of volcanic mountains towering high above the clouds and dwarfing all other features of the extensive prospect. Everything was steaming and dripping and gray, but there was a shimmering in the distance where Manila lay, as if the bay were in sunlight.

A dark spot ahead rising and falling as if it were suspended somewhere in the visible atmosphere which gave an unusual look to the water, now gave us something to speculate on. At times it looked as large as a warship, and then scarcely more massive than a clump of drift wood, so disturbing to the vision was the combination of mirage and vapor which distorted everything near the surface of the water. We had just decided it must be a patrol boat when it turned out to be a native dugout, the first indication we had come across that the land was inhabited, except, of course, the deserted lighthouse we saw on Cape Bojeador.

We ran along at full speed, leaving a wake of foaming waters, and entered the Boca Grande, following the same channel by which Commodore Dewey's fleet entered the harbor the night before the battle, and, as we opened out on the bay, a horizonless expanse of sea and sky was before us, unbroken by a single object and with no perspective of fleet and town which had been pictured in our minds. The patches of turf on Corregidor, the fresh earth marking the position of the batteries and the neat lighthouse with its group of buildings nestling at its base, and its attendant rock, were the only solid objects visible in this curiously unreal effect of atmosphere, for everything was now vibrating and floating in a silvery haze. Ahead of us, where we expected to see Cavité and our fleet and the towers of Manila beyond, was a blank glare of sunlit vapor.

While we were trying in vain to trace the course of the shore to the vanishing point, certain confused perpendicular lines came into view in the extreme distance and then a long level mass with a rigid contour, distinctly higher than the neighboring land, was disclosed by the shifting of the mist, and we recognized at once the port at Cavité. The perpendicular lines developed gradually into the masts of the warships, and presently their gray hulls were visible and the darker forms and more slender masts and funnels of other vessels, just abreast the fort. As we approached, one of the gray ships which we soon saw was the *Concord*, left her moorings and steamed out to meet us and with this escort we rounded the point, made our way through the line of the squadron, and dropped anchor between the *Olympia* and the point. A salute from the flagship announced the fact that the commander-in-chief had arrived and the dull echo of the great guns sounded along the great curve of the low

FORT AND EARTHWORKS, CAVITÉ, SILENCED AND CAPTURED BY ADMIRAL DEWEY

shore miles to the north where the domes and towers and palaces of Manila gleamed white in the sunlight, and carried to the Spanish forces an emphatic message that this was the beginning of the end, and to the foreign fleet grouped near the town, the more welcome news that the tedious wait for the final act of the drama would be broken speedily.

The little roadstead was filled with vessels of all sorts, from the aggressive monsters bristling with polished cannon to the peaceful-looking transports and dingy colliers. Steam launches hurried to and fro, native canoes with outriggers and curious sails caught the first puffs of the freshening monsoon and, half buried in foam, scurried from ship to ship with their loads of fruit. Scattered between us and the shore, almost within bow shot, the distorted and ruined upperworks of the sunken Spanish vessels showed high out of water, ugly but significant monuments to the efficiency of our fleet. A few hundred yards to the south of us, the town of Cavité with red roofs rising above the dark green masses of trees, the long gray walls of the fort, the bald façade of the arsenal looked exactly like a small Spanish or Italian seaport with its small landing place crowded with miscellaneous craft and groups of loungers on the wharf end.

A large party of visitors, many of them correspondents, came aboard and in a few minutes Admiral Dewey came up the steep companion-way as active as a midshipman, was welcomed by General Merritt as an old friend, and sat for an hour or more with him in his stateroom, while the visitors and our own company crowded around the door, some anxious to see the chiefs together, others awaiting a brief word with one or both of them.

Historic meetings of eminent personages are so often illustrated in the periodicals of the day and described with so much accuracy of detail that it has become very stale reading, but yet I cannot refrain from a brief comment on the contrast between the two officers, the one a soldier of long service with a record for conspicuous gallantry in scores of battles, and the other the most successful and popular naval hero of the day, whose remarkable exploit has raised him to a position in the estimation of the world and in the hearts of the American people in which he has no rival.

General Merritt is tall, of commanding presence and distinguished military bearing, the type of officer, indeed, for whom the phrase "every inch a soldier" might well have been invented. Admiral Dewey, on the other hand, is not above medium height, but his strong personality would be felt in any assembly of men. He has nothing of the traditional manner of the bluff and hearty sea-dog, and I doubt if anyone would be able to pick him out of a crowd as a naval officer.

Our journalistic visitors, some of whom had been on the spot since the 1st of May, were full of information about the situation, and rattled off the names, Bacoor, Parañaque, Tambo, Malate and Malabon, with bewildering fluency and quite confused us with their rapid description of the military situation in the neighborhood of Manila. In a day or two we ourselves unconsciously acquired familiarity with the names of the different important points along shore, and the topography of our limited field of activity became as well known to us as the drives in Central Park. From the anchorage the whole grand curve of the low shore from Cavité point to the houses of Malate, the southern suburb of Manila, is plainly visible, and not more than a half dozen miles distant at the extreme point, seems to be a clean, unbroken line of sandy beach with a level fringe of trees growing close to the high-water mark. The monotonous band of foliage is interrupted at long intervals by the roofs and towers of large churches, marking the position of the villages. Far in the distance a great mountain range pierces the clouds, and leading the eye away beyond the shining town disappears in the perspective. On the opposite shore the foot-hills rise abruptly from the water's edge, and to the north, far beyond the cluster of foreign warships, the wooded shores melt away into the distance and the faint outline of volcanic summits stretching across in a rank from east to west complete the grand amphitheatre of mountains which surround the beautiful expanse of the bay. Just where the level band of foliage on the shore ends and the houses of Malate begin stands a small but conspicuous white building which was pointed out to us as within the Spanish lines and a very short distance this side of it a spot of brown against the background of dark green marked the insurgent position on the seashore where we were told there was a brisk skirmish regularly every evening about nine o'clock.

The correspondents who had been living in comfortable quarters in Cavité or on the warships were so spick and span and tidy in their appearance that we did not need to be told that theretofore they had suffered no hardships of campaign, but it was a great relief to hear from them that everything had been waiting for General Merritt's arrival. Nothing had been done, in fact, towards active land operations, except landing the Second Brigade at Tambo, where the camp had been named after the admiral.

Towards evening Greene came aboard straight from Camp Dewey, sunburned and weatherworn, looking as if he had been through a long and arduous campaign. His campaign hat was battered, his gray linen uniform was mud-stained and bleached and the blue trimmings were faded, but he had an alert, keen expression which showed that all his energies were enlisted in his work and that the business was exactly to his taste. We secretly envied him his experience, brief and comparatively uneventful as it was, and to our eyes that uniform suggested a volume of anticipations and a multitude of reminiscences. To me came back like a flash the vivid memory of dreary weeks at Plevna and in the Danube valley, of the winter march across the Balkans, and the exhilarating campaign from Sofia to Adrianople, in all of which Greene, then United States military attaché to the Russian army, was a prominent figure, participating in every important movement and studying the war with a thoroughness and intelligence which gained him the admiration and respect of all in authority.

That evening was memorable on board the *Newport*. After our long voyage and our fever of impatience, we were finally at our goal and sure to be in at the death. As we sat on the deck in the darkness the electric lights along the water front of Manila sparkled with festive brilliancy and occasionally a dull red flash, followed at a long interval by the echo of a report, showed that the regular evening duel was in progress. To add to the dramatic effect, our lights were all extinguished by orders given by Commodore Dewey, and the powerful searchlights of the squadron played nervously over the water, and signals were interchanged constantly between the vessels of the fleet.

CHAPTER III

IT was settled that General Merritt with a small party should accompany General Greene ashore the next morning and have a look around the lines so that the commander-in-chief should have a correct idea of the situation and be able to decide on a plan of campaign. We consequently took a steam launch early the following day and ran in as close as we could to the beach where we saw the gleam of tents near the little village of Tambo hidden away among the manga trees and the palms. The surf was breaking so heavily on the beach that it was impossible to approach within hailing distance, but a captured Spanish boat was put off with a crew of mountaineers and we were rowed and poled and dragged through the breakers and then carried to dry land on the shoulders of the men. A general looks neither dignified nor picturesque riding pick-a-back, and I refrain from a realistic description of the landing of the first American governor-general of the Philippines, which had more of the hilarious than of the heroic in it. We walked by a narrow path through the tangle of bamboo and tropical undergrowth; past native huts perched high on stilts where naked children scampered about like monkeys and scantily clad adults stared at us from the platforms of their airy little habitations; past an almost pretentious two-storied, tin-roofed house from which was flying the headquarters flag, and out upon a broad, open plain three or four feet above the line of high water, extending north and south about a mile and a half long and less than a quarter of a mile broad without any break of importance. As far as we could see in either direction, this whole area was covered with shelter tents. The headquarters camp and the hospital tents were pitched between the fringe of trees along the shore and the plain, and a natural boundary of trees separated these groups of tents from each other and from the main encampment.

I have lived in scores of camps and bivouacs, in the swamps of Virginia, in the Danube morasses and on the arid hills of the Dabrudscha, in the snows of the Balkans, and in the ore fields of Roumelia, but a more curiously interesting panorama than Camp Dewey never met my eyes. The company streets were laid out from east to west and extended from the tree border perhaps two-thirds the distance to the Camino Real, or main road from Manila to Cavité, which formed the eastern boundary of the plain. The officers' tents were a little apart on the shore side of the camp ground, and the cooks' establishments, a confusion of shelters, pits, rude ovens and piles of fuel, were placed on the side near the Camino Real. The shelter tents were rigged up with great skill on platforms of split bamboo a foot or two from the ground, and sometimes a two storied framework was erected which housed four men more or less comfortably. The men soon learned the value of bamboo as a material for general use, and many of the tents were marvels of skilful arrangement and ingenious contrivances for comfort quite different from any articles of native manufacture. Unfortunately these shelters which were adequate for protection in fine weather, were but little better than nothing in the severe tropical downpours which visited this region almost every day and flooded the camp inches deep in very few minutes. Nothing short of a good duck tent with a well set fly would keep the wet out on these occasions, and even in the best tent it would drive through the ventilators and between the flaps and drench everything inside.

When we landed at Camp Dewey there had been no rain for some hours, and the ground was dry in spots but the paths and roads were canals of black mud. Walking was

TWO-STORY TENT OF COLORADO TROOPS, CAMP DEWEY

out of the question, the riding ponies were very small and few in number, and therefore *carromatos* or light two-wheeled spring carts in common use were brought to transport the heaviest members of the party. General Merritt and General Greene occupied one of these vehicles until it became too great a torture, for they could scarcely sit upright and it bumped and jolted and narrowly escaped upsetting several times, and jumbled the passengers together regardless of rank and its privileges, and then the former took to the pony I was riding, which was so small that the general could almost stand and let the animal walk under him.

We left the camp in as much state as circumstances permitted, the orderly and I on rats of ponies, leading the way, then a *carromato* with the generals followed by a second one with two other officers. It was not surprising that in this guise the commanding general was recognized by only few of the men. We splashed along for about a mile along the Camino Real, or rather in the Camino Real, for our horses were hock deep in the mud, until we came to a cross road which leads from the beach eastward and straight to the village of Pasay, and beyond this place wanders off with many windings through the rice fields and between dense hedges of bamboo to San Pedro Macati, a small village on the Pasig river, soon named by our men "Pete M'Carty's." A half mile or so beyond Pasay our engineers had built a bamboo bridge over a sluggish, muddy river, just where it flows out of a broad open marsh, and our pickets were posted along this road from the beach to this bridge, which was the limit of our area of occupation. From this bamboo bridge to which we succeeded in floundering on foot, we could look across the broad marsh cut up into a maze of rice fields and distinguish the course of the highway from Paco to Santa Ana, along which there were Spanish blockhouses and entrenchments, one or two of which were visible among the trees. The twin towers of San Sebastian church in Manila showed above the trees directly to the north, and the quaint belfry of Santa Ana made a conspicuous landmark further to the east, beyond which we could see the densely wooded elevations which form the backbone of the narrow strip of territory between the sea and the Laguna de Bay with here and there a white building or a church tower. The road beyond the bamboo bridge was held by the insurgents, who also occupied an irregular line of scattered rifle pits and detached entrenchments which practically extended along the edge of the open marsh skirting it to the north for half a mile or more and then turning abruptly west until it met the shore at a point about a thousand yards distant from the stone fort San Antonio de Abad, the chief stronghold of the Spanish in their whole line of suburban defences. The fourteen other forts or blockhouses which had been erected a few months before at various points of strategic importance were diminutive structures, but with their surrounding breastworks were formidable enough to cause trouble, although by no means so important as the great stone pile on the seashore.

Our pickets were having a rather dull time of it, for they did not have the excitement of watching the enemy, as the insurgents were attending to that duty a few hundred yards farther to the front. They did, however, have the doubtful entertainment of being exposed to a shower of Mauser bullets and shells whenever there was any Spanish firing, because they were well within the danger zone and, indeed, just where a large part of the missiles found lodgment. To protect themselves they occasionally had low embankments of earth stacked up in the hedges or bamboo clumps which had been built by the insurgents as they advanced, and as time went on it was found necessary to throw up breastworks around the huts which were used as guard-headquarters.

There was no firing on the day of our excursion, and not far in the rear of our pickets the natives were ploughing the

TYPICAL BAMBOO BRIDGE

paddy fields with the ungainly water buffaloes, and in the huts which are hidden away among the trees in a most extraordinary fashion and are sometimes as difficult to see as birds' nests, the women and children were engaged in their usual occupations. The only thing which gave us the impression that this was not a picnic was the actions of our outpost on the seashore, whither we proceeded from the bamboo bridge, retracing our route along the cross road. The soldiers were crouching behind a rude breastwork made of a log and some rubbish and now and then one of them would rise up and cautiously look over in the direction of the town. We walked out upon the beach and examined the ground with our glasses. A few hundred yards up the beach was stranded a great iron lighter, and near it we could see the white posts of a large garden gate which marked the position of the afterwards notable Capuchin house, at that time a hundred and fifty yards in advance of the insurgent lines. About midway between the first hulk and the sand-bag battery, which was a prominent feature under the gray walls of the stone fort San Antonio de Abad, was a second stranded vessel and just beyond this we could see an indentation in the seashore where a broad but shallow estuary enters the bay. We took careful note of these different landmarks, knowing that each one of them might later become of conspicuous importance in the advance. With the naked eye we could distinguish the small sand bags used in strengthening the parapet of the fort, and the embrasures of the field guns mounted there. We were in easy range of these pieces and indeed within easy killing distance of the Mausers, but our presence apparently was unnoticed, although we made a prominent group and tempting mark on the broad, gently sloping beach. Having pretty thoroughly studied the ground in the vicinity of this part of the Spanish defences, we returned to camp and to the ship without having heard a shot fired, just in time to escape the regular afternoon gale and tempest which burst upon the bay while *cascos* were along-side the *Newport*, half loaded with stores and ammunition and before the fleet of small boats and launches could reach harbor. In a few moments a dangerous sea arose and the *cascos* were knocked about a good deal and nearly swamped before they could be towed to Cavité for safety. The soldiers stowing the cargo were unable to get back to the ship, and the last we saw of them that day they were clinging to the rail of the boats for dear life, seasick and drenched with the chill rain. Several of the officers who had been on a visit to the squadron or ashore at Cavité made heroic attempts to board the *Newport* where plenty and comfort awaited them, and where they could dry their bedraggled plumes, but the sea was so vicious that it was impossible for the launch to approach the companion ladder, and after many adventures they found shelter ashore and slept in wet clothes, supperless, much annoyed at their initiation to the delights of campaigning in the tropics.

This was our first introduction to the caprices of the weather in the rainy season, and we shortly found that we could safely count on a smooth sea and sunshine all the early part of the day, and with quite as much certainty expect a gale and heavy showers in the afternoon. There was every reason, then, why all operations conducted on the water should be undertaken in the early morning and particularly the landing of the troops on the open beach. This was seldom done as I shall presently show.

The following day, the 27th of July, the great lumbering *cascos* were towed back to the ship and all our men put aboard, the Astors on one boat and the batteries of heavy artillery on the others, with all their camp equipage. The usual mode of proceeding was to tow the *casco* within a short distance of the beach, where she was dropped and, throwing over an anchor to keep her head to the sea, paid out cable and drifted slowly through the breakers where she stranded

ASTOR BATTERY BOARDING CASCO TO GO ASHORE FROM THE *NEWPORT*

and lay until the next tide. These useful vessels are very strongly built and will stand a great deal of hard usage. This plan worked all right when the cable was strong and the anchor held. Our men were sent ashore rather late in the day, and reached the landing place in the height of the afternoon blow. The regulars got ashore all right according to programme, but the Astors' *casco* parted her cable, drifted broadside on, swamped and was broken up. All the stores were soaked, the ammunition chests flooded and the powder in the metal cases was almost all wet and spoiled. The men got ashore without accident, and made camp before suppertime, but they were not a little humbled to find themselves within striking distance of the enemy, with no effective weapons but their revolvers.

It was now apparent that the difficulty of the situation for a correspondent which was enormously increased by the rainy season, lay chiefly in the irregularity of communication between the camp and Cavité. The cable was cut and all telegrams as well as letters were taken at intervals by a government despatch boat whenever the commodore thought necessary to send her to Hong Kong. It was the regulation that all telegrams were to be passed by a censor on the *Olympia,* and it was quite on the books that one might miss the despatch boat by sheer inability to get aboard. Personally, I could not then nor can I now see the necessity of rigorous censorship at Manila, when all damaging information could be sent to Hong Kong in a private letter and be transmitted from there to Europe quite as expeditiously as if it had been put in the form of a cable message at the beginning. Besides there was no information to be sent which could possibly be of assistance to the Spanish cause. The censorship, however, was rigidly maintained, and it was even projected to exercise this power over letters as well as telegrams. This I know because I heard an officer in high authority seriously discuss the question and express his determination that it should be done. The matter of communications was settled luckily for me to my entire satisfaction through the kindness of Mr. Joseph L. Stickney, the New York *Herald* correspondent, who had been ordered to Spain. He had hired a medium-sized steam launch called the *Albany* from a Captain Plummer, a native of Rochester, New York, I believe, who had been for many years in the stevedore business in Manila. This he turned over to Mr. T. H. Reid and myself for our joint use in serving the New York *Herald* and the *Times* of London. Mr. Reid had come down on the *Esmeralda* for the *Times* and his own paper the China *Mail,* and had arrived in time to see the second act in the fight. He was perfectly familiar with the ins and outs of the business in Manila bay, and I proposed to him that, inasmuch as we had interests in common, we should divide the field, he to take care of everything on the water and I to look after the land campaign, the *Albany* to serve as a means of keeping us in constant touch with each other. She was as stanch and fast a little craft as could be found, even in that home of the steam launch, Hong Kong, and carried a reckless and harum-scarum crew of four natives and an indefinite number of women and children who swarmed the untidy deck abaft the engine and were always cooking and washing there. The captain was not over enthusiastic about work, but was indifferent to exposure, cherished a firm belief that no sea could swamp the *Albany,* loved adventure, and had only one prominent ambition, which we persistently failed to gratify, the possession of a revolver. Altogether it was just the craft and quite the proper crew for our purposes.

The men from the *Newport* safely established in camp and nothing yet being heard of the remainder of our fleet, we had the inclination to look about Cavité, where General Anderson some weeks earlier had established his headquarters and where there were about 2000 of our troops. The town, which near the water front is, to the sea-worn eye, rather pretty, with an abundance of shade trees and open grassy spaces with flowering shrubs and park seats, covers the low promontory as far as a narrow neck about three-quarters of a mile to the south, with the exception of the large space on the north and west occupied by the fort and arsenal. It is a typical Spanish provincial town, a jumble of bald and ugly houses and a maze of squalid and dirty streets. The bombardment of our fleet had not left any very prominent scars, although shells had burst in some of the public buildings. The most of the damage done to the place was at the hands of the insurgents who had busily looted there on several occasions. Attractive as it was at first sight, as we walked up through the arsenal grounds which were busy with hundreds of workmen engaged in all sorts of repairs and crowded with soldiers, I soon got to loathe the place on near acquaintance for its shabbiness and cheap and artificial character. The columns and arches which looked so fine and solid through the trees, turned out to be poor stucco work; the great statue which rose high above the level green turf on a grand pedestal and gave a finished and park-like appearance to the little square, proved on nearer examination to be rather an unskilfully carved wooden affair, much besmeared with paint, and on a base which might pass as a bit of theatrical property. In bright sunshine the green mould which stained everything, creeping up the walls, accenting all the joints and spreading over all perpendicular surfaces in great patches, varying from intense purplish black to vivid metallic greens and yellows, was picturesque enough to look upon from afar, but close at hand, and particularly in the rain, it seemed repulsively noxious. Besides, its picturesqueness is monotonously obvious like the brush work of the conventional scene painter.

The insurgents who were mixed up with our troops in a most extraordinary manner, having their own guards inside our zone of occupation and pre-empting most of the best houses in the place, held, in the casemates of the fort and in adjoining dungeons, a large number of Spanish prisoners, who were in a most wretched plight from starvation. This fact was soon reported to General Merritt, who immediately took steps to relieve their distress.

I went with Colonel Brainard and Major Cloman of the Commissary Department to investigate the condition of these prisoners before anything was done for them, and we found that they were, indeed, dying for want of proper food. Many of them had suffered from fever and were unable to digest the boiled rice, which was, so far as we could find out, the only ration served out to them, and by no means in adequate quantities. The large majority of them were horribly emaciated and weak, and were scarcely able to stagger around the court yard. Those who had money to buy bread and other simple articles of diet, which were sold by native women in the very entrance of the prison, were fat and hearty, and frankly boasted that their condition was due to their ability to buy food. General Merritt ordered rations to be distributed to them, and this was done promptly. In a day or two Aguinaldo sent a protest against feeding his prisoners, but no notice was taken of it. He then removed them somewhere out of Cavité. I saw, later, a batch of 150 to 200 Spanish prisoners marched along through the bamboo swamps and the officer in charge told me they were going to be employed in digging entrenchments. This might have been the fate of those at Cavité, although it is quite possible that they were disposed of otherwise. I was told that about twenty-five of those who were fed by General Merritt's orders reached Cavité one day two or three weeks later, in a native boat. They were all more or less disabled by wounds and bore other marks of hard usage, and reported that the native guard had attacked them suddenly, and that they had barely escaped with their lives. There was

HOUSE OF THE COMANDANTE, CAVITÉ

no means of confirming this tale, and they were sent to Manila and kept with the other prisoners.

About a month before we arrived Aguinaldo and his friends had established a provisional revolutionary government, the seat of which was at Cavité, and he as the figure head and active leader had issued a proclamation, of which the following is a translation:

"MESSAGE OF THE PRESIDENT OF THE PHILIPPINE REVOLUTION

"If it is true that political revolution is the violent means employed by people to revindicate the sovereignty that naturally belongs to them and which has been usurped and trampled under foot by a tyrannical and arbitrary government, no revolution could be more just than that of the Filipinos, because the people have had recourse to it only after having exhausted all pacific means that reason and experience could suggest.

"The former Castilian kings looked upon the Filipinos as a kindred people united to Spain by a perfect solidarity of views and interests, and by the constitution of 1812, promulgated in Cadiz at the time of the Spanish war of independence, these islands were represented in the Spanish Cortes. The interests of the monastic orders, however, which have always found a strong support in the Spanish government, were opposed to the fulfilment of this sacred obligation, and the Philippines were excluded from the Spanish constitution, and the people were left at the mercy of the discretionary or arbitrary powers of the governor-general.

"In this state of affairs the people asked for justice, and begged the government for the recognition and restitution of their secular rights, which should gradually and progressively assimilate their position with that of the home country. Their prayers were unheeded, and their sons received as a reward for their abnegation, deportation, martyrdom and death. The religious bodies, whose interests always opposed to those of the Filipinos, the Spanish government has made its own, laughed at the claims of the Filipinos, and replied, with the knowledge and permission of the government, that Spanish liberty had cost blood.

"What other course then remained to the people but to insist, as they ought, upon the recovery of their stolen rights? Nothing was left but force, and, convinced of that, they resorted to revolution.

"And now they no longer limit themselves to asking for assimilation with the political constitution of Spain but ask for a complete separation, strive for independence completely assured that the time has come when they can and ought to govern themselves.

"Thus they have constituted a revolutionary government with wise and just laws, suited to the abnormal conditions confronting them and which, at the proper time will prepare them for a true republic. Thus, taking for its only justification the right, for its sole aid, justice, and for its only means honorable labor, the government calls upon all its Filipino sons without distinction of class, and invites them to unite solidly with the object of forming a noble society, ennobled not by blood nor by pompous titles but by labor and the personal merit of the individual—a free society where there is no place for egotism and personal politics which wither and blight, nor for envy and favoritism which debase, nor for charlatanry and buffoonery, which cause ridicule.

"No other course is possible. A people that has given proof of fortitude and valor in suffering and in danger, of industry and learning in time of peace, is not made for slavery. This people is called to be great, to be one of the strong arms of Providence in directing the destinies of humanity. This people has sufficient energy and resources to recover from the ruin and humiliation in which it has been placed by the Spanish government and to claim a modest but worthy place in the concert of free nations.

"Given at Cavité June 23, 1898.

"EMILIO AGUINALDO."

This flowery production was widely circulated and had a great effect on the imagination of the people who, in the elation of their present success in investing the town and in their belief that the United States was beginning a campaign in the Philippines in order to free them from Spanish oppression, shortly came to think that they were already a nation. The incident of the feeding of the Spanish prisoners before mentioned is a fair indication of their attitude in respect to the American military authority which we discovered on our earliest acquaintance with them.

CHAPTER IV

Two days after we arrived in Manila bay I moved over to Camp Dewey and, having no tent, planned to take up my quarters in one of the native huts near by. Wandering through the headquarters camp on my way to the village, I happened to pass the front of a fine, large, new tent with an ample fly. The cheery voice of Colonel Potter of the Engineers greeted me with:

"Where are you going to tie up?"

"Under some *nipa* thatch, I expect," was the reply.

"Haven't you got a tent?"

"Not a yard of duck!"

"Then come in with me. My tent-mate is ordered somewhere else, and I am quite alone and dying for company."

He was not obliged to repeat his invitation or to emphasize it, and I was soon installed in most comfortable quarters which were quite large enough to swing a cat in and were extensive enough to cover Colonel Potter with room to spare, and he was the largest man in the expedition, by inches I should judge, and with a heart in proportion, as I came to know on more intimate acquaintance with him.

The different organizations in the Second Brigade were encamped in the following order: At the extreme north was a company of United States Engineers under command of Captain Connor; then came the two batteries of the Third Regular Heavy Artillery, the Astor Battery, the two Utah Light Batteries, the First California Volunteer Regiment, the First Colorado Volunteer Regiment, one battalion of the Eighteenth Regulars, the First Nebraska Volunteer Regiment and the Tenth Pennsylvania Volunteer Regiment.

UNITED STATES CAVALRY DRILLING ON THE BEACH

The ground on which the headquarters tents were pitched was a little lower than the peanut fields where the main camp stood only a few rods distant and even this slight difference of level made the latter site much more desirable. An intricate network of ditches was dug to carry off the water which stood long after every rain. These were dangerous pitfalls at night and between the tent ropes which were invisible in the darkness, and these chasms a night wanderer about our camp had a sorry time of it. The main thoroughfare from the Camino Real to the beach, little more than a path, led past our tent, and the station of the headquarters guard was on the other side of this, together with the depot of the commissariat.

Major Bell of the Intelligence Department pitched his tent opposite ours and stretched an extra fly between the two so that we had a comfortable joint veranda, which, being handy to the entrance of the camp and a very agreeable shelter at all times, was a popular lounging place for our friends. This most efficient and energetic officer was always on the rush and never really happy unless he was sneaking about somewhere in the jungle near the enemy's lines, and he counted among his many duties the examination of spies, deserters and the natives who had found their way out of the city. In this task he was assisted by Major Bourns who had spent two or three years in the Philippines as an ornithologist with the J. B. Steere expeditions, understood the native character thoroughly and spoke Spanish and a little Tagalo. There was frequently a small drama in progress under our canvas portico and many were the wild tales we heard of sunken mines along the Luneta, of barbed wire stretched through the thickets and of wonderfully ingenious defences invented by the Spaniards. The highly colored adventures were related with every expression of truth and perhaps were fairly accurate, some of them. The best information probably came from our own scouts who were enterprising and courageous beyond praise. Their task was no holiday one, for the whole country was not only sodden and flooded, and in places absolutely impassable even on foot, but the tangle of bamboo and undergrowth in front of the enemy's works was absolutely impenetrable. Captain Grove and Lieutenant Means of the First Colorado Regiment, Lieutenant Bryan of the Second Oregon and many others did most valuable work in this line and the tale of their exploits would make as good reading as the most exciting military romance.

The Camino Real near the camp became speedily a temporary native bazaar with booths and shops and peddlers and it was always crowded no matter what the weather was. The enterprising Filipino soon discovered that the American soldier was free with his coin and was slow to acquire the Oriental custom of haggling. Consequently everything that could be scraped together in the way of fruit, vegetables and articles of native manufacture were brought to camp for sale at inflated prices. The money difficulty was always present and caused no end of annoyance. When the troops of our expedition landed they had nothing but United States silver and gold and this the natives would often take only at par although the dollar was worth more than double the Mexican coin of the same size and designation. Trade flourished feebly and spasmodically until there came into circulation a sufficient amount of Mexican and Filipino coins to ease the pressure for this currency. At the best of times small change was very scarce, probably because the native knew it was somewhat to his advantage to be unable to give change when there was a chance of working off stock in its place. There was no system of providing the men with money of the country, for the paymaster is not empowered by the Army Regulations to act as money changer. Therefore the urgent and constantly increasing demand for Mexican dollars in exchange for United States coin, while it was not ignored by those in authority, was never met by any system of relief.

CAMINO REAL, NEAR CAMP DEWEY

If an officer could get transportation to the *Olympia* he could get money changed at the market rate but very few were able to avail themselves of this privilege. Colonel McClure, the paymaster-in-chief, was so far blind to the text of the Army Regulations that he distributed many thousand dollars in exchange to those who he knew were in need of it, but his stock was not inexhaustible and this was only a slight relief. I am indebted to him for many favors of this kind for I never went on board the *Newport* without bringing a haversack full of Mexican dollars back to camp with me. Having inadvertently established a reputation as a money changer, our tent was often besieged by a line of men, each one with a gold piece to change and each one with a very good reason for wanting Mexican money. My pile of shining new dollars would disappear in an hour and I would be left without a silver piece to bless myself with. Much of the money was spent, of course, for luxuries and probably some was exchanged for the poisonous liquors which the natives had on sale, but a great deal was actually needed for payment of native labor, for the purchase of bamboo platforms which were prime necessities of comfort and health, for buying wood, forage, milk and other produce.

Drinking water and fuel were neither of them easy to obtain. Strict regulations about boiling water for drinking purposes were in force and every effort was made to induce the men to drink this only, but it was often absolutely impossible to keep up the supply, because the appliances for boiling water were none too numerous and wood was so scarce that sometimes there was not enough for cooking the regular meals. The operation was an additional burden on the cooks who naturally did not relish being compelled to start a fire, hours earlier than would have been necessary for the breakfast, in order to boil water for the day. Cooks cannot be expected to be sanitary enthusiasts and probably they avoided this task as much as they could with safety.

The supply of fresh water came from wells, little more than shallow pits dug in the soft earth. It was only necessary to dig down a foot or two and water was found which looked pure enough and was not unpalatable. Simply bringing it to a boil which was the usual practice, was of very little use as many found out. It took at least a quarter of an hour's boiling to destroy the harmful properties of this marsh water. Colonel Potter was seriously ill from drinking water which I brought myself from the supply of the headquarters mess. We found after the illness developed that this water, alleged to be boiled sufficiently, grew absolutely putrid if left standing over night. After this experience I arranged an elaborate system of bamboo gutters and spouts around our tent, and having secured a number of large tin hardtack boxes, caught many gallons of rain water every day. This was undoubtedly safe to drink and was very popular in the headquarters camp, as I soon discovered, because if the tent was left unguarded an hour the supply evaporated entirely. When the canvas dried a little and the guys slackened up the gutter system got out of gear and would not work, so if a downpour came on in the night I had to go out and rearrange the bamboos. This was sure to result in a thorough drenching, and, much to the amusement of the guard posted near by, I adopted the plan of attending to the gutters clothed only in a pair of native clogs. Thus I combined an exhilarating bath with an irksome task.

Considering the quality of the water, it is remarkable how little illness resulted from its use, for less than three per cent. of the men were on sick report at any time. Almost all of us in the headquarters camp had a brief turn of malaria or some kindred ailment. In most instances it was simply a headache, lassitude and general *malaise* for a day or two and then wore off. It was a great surprise to find that exercise and strong food were healthful in that climate and our experience in camp contradicted many theories about the insa-

BATHING PARADE—UNITED STATES CAVALRY

lubrity of the Philippines. We were practically living in a marsh, were almost always wet and were frequently exposed to cold rains at night and to the powerful sun at day and all without feeling any particular ill effects from these rough experiences. Active life and excitement had doubtless a great influence on the health of the men, for the record was by no means kept up after the fall of Manila, when they fretted at the enforced idleness and grumbled constantly at the irksome garrison duties.

With commendable forethought printed slips, with simple directions for preserving the health in the tropics, had been distributed among the troops, and on the *Newport* the sergeants read these aloud to the men once a week so as to impress them thoroughly with the importance of following the rules. Actual experience justified many of these suggestions, but it was a standing joke in the camp that the medical authorities earnestly recommended an immediate change of wet clothes for dry ones. At one time the theory that fat meat of any kind was injurious in tropical climates took a practical turn and no pork was issued. The consequence was that there was a sudden famine of this necessary article and absolutely no fat for cooking. Such a general outcry was raised that the regular supply was soon issued again. The only ration which was generally unpopular was the canned salmon and this because a large proportion of the men were always ill after eating it. Everything else, so far as I know, was considered palatable and there was certainly less grumbling about food than usual among soldiers.

As far as our personal discomfort went the greatest annoyance was the condition of our boots. We all regretted following the advice of a magazine writer who declared that rubber was of no service in the climate of the Philippines. A pair of india rubber boots would have been a godsend in camp for we often could not step outside the tent without paddling in the mud. If any one had a pair of dry boots in

Camp Dewey I did not see them. Even the canvas barrack shoes distributed at the camp were all wet in the cases. Every leathern article was always mouldy and the boots taken off at night would be decorated before morning, inside and out, with a beautiful pattern of this blue fungus. Clothes were never expected to be dry. We might get a chance to dry them in an hour or two of hot sunlight, but, except for the grandeur of the thing, it was scarcely worth while to trouble about it for they generally got wet again immediately. The tropical sun was not to be trifled with as we soon discovered, for the rays seem to have some special penetrating quality unobservable in a temperate zone and if the head were exposed without the proper covering a most uncomfortable sensation followed. The campaign hat of the soldiers was, all around, as adequate as need be, in the rainy season, at least, and although it took shapes never dreamed of by the manufacturer, it kept off both sun and rain remarkably well. The helmets made in the United States usually melted like frosting on a wedding cake and became masses of pulp.

The difficulty of providing fuel for cooking was, as I have said, exceedingly great, and it increased daily until the problem became most serious. It took a great many cords of wood a day to keep the fires going for the brigade and when General MacArthur's force reached camp there was well nigh a famine of this necessity. The fuel in common use in Manila is billets of hard dry wood of irregular size and shape, generally less than a yard long, which is brought on pony back from the mountains and shipped in *cascos* from the inlets and rivers. There was no supply of this to be procured until near the end of our stay in camp and the fatigue parties went farther and farther away each day in search of dry trees or timber or any combustible material fit for supplying the fires. The insurgents had plenty of wood which they forced the natives to bring them. We were so

GENERAL F. V. GREENE'S HEADQUARTERS

legal-minded that we treated the natives much the same as we were accustomed to treat the farmers in the vicinity of the state encampments. We took what they were willing to sell at war prices and paid cash for it. If the native refused to part with his property we went to look for the article elsewhere. The Malay cannot comprehend the disinclination of the European to exercise authority based on superior force alone and he puts this down to cowardice. The deduction is obvious.

One afternoon General Greene sent for me and, as I mounted the steep stairs leading to his quarters, he asked:

"Would you like to see a scrap?"

"Rather," was my natural reply.

"Then follow a company which has just gone up the Camino Real. The insurgents have arrested some of our men for taking firewood from a ruined house and their combs are very high and red and I am afraid there is going to be trouble."

I paddled off as rapidly as I could through the mud and into a bamboo lane after the little force which was moving at quick time. Before I succeeded in overtaking them they had halted and were parleying with a fat interpreter belonging to Aguinaldo's staff. Presently a little group of men half Filipinos and half Americans came in sight and we gathered them all in and marched them back to camp to the great excitement of the natives. The rotund interpreter argued that they were only pointing their Mausers at our men for fun, that they were not loaded and so on, but the half dozen villainous-looking insurgents were disarmed and haled before General Greene who heard the story from both parties and then let the culprits off with a warning to the interpreter to make it known that if our men were found taking wood or any other material without payment or against the will of the owners they would be dealt with on complaint, but, that if the insurgents undertook to interfere with the

United States soldiers by force he should consider it an insult to our arms and should act accordingly.

This incident is only worth the telling as an indication of the strained relations which existed even at that early date between the two armed forces. The natives who threatened our men with loaded weapons had no authority over this property they were attempting to protect. They only made the bluff on general principles, native versus white man. It was at that time much easier to account for the prejudices of the natives than for the sentiments of our men towards them. The Tagalo is an extraordinarily conceited individual and the soldiers often used to say: "Those little fellows think they own the earth." The insurgents, who are mostly of this race, resented the presence of our troops because they were keen enough to understand that there was danger of their being foiled in their long cherished scheme of plundering the rich town of Manila. The common idea held by the insurgent army may or may not have reflected the sentiments of the leaders, but, judging from the demands of Aguinaldo after the capture of the town, it is certain that one great stimulus offered to the native soldiers was the promise of loot. At the mention of the word Manila the insurgent was sure to brighten up and to draw his hand across his throat and to mention the Spaniards in terms of obloquy on the character of their ancestors. There is very little doubt that, if they had succeeded in taking the town before our army arrived—and they made a herculean effort to do this—they would have committed untold atrocities. The Spaniards knew they could expect no mercy from them, and fought desperately. Nevertheless, the insurgents, practically without artillery, accomplished wonders in forcing the enemy to retire to their inner line of defences.

Until the campaign before Manila I always believed it to be an elementary military axiom that if two armed bodies jointly occupy a territory they must be either enemies or al-

UNITED STATES LIGHT ARTILLERY DRILLING ON THE BEACH

BATHING FOR MAN AND BEAST

lies. In the investment of Manila the insurgents were not recognized by us in either of these capacities. The difficulties in the way of formally recognizing them as belligerents are readily conceivable but I am quite unable to explain why we did not in the very beginning make them understand that we were the masters of the situation and that they must come strictly under our authority. Even the Army Regulations might possibly provide for a means of making use of them in the same way as Indian scouts were employed in the Western campaigns. Aguinaldo had assembled an effective force and had completely invested the town from Caloocan on the north to Maytubig on the south and yet no official notice of him was ever taken, although he repeatedly made urgent requests to be recognized as an ally or at least to be notified of his acknowledged status. He never called upon General Merritt and although the latter passed through Bacoor, Aguinaldo's headquarters, they never met. The province of Cavité was entirely in the insurgents' hands when we arrived. They largely controlled the water transportation for they had possession of all the private steam launches except two, and almost all other craft except a few *cascos,* and on shore they had most of the available ponies and *carromatos.* At this time the main body of their army was concentrated in this province and that was the moment to settle once for all the mutual relations between the two forces. It must have been patent to those in authority that the ill feeling which germinated there was increasing daily and would finally result in mischief. Those familiar with the Malay know that one of its strongest characteristics is an implacable spirit of revenge and that nothing is more actively provocative of this feeling than a real or imaginary slight or an act of injustice. As time passed and their position as successful antagonists of the Spaniards was not recognized, they began to grow aggressive and to comfort themselves with an obtrusive arrogance of manner. Of individual acts proving their real feeling there are a thousand instances to be cited and while their profession of friendship became more and more effusive and verbose it ceased to carry any assurance of sincerity. Officially, they committed themselves in only one direction while we were at Camp Dewey. They refused to let any white man enter their lines without a pass from Aguinaldo. Their camp gossip was always derogatory to the American troops and many stories were in active circulation regarding the cowardice of the strangers. Having been made more or less of a confidant on several occasions because, as I represented an English paper I was presumed to be of that nationality, I was several times told a story of an American soldier at Cavité who took an orange from a market woman's basket and ran away for dear life when she attacked him to recover her property. Of course the American pickets were posted behind the insurgent line because they didn't dare to go any nearer the enemy and thus a fabric of tales was woven to bring discredit to the valor of the American soldier.

It was an interesting sight at Camp Dewey to see the insurgents strolling to and from the front. Pretty much all day long they were coming and going, never in military formation, but singly or in small groups, perfectly clean and tidy in dress, often accompanied by their wives and children and all chatting as merrily as if they were going off on a pigeon shoot. The men who sold fish and vegetables in camp in the morning would be seen every day or two dressed in holiday garments with rifle and cartridge boxes strolling off to take their turn at the Spaniards. There was no restriction of age in that service and none of size, for at the best the race is of small stature, and the men looked like children in contrast with the stalwart giants of the Western regiments. Any boy who was strong enough to carry a rifle and ammunition, even if he were unable to level the weapon properly without resting it on the earthwork, was as good a soldier

IN THE INSURGENT TRENCHES

as the next man. When they had been at the front twenty-four hours they were relieved and returned home for a rest. They generally passed their rifle and equipments on to another man and thus a limited number of weapons served to arm a great many besiegers. They had no distinctive uniform, the only badge of service being a red and blue cockade with a white triangle bearing the Malay symbol of the sun and three stars and sometimes a red and blue band pinned diagonally across the lower part of the left sleeve. The plundered arsenal at Cavité provided thousands of them with Spanish uniforms made of finely striped blue linen and these were much affected among them, particularly by the officers. A revolver with a cord to go around the neck was the most prominent badge of rank and much more esteemed than the sword, although most of the officers proudly wore both.

During our short acquaintance with them in camp there were few casualties in their ranks notwithstanding the fact that scarcely a day passed but they expended a good deal of ammunition. Personally, I only saw a half dozen wounded men. Their organization was not apparent and it is scarcely probable that they possessed at that time any complete record of the numerical strength of their force or had anything like brigade organization, even if they were broken up into regular battalions. They were never observed to drill and were rarely seen to march in large detachments. Occasionally at Aguinaldo's headquarters at Bacoor where there were several excellent native bands a gala parade was organized and every available man was turned out. On these ceremonial occasions the young leader and his staff were most resplendent in gold lace and trappings and the review was conducted with a pomp and style calculated to impress the native with the power of the dictator and the high quality of the army at his command. The troops certainly made an excellent appearance. Many of them, to be sure, had belonged to the native volunteer force and had acquired a certain amount of training in that way. The recruits were soon hammered into shape by the veterans of the rank and file and by the officers who did not waste many soft words on them, at least until they had sufficiently impressed them with the extent of the official authority—a method of training which the Malay is capable of understanding. I was often told by the under officers, many of whom were men of a certain education having studied with the priests, that their men were perfectly obedient to orders and that it was only necessary to make them appreciate the fact that the officers had supreme power over them and they made the most devoted soldiers.

There was no visible Commissary or Quartermaster's departments, but the insurgent force was always well supplied with food and ammunition and there was no lack of transportation. The food issued at the front was mostly rice brought up in *carromatos* to within a few hundred yards of the trenches when it was cooked by women, perhaps in some large and now disused cock-fighting theatre which remarkable structures of bamboo and *nipa* are found everywhere in the country. Each man had a double handful of rice, sometimes enriched by a small proportion of meat or fish, which was served him in a square of plantain leaf. Thus he was unencumbered with plate or knife and fork and threw away his primitive but excellent dish when he had "licked the platter clean."

It was noticeable that the insurgents carried no water bottles nor haversacks and no equipments, indeed, but cartridge boxes. They did not seem to be worried by thirst like our men and were quite as averse to drinking water as the ponies are. However hot and thirsty these animals may be they will never drink out of a pool or a stream, not for reasons of health, to be sure, but because they are accustomed to drink water which has been sweetened with coarse molasses popularly called honey. The only times I saw the natives drinking water they were eating lumps of brown sugar at the same time. We remarked constantly on the cleanliness of the insurgents and of the natives in general. When our men would be smothered in mud and bedraggled almost beyond recognition, the insurgents would look as clean and well cared for as if they had never left their huts. One reason for this was that they built shelters everywhere along their trenches to keep off sun and rain and had platforms to stand on as well, a practice which added a great deal to their comfort and considerably increased their efficiency at the front.

No baggage or supply trains were ever seen. When a detachment was moved from one point of the country to another it would be followed, perhaps by a buffalo sledge or a *carromato* or two with a few extra rifles and possibly the officers' kit, and that was all. Some of the men had small bundles but the majority carried rifle and cartridge boxes only. They needed no tents for they pitched no camp but scattered through the bamboo and occupied the native huts which are everywhere as thick as toadstools and they got their rations where they happened to be. This method of life is possible, of course, for the native alone, for no white man could exist on the food they flourish on or long resist the many diseases which prey on all foreigners who do not keep up the habit of taking strong nourishment, and, moreover, plenty of exercise.

There was a small variety of pests in the way of insect life in the camp, and those noxious creatures of which we had read so much about in the magazine articles did not materialize to any great extent. There were no mosquitoes and very few flies, but the red ants made up in numbers and activity for the absence of other crawling things. Everywhere in the Philippines the ants swarm in enormous quantities and active armies of them are always on the move, crawling in a busy line around the windows, up the walls, along the floors and massing in all the most unexpected corners. In camp one of these hostile expeditions would suddenly appear crawling up the posts of the bamboo platforms and then the only thing to do was to turn out everything and to arrange the uprights in tomato cans half filled with water or, better, with petroleum. The small red ants have a vicious sting and are exceedingly active in their attacks, causing their victim to dance suddenly with a fiery sensation on many parts of his body at once. The frogs were the greatest nuisance of all for, although they neither bit nor stung nor crawled over the person, they were the cause of many a sleepless hour. The moment it began to rain, particularly at night, they immediately set up a most deafening noise and made a racket out of all proportion to their size, for they were tiny translucent things quite innocent in appearance. They were silent and invisible until the rain began and then they sprang into existence on all sides, by choice under the bamboo platforms where they kept up a strident and irritating chorus quite deafening and loud enough to make conversation impossible. In Manila I have known them to make so much noise in a shower that I could not hear my pony's footstep on the pavement.

The camp was very early astir. Long before sunrise the first bugle calls sounded and there was certainly not light enough to dress by when the blare of these instruments shattered the morning air with a medley of unpleasant sounds which, judging from our own feelings, must have shocked the musical sense of the natives, who are gifted with a remarkable appreciation of harmony. The discord of the bugles was an effective sleep-destroyer and was always followed by a volley of raucous expletives echoing from the shadowy interiors of the headquarters tents, and, when the quickstep was resounding over the plain, there were accompanying noises indicating hasty toilets, great splashings of water and a series of emphatic remarks as the wet garments were put on one by one and the struggle with the boots began. Breakfast in the general's mess was promptly at seven and his colored servant let no laggard dally too long over his matutinal polish but worried him into habits of punctuality at meals. I hope that no one will notice that I do not speak of the bill of fare.

The dress parade of the different regiments was the great popular event of the day in camp and never ceased to be of the greatest interest, for the dramatic elements of the ceremony were impressive and inspiriting. Crowds of natives assembled near the parade grounds and marveled at the brown clad giants who had come from that far off republic, a country as vague and mysterious to their comprehension as if it were a part of another planet. Stalwart and hearty specimens of manhood were these soldiers and our hearts throbbed with admiration and patriotic fervor as we watched them march out with vigorous step and form the line. The warm haze of the tropical atmosphere glorified the landscape and the setting sun gilded the feathery tops of the bamboo and the symmetrical branches of the palm trees and made the dense foliage of the great manga trees vibrate with contrasting tones of violet shadows and orange lights. The Stars and Stripes flew from a tall bamboo in the headquarters camp, and as the band played the "Star-spangled Banner" and the flag was lowered, every one remembered the significance of the emblem and felt individually responsible for the perpetuation of the great idea it represented. We uncovered our heads with undisguised emotion, moved by the universal sentiment. The natives, too, began to learn that this ceremony was no perfunctory duty and we of the spectators who were among them took pains to impress upon them that they also should respect the flag as we did and they soon took off their hats whenever the national anthem was played.

Quite as impressive in another way was the mass celebrated in the open air by Father McKinnon, chaplain of the First California Regiment, under the shade of a wide spreading tree. There hundreds of devout soldiers knelt in prayer and the soft murmur of the foliage was the harmonious accompaniment of nature to the pleasant voice of the priest.

Out of consideration for the natives who frequented the beach which was practically the village street, sea-bathing was prohibited except early in the morning and late in the evening. The tide rose but once a day, and at high water when the wind was strong, the waves dashed over the roots of the trees and flooded the adjacent low places so that the beach was impassable. At all other times it was a busy promenade and our favorite diversion was to walk there and watch for the *Monterey* for it came to be known that no advance would be made until the squadron was reinforced by this impregnable vessel. Manila, when the air was clear, seemed almost within rifle shot and was always interesting to study. The flags of different nationalities flying over the houses along the shore, the fleet of foreign war vessels and the constant coming and going between them and the town encouraged constant speculation on the condition of things inside the Spanish defences.

CHAPTER V

THE quartermasters had novel and unexpected difficulties to contend with and situations, never contemplated by the compilers of that wonderful code of laws, the Army Regulations, continually obtruded themselves and had to be met often in a way which was not a gentle shock to the conventionalities of the system. The separation of the Commissariat and the Quartermaster's Department is, I am convinced, a great mistake and, under any circumstances, adds greatly to the complications of supplying an army. Even in the brief campaign near Manila where the situation, although by no means simple, presented no extraordinary difficulties, this fact was certainly prominent. In the British service, in case of movement of troops by sea, the navy takes entire charge of the transportation from high water mark at the point of departure to high water mark at the landing-place, and the army quartermaster has nothing to do but to carry on his regular and accustomed duties on shore. With us it is entirely different. The transports were hired, fitted up and loaded and the troops embarked and landed by the Quartermaster's Department.

At Cavité the chief quartermaster, Colonel Pope, had, figuratively speaking, not a leg to stand on. He was absolutely without means of transportation and, for a time, could not procure so much as a row boat for his own use. The first expedition under General Thomas M. Anderson had taken quarters at Cavité, and the second under General Francis V. Greene had successfully landed at Tambo, at a point well within range of the enemy's guns, by the way, some six miles by sea and sixteen by land from Cavité. Both these landings were made while the weather was fine and without an accident of any kind. Commodore Dewey provided a captured Spanish tug-boat, absurdly misnamed the *Rapido,* which was used to tow the *cascos* to the shore. Landing at Cavité was, of course, possible in all weathers, but at Tambo it depended on the direction and strength of the wind and sometimes for days together not even an outrigger canoe could live in the sea of the bay and no boat could run the line of breakers along the beach. It readily occurs to any one that an obvious provision against complete isolation of Camp Dewey in bad weather would have been to open communications by way of the land and if we had been facing an active enemy this would have been done of necessity. The road was certainly bad, but it was always passable and although the *carromatos* were light and small and bore no resemblance whatever to the conventional army wagon they were the only vehicles except the buffalo sledge which it would have been practicable to employ on the muddy highways for there were no mules or horses to be had and small ponies alone were in use. Compared with camel transport a *carromato* train would be most satisfactory. The only thing to be considered was the number of carts, which after all would not have been so enormous, as we found later when all the stores were hauled from Parañaque to camp in *carramatos.*

There was no field telegraph with the first and second expeditions and no line was run from Cavité to the camp until about two weeks after we arrived. This delay was due, first, to the fact that the transport which brought the material was among those which followed us and, second, to the impossibility of unloading the wire and other articles until some of the cargo had been sent ashore. The only communication with the camp was therefore, in the case of heavy weather, by means of signalling. There was always anchored quite near the beach the small captured gunboat *Callao* and, some

"RAPIDO" TOWING CASCOS WITH NEBRASKA TROOPS ASHORE FROM TRANSPORT SENATOR

distance farther out, one of the cruisers was posted as a guard-ship, and in case of emergency these vessels were to transmit signals from the signal-station on the beach to the *Olympia*, whence the message would be sent to General Merritt, whose headquarters remained on the *Newport*. Fortunately nothing serious resulted from this isolation.

The insurgents possessed all the private steam launches with the exception of the *Cañacao* which Commodore Dewey courteously put at the disposition of General Merritt and the *Albany* which Mr. Reid and I controlled. After various ineffectual attempts to secure means of water transportation, Colonel Pope finally persuaded the insurgents to part with one of their numerous launches and when it appeared it was plainly evident why they consented to let it go. It was an open boat, overladen with a boiler and engine which were insecurely fixed in place and, altogether, she was as dangerous a craft as ever navigated the bay. She lasted but a few days and then swamped. Fortunately, Colonel Pope was not on board at the time although he had risked his life on many perilous trips in the boat.

The *Rapido* belonged to the navy and would take no orders from the army except through the proper officer of the fleet. This we discovered on one occasion when General Merritt directed Colonel Pope to secure her in order to take some sick men ashore from the transports. We had the temporary loan of the *Cañacao* and started to head off the *Rapido*, which was towing some *cascos* in the direction of the camp. It was Colonel Pope's intention to order the captain of the tug to anchor the *cascos* and make a trip or two to Cavité with the invalids. The captain paid no attention to our energetic signals, but ran some distance before we ranged alongside and he slowed down. After some preliminary conversation which was rather staccato in movement, the captain yelled:

"Who in the devil are you, anyhow?"

"I'm Colonel Pope, chief quartermaster," was the reply.

"To hell with the Pope!" came back the sonorous retort. "I take my orders from Commodore Dewey. Get out of my way or I'll swamp you!" And he went on at full speed before we could get our boathook out of his rail, and we retired disconcerted and chagrined. This incident does not go to show that the navy was not ready and willing to assist the army at all times but only indicates the method of co-operation which was in practice. Of course I could only judge from the outside what were the official relations between the two branches. There was undoubtedly only one main object in view—namely, to finish up the job as expeditiously and with as little loss of life as possible. The side issues were that the navy had a record to keep up of not having lost a man or having a ship damaged, and the army had to have a chance to stretch its legs and square its shoulders and to make a reputation. Whether there was any necessity of a demonstration by land is another question which every one can settle for himself. My own opinion on that point is unalterable and the only argument I heard against the value of logical deduction from facts as they stood, which is worth repeating, is an epitomized statement of the case from the purely military point of view. In the course of a long discussion in which I stoutly maintained the opinion that Manila could have been taken without the loss of a man by a threatened bombardment and the quiet landing of a force of occupation, an officer of high rank said with not a little acrimony:

"That would have been ridiculous! It is absolutely opposed to precedent and to military principles that a town should be captured in that way. When land and naval forces are in combined action, the army must conduct its operations ashore."

A whole *carromato* train could have been driven through this argument but I saw I was trespassing and although I had the support of several of the officers present, I preferred to drop the subject.

The officers of the two services were the best of friends and if the army did not get all the help it needed it was because there was no distinct and definite request made for assistance. From the point of view of an outside observer it seemed as if there was a disinclination on the part of the army to ask the navy for favors as if it were derogatory to the dignity of the older branch of the service, and that it was only done as a last resort. There were many ways in which the sailors could have been of incalculable assistance. For example, it happened that most of the soldiers were from the West and from interior states and consequently unfamiliar with boating. The surfmen at the camp landing were mountaineers, many of whom had never handled an oar, They managed the operation with the greatest good will and a tireless and enthusiastic spirit which largely made up for their lack of practice. Landing in the surf requires sound acquaintance with the management of a boat and it could not be expected of these landsmen that the experience of a single week could convert them into trained sailors. They seldom came ashore without half filling their boats, from sheer inability to keep the bow to the breaking surf, and soon nearly all the boats were stove and lost. They were cumber· some and heavy affairs, originally belonging to the Spanish fleet, but were not ill adapted to the work.

Whenever a rowboat from the navy landed in the surf it was a great object lesson to the soldiers for she came riding in like a duck and ran up on the beach without shipping a drop of water. Skilful boatmen would have spared the soldiers much trying exposure and prevented the loss of quantities of valuable material. I was told by one of the quartermasters that he made a personal request to the commodore for the loan of some launches, which was granted so cheerfully that he was almost emboldened to ask for a detail of surf boatmen, but refrained as he did not wish to ride a free horse to death.

A suggestion for the construction of a landing stage on the beach was made to General Merritt shortly after his own experience on the shore and he ordered one to be built. There were a number of large iron lighters loaded with stone anchored near the wharf at Cavité and somewhere there was said to be a large quantity of deck planking. Here, then, was just the material which would appeal to an experienced engineer like the officer who took it in charge, who was accustomed to deal with solid masses and heavy weights.

The original suggestion was that a bamboo structure should be erected, similar in all important details to the ones which project far out into the shallow water off Malate and resist the action of the sea and wind by reason of their flexible construction, their height above the water and the little resistance which the bamboo piles offer to the waves. If this had been done a landing could have been made in all weathers, not perhaps the landing of heavy material when the sea was running very high, but a small boat could always have deposited its passengers there in safety. This scheme for a bamboo wharf was rejected and a project for building a solid pier, or rather a solid pier end with a shore connection built of timber, was adopted and preliminary steps were taken to carry it out. The commodore gave permission to use the lighters for this purpose and the lumber was forthcoming. It is all very well to have material if you have not got the tools, and a trifling defect in the arrangements nipped this enterprise in the bud and we had no landing after all. To make a start, one of the lighters was towed across the bay and anchored near the spot chosen for the position of the caisson. The usual afternoon blow came up and her ground tackle would not hold. She drifted inshore and was rescued only with the greatest toil and difficulty. It was then seen that even if the caisson was built of the

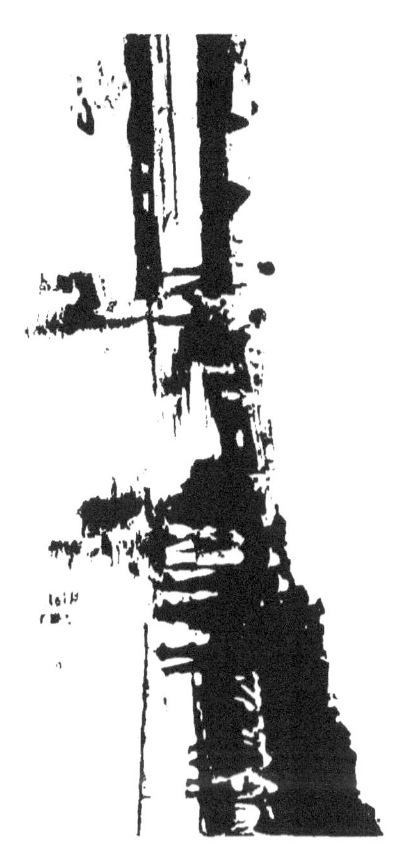

two sunken lighters the combined force of the tide and the waves would doubtless break it up in one day and besides that it would probably not be finished until after the town was captured. The permission to use the lighters, I believe, was withdrawn after this first attempt, and nothing more was heard of the plan.

Meanwhile the landing of men and supplies went on at the beach and with constantly increasing danger, for the monsoon blew stronger and stronger every day. It was usually quiet enough in the morning when the *Rapido* towed back to Cavité the empty *cascos*, but somehow the landings were almost always made in the afternoon when there was sure to be a blow.

The final important landing on the beach was made after the arrival of the transports of our expedition when five companies of the Fourteenth and four companies of the Twenty-third Regulars were sent over from Cavité, and the *Rapido*, with a string of five *cascos* in tow, arrived off the camp in the height of a gale. Each boat was full of cargo and black with men, and we watched them with some anxiety as, one by one, the great unwieldly hulks were dropped off the line and swung into the breakers. The ground tackles held for a short time then one *casco* suddenly parted her cable and she drifted rapidly ashore, broadside on, with the heavy seas breaking over her from stem to stern. The mat awnings vanished and then the bamboo platforms along the sides and when she struck the bottom she was a wild confused mass of human beings, timbers, boxes and seething waters. Many of the men were seen to strip off their clothes before she struck and plunge into the water and swim for it and, when the shock of grounding came, scores tumbled over the sides and waded ashore. She thumped and rolled and began to go to pieces at once and it seemed impossible for the men to escape injury from the floating boxes and wreckage dashed about by the waves. She was soon hard and fast and all the men were safely ashore except a few who remained to struggle with bales and packages which had not been washed out of the hold. Almost before she was deserted, wood details from the camp swooped down upon her shattered carcass and in a few minutes she was distributed piecemeal among the camp fires and nothing remained but her enormous keel, which resisted the attacks of the axemen for hours after the tide went down. The second and third *cascos* had rather better luck, as the crews managed to keep them head on and they grounded in the proper way, one at least being got off at the next tide. But they were filled with water immediately after they struck, and the men and all their paraphernalia were as wet as if they had been at the bottom of the sea.

The first man to come ashore was a bandsman with his great tuba and, as he waded through the surf holding the shining instrument high above his head, sometimes smothered with foam, with no part of him visible but his extended arms, he looked like some strange sea-god of classical fable. Profiting by the example of their comrades on the first *casco*, many of the men now took off their clothes, bunched them up and, with the bundle in one hand and rifle and equipments in the other waded ashore. Often an extra heavy wave would wrest the bundles from their grasp, but they always managed to come ashore with rifle and ammunition.

This instinctive care of weapons reminded me of a somewhat parallel experience in the lower Danube during the Russo-Turkish campaign. We were crossing the river just above the Turkish lines in two flatboats heavily laden with men and stores. A strong wind was blowing up stream and, meeting the rapid current, raised a nasty sea which swamped one of the boats in shorts order. We were so busy with saving our own skins that we were unable to help, and all in the other boat were lost except one man whom we saw bobbing down the river holding his rifle in his right hand.

GENERAL MERRITT AND STAFF ON THE BEACH AT TAMBO

Sometime after we landed this man turned up, having just managed to reach the shore. We asked him why he did not throw away his rifle to give himself a better chance.

"What should I have done if I had got ashore inside the Turkish lines without my rifle?" was his reply.

On the Tambo beach that day the brigade quartermaster, Major Jones, a man of extraordinary energy and tireless activity, was seen everywhere in the confusion of waters, helping this one to struggle ashore, directing those who had not yet left the boat and generally making heroic efforts to minimize the extent of the disaster. The shore near the landing presented as strange a panorama as the one described in the romantic episode of the capture of Lung Tung Pen. Stalwart men, as naked as they were born, wandered around among the natives quite unconscious and casual, hopeless of recovering from the greedy waters anything to cover themselves with. Here a half-drowned man was led along by his comrades toward the hospital, there a bedraggled warrior was preoccupied with an elementary toilet, vainly trying to haul on his soaked garments. Others were hanging their wet clothes on the bushes to dry; careful men were already cleaning their rifles, and those who had not shed their garments were helping the natives carry the stores out of reach of the rising tide. Everything was thoroughly drenched, even the company chests with the books and papers, and all stores which were not in water-tight tin cases were spoiled. The general appeared on the scene, and it was a ludicrous caricature of military etiquette the picture of a literally un-uniformed soldier at the salute as this officer passed. A knapsack was quite full dress on this occasion. For an hour afterwards tall white nudities were seen straggling away off among the tents seeking the camp ground assigned to the detachment just landed.

After this incident, Parañaque was chosen as a landing place, both because it was within a mile and a half of camp, and because a river entered the bay at that point. This river was navigable for *cascos* and small craft as far as the bridge of the Camino Real, a quarter of a mile or more above the mouth, and made a quiet little harbor, provided, of course, the bar could be crossed.

I happened to be trying to land here from the *Albany* with Major Thompson and some men of the Signal Corps, on the afternoon, when a battalion of the Thirteenth Minnesota Regiment was going ashore, and as the launch drew too much water to cross the bar we were obliged to go farther up the beach to Bacoor in the lee of Cavité point. Colonel Pope had managed to hire a side-wheeler called the *Kwonghoi*, which shabby craft had little that was shipshape about her except the name in gilded Chinese characters, but was a most useful adjunct to the meagre appliances under control of the Quartermaster's Department. She was anchored just outside the line of breakers, and three small navy launches, each with a large row boat in tow, were making frequent trips between the steamer and the shore. The sea was very high and breaking heavily on the bar, and on each trip it seemed absolutely certain that the boats would come to grief for the one in tow was jerked along, sometimes almost broadside on and again they would both disappear entirely in the trough of the sea, and then rise again against the sky. The expert sailors were familiar with this sort of work, and only one boat was swamped during the operation. The officer in command of the troops—Colonel Reeve, I think it was—with admirable forethought, insisted that a case of hardtack should be taken ashore in each boat, because, as he said, he was not going to let his men land as some others had done with no rations for the night and no prospect of getting any. This extra load proved to be no handicap, and the enterprising officer put in more and more each time until the row boats were half full of boxes as well as crowded with men. In this way the detachment reached camp with all their outfit and several days' rations intact. This landing was one of the most successful of all, and was managed by Major Wadsworth, a volunteer quartermaster.

Bacoor, as I have just suggested, was by far the best landing place, on account of its sheltered position, and this is probably one reason why Aguinaldo selected it as his headquarters. The sea did not run heavily near shore and a native dugout could weather the breakers in any gale short of a typhoon. It had the disadvantage, however, of being about six miles from camp, and the road was none too good between Bacoor and Parañaque, Major Jones, who had hired a large number of *carromatos* and ponies, and had an extensive corral at Camp Dewey, put a large force of natives at work on this road, corduroying it in some places with bamboo and draining it wherever it was practicable, so that it was kept in a fairly satisfactory condition. The insurgent and native traffic over this road was far more active than our own, but they made no recognizable effort to assist in this enterprise. The work was not carried out very thoroughly, probably because the inevitable fall of the town was imminent. Between Parañaque and camp the road was much better, and was generally as crowded as Broadway on a spring afternoon, with strings of *carromatos* laden with stores, with an endless procession of armed insurgents and groups of our soldiers always on the move. Parañaque is quite a large village, mostly of bamboo and *nipa* huts, but with a goodly number of substantially built houses and a large and picturesque church riddled with Spanish shells. Bacoor is much more of a town, but rather knocked about by the numerous fights which have taken place there. We had a few men of the Signal Corps stationed near the shore at the latter place, but it was not considered necessary to occupy the village with any significant force. Besides, we were on terms of amicable enmity with the insurgents and this their special covert.

The routine of the Quartermaster's Department did not, I

am free to say, interest us enough to tempt me to pay much attention to the workings of the organization, except to notice the trouble which constantly arose from the separation of it from the Commissariat. Then, too, criticism was often disarmed by the enthusiasm and energy which every one put into his appointed task. In the cool light of the perspective of time, I fancy the ultimate judgment of those among us who most criticised this department would now be that the chief difficulty lay in the status of this branch of the service, and in the unwillingness to invite the extensive co-operation of the navy. My previous experience in war had fixed in my mind the notion that the quartermaster-in-chief was the most important man in the outfit; that he was an independent autocrat who had practically unrestricted powers to carry on his work; that he could employ public funds at discretion, requisition anything which was of vital importance and, in general terms, use any means within reason to perform the task on which the efficiency of the army absolutely depended. I never had the heart to search that wonderful book, the Army Regulations, for an exact definition of the status of this department in our army, but from my own observations I concluded that it had less authority than in any other army with which I have been associated.

It is quite possible that some requisitions may have been made on the natives for labor, for supplies or for transport, but I never happened to hear of any. I know that at Camp Dewey Major Jones had considerable difficulty in hiring *carromatos* and transport animals, and the natives would often escape him after they had only carried out part of their contract, knowing that no penalty was attached to this act. There were plenty of natives ready to work, and each morning at daybreak there assembled a motley gang of several hundred near this officer's tent. They were marshalled up, and all those who had *bolas* or any other effective culling instrument or any agricultural implement suitable for road

NEBRASKA REGIMENT WADING UP THE SHORE

repairing, were hired at fifty Mexican cents a day, about three times the ordinary wages. The only shovels and pick-axes in camp were those few which belonged to the different organizations. There were over ten thousand entrenching tools in the transport *Morgan City,* but these were not landed until a day or two before the capture of the town. Neither were the much needed sand bags brought ashore until the very last.

Major Jones, with characteristic enterprise, established an open air manufactory of bamboo platforms for the tents, and a score or more of native carpenters were always at work, cutting and slashing at green bamboo poles, preparing the different pieces and lashing them together with rattan. I learned the advantage of occupying a tent with an officer, for after trying in vain to hire some one to build us a platform, large and strong enough to hold my colossal tentmate and myself, I found one day a fine structure of extra strength in place under the canvas.

I asked Colonel Potter how he managed to get this made.

"R. H. I. P.!" was his answer, with an amused expression. (Rank has its privileges.)

In a few days most of us succeeded in buying ponies at war prices from the natives, and we had quite a collection of sturdy little animals and a curiosity shop of old junk which passed for saddles and bridles. The Filipino ponies are very small and stocky, and have considerable endurance, although not so much, I am sure, as they have the credit for. Nearly all those in general use are stallions, and they are generally tremendous fighters, kicking and biting one another vi-ciously, although quiet enough to ride and drive. It has been a favorite entertainment of the inhabitants, both white and native, to pit the most vicious of these brutes against one another in the ring, a sport quite as edifying as cock-fighting and much less conventional. The price for ordinary ponies before the occupation was from $25 to $50 in Mexican currency, but the value rose at once after the demand for them began, and we seldom got them for less than double these figures. We never saw or heard of any Filipino cavalry, and the Spaniards had only a very small force of mounted men.

CHAPTER VI

FROM my account of the inspection of the lines by General
Merritt and General Greene the day after we arrived, it will
be gathered that the insurgents occupied all the available
strategic points along the front as far as we went, and the
problem, since General Merritt promptly and wisely decided
that the advance must be made over the territory near the
bay, was how to get possession of that part of the insurgents' lines nearest the shore without complicating relations
with Aguinaldo, whom the general was determined to ignore.
This was unquestionably the best field of operations, for it
did not require a change of base and had the inestimable advantage of lying in full range of the guns of the fleet.

On the afternoon of the 28th, General Greene received a
verbal message from General Merritt suggesting that he jug-
gle the insurgents out of part of their lines, always on his
own responsibility and without committing in any way the
commanding general to any recognition of the native leaders
or opening up the prospect of an alliance. This General
Greene accomplished very cleverly, dealing with the natives
exactly in accordance with their own methods. He sent for
General Noriel who commanded the force on the extreme
left, who promptly responded to the polite summons. He
then, **after** the usual interchange of courtesies, called attention to the fact that, at the point directly opposite the Spanish
fort, San Antonio de Abad, the strongest position of the enemy's lines, there was no artillery in place except an obsolete
ship's gun which, although of large calibre, was absolutely
ineffective, as it had not inflicted the slightest damage on the
Spanish defences, even if it had ever touched them at all.

This statement the visitor agreed with. Then General Greene proceeded to explain how much more it would be to the advantage of the besieging parties if the fine batteries of modern guns which were lying idle in Camp Dewey should be posted there, which would be promptly done if the insurgents gave permission to occupy the left of their line for about four hundred yards east of the shore and across the Camino Real.

General Noriel expressed himself in accordance with this view of the situation, and was ready to withdraw from that part of the front provided Aguinaldo would consent to it. At the close of the interview he said he would telegraph immediately, requesting authority to make this concession.

The reply he received from the astute leader was probably unfavorable, for he sent his chief of staff post haste to Bacoor to present the case verbally. About half past two in the morning that officer came back bringing the desired consent with a condition attached that General Greene must give a written receipt for the entrenchments handed over to him. This looked very much like a bargain concluded over a signature, and was a little more formal than General Greene thought advisable. He agreed, however, to write Aguinaldo on the following day and, meanwhile, as there was question of only a simple formality, he proposed to occupy the desired position in the early morning in order to save time. General Noriel made no objection to this arrangement and, consequently, at eight o'clock on the following day, one battalion of the Eighteenth Regulars, one battalion of the First Colorado Volunteers, and two guns from each of the Utah Light Batteries, were moved up to the front and the natives retired from their positions there without protest.

I understood at the time that General Greene sent Aguinaldo a carefully worded letter stating that he had occupied a specified part of the line, but I cannot vouch for the exact

FRANCIS V. GREENE

text of the communication. The insurgents were thus beaten at their own game, and our front was established exactly where we wished it without antagonizing our neighbors and without committing ourselves to anything except to defend the position we had occupied.

The earthworks at this point consisted of a shallow ditch about seventy-five yards long, dug straight across an open meadow between the border of trees along the shore and the Camino Real, with a platform and shelter near the middle of the low embankment where a small post had been stationed. Further, alongside the road to the west, was a small and rudely constructed embrasure in a clump of large bamboos, where the ship's gun was mounted, and down the road, a few yards nearer the enemy, a covered rifle pit. From all this part of the line the stone fort and the sandbag breastworks of the enemy were in plain sight across an open territory which was broken by a few small trees and covered with a tangle of long grass, reeds and undergrowth. East of the highway, which up to this point ran between dense bamboo hedges, there was, first, a narrow marsh quite surrounded by trees, then a bamboo thicket with an occasional hut and small garden and a succession of small jungles reaching as far as an impassable swale which extended southward nearly to the Pasay crossroad and was nowhere nearer the shore than twelve hundred yards.

The northern end of this morass was crossed by a stone dam, directly in front of the Spanish Blockhouse Fourteen, and here was posted the enemy's most advanced picket. Through the region just described the insurgents had an occasional small rifle pit, and they were established in several huts which happened to have stone foundations, which made an excellent protection. Our lines were gradually extended through this whole region, although it was not in the original concession, and extensive earthworks were constructed at various points.

About one hundred and twenty-five yards in front of the ditch first spoken of, stood a white house of two stories, the lower one of brick and the upper one of bamboo wattle and stucco, with usual shell windows on all sides and a spacious belvedere on the roof. From this building an excellent view could be had over the whole ground in front almost as far to the east as Blockhouse Fourteen, and the Spanish lines, only eight hundred and fifty yards away, were plainly visible to the extent of nearly a thousand yards. The house-contains a large chapel in which, among other things, was a large wooden statue said to be of Saint Francis, and from this circumstance it was commonly and erroneously called the Capuchin Convent. Among the trees near the beach were two other residences, one which had been the summer resort of an Englishman residing in Manila, and hence wrongly called by the soldiers the English Club, and the other had been formerly occupied by a Spanish merchant. In the first of these two houses was a piano in fairly good order, the only piece of furniture left except a fine green-glazed Shanghai bath tub, ornamented with figures in relief. This little settlement was called Maytubig. No apparent reason existed for the location of the insurgent earthworks, and General Greene decided at once to build a new and more solid entrenchment to extend on one side of the white house, past a small hut and to the beach where stood a garden gate, spoken of before, and where the great iron lighter was stranded on the beach, and in the other direction to cross the Camino Real and terminate at the edge of the marsh or swale. The great difficulty in constructing the breastwork was the character of the soil, which was a light, friable loam, and almost impossible to stack without the use of sandbags, which had not yet been landed from the transport. Moreover, water was found within sixteen inches of the surface, and, in order to make an embankment of proper height, the top of the ground had to be taken off to the depth of a spade

TYPICAL SPANISH EARTHWORKS AND SHELTER

and carried to the pile. The clods of turf obtained in this way made it practicable to build the breastwork very nearly right in profile, although a heavy shower would wash down a great deal of it. The gun embrasures, two on each side of the house, were built by using revetments of bamboo poles.

I went up to the lines shortly after daybreak on the morning after the occupation, in company with Captain Mott, who was temporarily attached to General Greene's staff, and Lieutenant Shieffelin, the general's aide-de-camp. The Colorado battalion, under Colonel McCoy, had not been relieved, and the men looked none the worse for their hard labor of the last twenty hours. The officers and soldiers were alert, cheerful and full of energy, and naturally not a little proud of their achievement, which was really extraordinary and worthy of all praise. They had moved thousands of cubic yards of earth, and had practically completed a breastwork nearly two hundred yards long and about five feet above the general level between the beach and the white house, besides making a beginning towards the road. The Utah men had thrown aside the ship's gun, and two of their pieces were temporarily placed in position in the little insurgent earthwork. There was some desultory firing that morning, but none to hurt, and the Spaniards had made no real attempt to prevent the construction of the new entrenchment, although it was in plain view and in easy range of their guns. The music of a bullet would frequently be heard, and we were told to go along round-shouldered, but our men were not replying to the fire, although they were much tempted to christen their Springfields. Just as we were leaving, a tall Colorado man with the eye of a born hunter said to an officer:—

"For God's sake let me have a shot at that fellow!" pointing at the same time in the direction from which a bullet appeared to come at frequent intervals. "Go ahead and kill him if you can!" was the reply. The soldier's expression was a study. He crawled up on the parapet and watched as one watches a deer, apparently expecting to catch sight of his enemy, somewhere near by in the bamboo. The chances were that it was only some restless picket who was firing at the white house on general principles.

We were out that morning on a tour of general inspection along the front as far as the insurgents would permit us to go, and it happened that a so-called attack had been planned by the natives, to come off at eight o'clock. After leaving our front we were obliged, being mounted, to retrace our steps a short distance and follow one of the many lanes in the thicket in order to reach a point where the insurgents had a large bronze gun which they were continually letting off day and night. We found this gun in position in a much overgrown lane running north and south. Fifty or sixty men were scattered about in the thicket near by, and the gun crew were engaged in loading. The young officer in charge received us most courteously, and after he had sighted the piece, I asked him what he was firing at.

"Singalong," he answered, pointing to the north.

Looking in that direction, I could see nothing but a tangle of bamboo, much cut and broken by shot and shell, and could discover no opening in the screen of small branches and smooth boles.

"Where is Singalong?" I asked.

"Oh, just over yonder!" he said, and prepared to fire.

Following the example of the others, we crouched on the ground, not quite knowing what was going to happen. The only protection in front of the gun was a low bank of earth perhaps three feet high. We sat, as it happened, behind a pile of powder bags which were stacked near a small clump of bamboo and covered with a mat.

The shell went tearing through the treetops and we heard it burst in the distance. In a half minute, as if by preconcerted arrangement, a return compliment came flying over

us. Immediately, without orders, the whole party sprang up and fired a ragged volley into the landscape and then crouched down again. This was answered by a perfect swarm of Mauser bullets which cracked in the bamboo like revolver shots, or went singing away to the rear to stir up our pickets there. Then the natives began to fire at will, and a sharp fusillade was kept up for a time on both sides. At last it gradually died away and stopped entirely. The officer loaded the gun again and all sat down and lighted cigarettes.

We now had an opportunity of examining the piece which was of bronze, with ornamental scrollwork on trunnions and body, and with a breech like a modern Krupp. It was marked "14 centimetres," numbered "3670," and inscribed: "Barcelona, 19 de Abril, 1803. Fondicion de Artilleria de Sevilla. Transformado in 1877." On the trunnions were the words, "Bronzes refundidos," and near the muzzle in an ornamental scroll, "Originario." It certainly deserved the latter title.

During the lull which succeeded this flutter, we jogged along the narrow byways towards the Pasay road, which leads from the village of that name to Paco, by way of the village of Singalong. As we proceeded we heard the natives calling out from their hiding places among the bushes: *"Bombas! señor. Bombas!"* to warn us that shells were flying here, but we saw nobody until we came to a rifle pit built alongside the Pasay road, and half across it, next to a hut with a stone foundation. It was now raining and we took refuge with our ponies under a shed in the rear of the hut, in the company of a half dozen insurgents and a Spanish deserter who had joined their ranks.

Across the road, perhaps a hundred yards in front of us, was a strong barricade, behind which was mounted on a heavy wooden carriage, a great columbiad, similar to the one near the seashore. No men were stationed there, but a dozen or more were in the rifle pit and behind the house, and many others were scattered through the bamboo behind the dense clumps. Suddenly we heard the boom of the bronze gun we had just left, and then a flight of shells came through the treetops and volleys, and a sputtering, followed in the same order as before, a proceeding in which all took part. Just before we arrived a shell had burst near by, and a small fragment had scored one young fellow across the chest, making a deep scratch four or five inches long. He was very proud of this, and displayed it for our benefit. To our surprise we saw no other wounded man, and it was difficult to understand why casualties were not frequent, there was such an incessant singing and cracking of bullets.

The regular lull did not last long this time, and before we could mount, the racket began again and continued with very brief intervals for an hour or more, so we were compelled to lie low like the others and wait, passing the time as best we could with camp gossip. At last, about eleven o'clock, the men said it was breakfast time, and part of them started down the road towards Pasay. We prepared to follow, but while we were unhitching our ponies the fusillade began again, and the squad came tumbling back, laughing as if they had been caught in a sudden shower. We finally got tired of the game and weary of seeing nothing, and rode off down the road, quickening our pace as we heard the little missiles in the air, and soon dodged into Pasay, where the streets were deserted and everybody in shelter because some men had been hit there. The insurgents had about three hundred and fifty men in the firing line that morning, covering a front of half a mile or more, and they wasted about eighty shots per man. Thus they celebrated their retirement from Maytubig. From the rifle pit on the roadside where we passed the morning, or, better, from the barricade up the road, it was possible to sneak through gardens and in the shelter of hedges up to a little hut which stood on the east

INSURGENTS FIGHTING IN UNDERGROWTH

side of the road near the corner where it makes a sharp turn to the right. Underneath the hut there was a low embankment of earth and, crawling behind that and discreetly looking over, we could see Blockhouse Fourteen right opposite across an open space only one hundred and eighty yards distant. The number "14" on a square of tin was prominently displayed on the front as if to inform the besiegers that they must call it by its proper designation. The little structure was exactly like all the others which had been built in haste a short time before. It was two stories high, made of two-inch plank, and with a small cupola or lookout on the apex of the pointed roof. It was only about twenty-five feet square, and of proportionate height. The second story was protected by a jacket of cement held in place by planks, with frequent loop holes. The lower story was half hidden by a high sandbag breastwork with ditch outside, and the general line of earthworks, which ran straight from the corner of the cemetery near the stone fort and was continuous with the exception of a break at the stream flowing from the dam across the morass, turned abruptly around the blockhouse at an acute angle and disappeared in the bamboo. Some field guns were in position to the east of the blockhouse. The works to their whole extent were provided with comfortable bamboo platforms and *nipa* shelters, and were strengthened every few yards by solid transverses.

When there was no active firing it was possible to mount to the floor of the hut which was fixed at a height of about five feet from the ground on stout posts which were planted in the earth and extended to the eaves. The slightest noise or a careless exposure would draw the Spanish fire, and a shower of bullets at this close range would riddle the walls. This had been done so often that there was not a hand's breadth of surface which did not have one hole or more in it. Scores of bullets lay on the floor, where patches and spatters of dried blood testified to real tragedies which had been enacted on this diminutive stage. I never ventured into this advanced place except on one occasion a few days after our visit to the rifle pit near by. At that time the insurgents were building a small masked earthwork between the hut and some other buildings not far off, where the Astor Battery took their position on the day of the capture of the town.

Work on the entrenchment at Maytubig continued without interruption all day Friday, Saturday and Sunday, and by that time it was finished across the road and a short distance beyond where it terminated in a bamboo hedge running north and south. The four guns of the Utah batteries under Captains Young and Grant were in position with as good embrasures as it was possible to build without sand bags.

On Sunday, the 31st of July, sharing the general belief that there would be no excitement at the front, as our men had orders to act strictly on the defensive and to refrain from firing unless they were attacked vigorously, I went aboard the *Newport*. The *Albany*, by arrangement with Mr. Reid, was to be sent for me at one o'clock, to take me back to camp. She did not appear at the appointed time and, as there was no communicating with Cavité by boat or by signal, there was nothing to do but to wait. At two o'clock I thought the delay was a piece of good luck, for the smoke of a steamer broke the horizon beyond Corregidor and soon our transports came in sight, the *Indiana* leading and followed by the *Morgan City*, the *Ohio*, the *City of Para*, and the *Valencia*. Cheer after cheer was exchanged as the vessels, black with men, one by one dropped anchor and signalled to the *Newport* their brief reports of the voyage. There was no unusual illness and only five men had died on the trip.

The transports were scarcely anchored before we noticed a great column of smoke rise from Manila somewhere in the direction of the business quarters, and it increased in volume until it seemed as if the whole district north of the Pasig must be on fire. Every few minutes great spurts and jets of flame would rise suddenly, like the eruption of a volcano, and the whole landscape to the north was soon hidden by a slowly drifting screen of black smoke. The conflagration lasted for three or four hours and then gradually subsided having spread, as far as we could judge, over a very large tract.

The excitement of the afternoon so preoccupied my attention that the non-arrival of the *Albany* did not worry me much until toward evening, when I began to suspect that the wily native skipper was up to some trick. It afterwards turned out that he had discovered, early in the morning, that an important bolt was missing from a part of the engine, and he could not move until he had got another one made. We had been working him too hard.

When the sun set, I found myself a prisoner for the night, because no craft was permitted to move in the bay after dark, except the patrol boats. The evening was wet, and we were allowed no lights in the saloon, so we sat and chatted for hours in the darkness, for some reason or other feeling disinclined to go to bed. Shortly after eleven there was the sound of heavy firing at the front, and sometimes we could see long continued flashes among the trees, apparently at Maytubig. This went on until long after midnight, and then ceased. The trickery of the captain of the *Albany* had lost me an interesting night on shore.

Awakened very early in the morning by an indefinable sense of anxiety, I took a shadowy breakfast with Colonel Pope, who had been ordered to go to Cavité at daybreak. I was, of course, only too anxious to accompany him, and we went on deck and watched for a launch. None appeared. Finally, hearing General Merritt moving about in his room, I went there and asked him if there was any possible means of communicating with Cavité, offering as an excuse for my early visit my anxiety to get to camp to learn about the affair of the night, and remarking at the same time that Colonel Pope, who had been directed to go ashore at daybreak, was unable to leave the ship for lack of transportation. He replied that there was no means of getting word to Cavité until the *Cañacao* came, and that if I wanted to go to camp, I would do well to accompany General Babcock on the *Concord*, which was going to pick up some of General Greene's officers and run up to Malabon to see if it were practicable to land troops there. I was only too glad to accept this offer, and landed in the camp from the *Concord* about nine o'clock.

The following day there was a signal service established between the *Newport* and Cavité.

In twenty-four hours the greatest change imaginable had come over the men in camp. We saw and felt it the moment we landed, even before we had been told the story of the night. There was no longer that look of the excursionist about them. They were as restless as ever, but no one was playing pranks or retailing stale jokes. They were thinking of something else. The hospital tents, crowded with wounder, many of them in a bad way, were now the centre of interest. The operating table was still busy. The surgeons were serious and preoccupied. They were half worn out with the labors of the night. Surgeon-Major Crosby and his assistants had been operating for hours, standing ankle deep in the water which flooded the hospital tents.

The picnic was over. Everybody felt this, and it was a salutary feeling. The men were learning that war is a serious business, which it is. Very few of those at the front during the night had ever been in action before. The experience was very trying, but it made men of them. They could no longer be called "tin-soldiers", they felt like veterans, for they had stood fire, and fire in the darkness too, and on strange ground.

What had happened was this: Shortly after eleven o'clock, in the height of a tempest, the enemy suddenly opened a terrific fire all along the line, with both artillery and infantry. The Tenth Pennsylvania Volunteers and four guns of the Utah Light Batteries were in the trenches. For a moment they did not reply, as they were ordered strictly to act only on the defensive, but the firing indicated a determined effort to drive them cut, and they returned it vigorously, aiming at the flashes as well as they could. The darkness was impenetrable, a gale was blowing and torrents of rain were falling. The men were unfamiliar with the ground in front of them, and few of them knew the general plan of the enemy's lines. The officers had maps, but in the storm they were of little use. All the guide they had was the apparent direction of the firing, and this was often deceptive. They expended a great deal of ammunition to be sure, but probably no more than the enemy, who had been fighting for months, but they carried themselves like veterans and never dreamed of yielding an inch of ground. By the direction of the bullets which came in great numbers from the right, it was believed that the Spaniards were advancing to attack the flank which was unprotected, the entrenchment ending without a returning angle at the edge of the open marsh just beyond the road. When the bullets struck the house or the breastworks, or the bushes in front, they made a cracking noise like the sound of a Mauser rifle, and this made the men think the enemy was close at hand. In the darkness and storm the mistake was natural. Colonel Hawkins decided then to throw out a force on the right to meet the supposed flank movement, and Major Cuthbertson led E, D and K companies out into the marsh where they stood for a long time, exposed to a severe fire, unable even to see the flashes of the enemy's rifles on account of the screen of trees, and lost man after man. Their cartridge belts were almost empty, but they held their ground until it was evident that the enemy was not advancing. Meanwhile messengers were sent to the camp through a zone of fire seven hundred yards or more in extent, with urgent calls for ammunition and supports.

When the first of these men came floundering back to the Pasay cross roads where H Battery of the Third Regular Artillery was on picket and in reserve under Lieutenant Krayenbuhl, that force was all ready to move to the front, and promptly did so, sending word back to camp that they had gone on. One man was wounded mortally before they started. The Second Battery of the same regiment, under Captain Hobbs, turned out as soon as the firing was heard, at the order of Captain O'Hara, commanding the battalion, and was on its way to the assistance of their comrades before word to move reached their camp from headquarters.

The messengers arrived from the front, reporting that the Pennsylvanians were wiped out, and that the ammunition was gone, but that the position was still held. *Carromatos* with a fresh supply of cartridges were hurried away, and the hospital corps went in search of the wounded at the field hospitals already established in the trenches. The greatest activity prevailed in the camp, and every man was eager to be ordered forward, undeterred by the discouraging reports of the fight.

General Greene, while he did not fully credit the somewhat hysterical information he received at first, knew, of course, that a sortie was possible, and ordered a battalion of the First California Volunteers into the trenches, and the remainder of the regiment, with the First Colorado Volunteers, to advance to a point just outside the danger zone, where they would be held in reserve. The firing became more regular and less continuous and slowly diminished until it ceased altogether. The general was in the trenches himself during the latter part of the trouble, and for an hour or two after, and was fully convinced that no sortie had been made.

The trip of the *Concord* to Malabon, which was temporarily interrupted by the visit to camp, when there was some delay in finding the officers to accompany the little expedition, did not turn out to be productive of any more valuable results than the confirmation of the report that the bar off Malabon was impassable in heavy weather. We cruised along a mile or two from the shore, past the scene of the previous night's conflict, past Malate, Ermita, the walled town, the breakwater off the mouth of the Pasig, the suburbs of Binondo and Tondo, successively, and up to a point in the low coast where a great area of white water marked the dangerous bar. Then we turned back past the fleet of foreign warships to the anchorage at Cavité, and I returned to camp, landing this time with great difficulty, in plenty of time to interview the heroes of the first fight before nightfall.

My friends of the Third gave me the most lucid and complete account of the affair, and the officers stoutly maintained that not a man of the enemy had left the shelter of the earthworks. This was also the impression of the rank and file, many of whom told how they had at first mistaken the crack of the bullets for the report of a rifle close at hand. Not one held out that he had caught sight of a moving object in front of the lines. Captain Hobbs, who bears the marks of the Wilderness campaign, where he was twice wounded seriously, had a curious experience which quite upset prevailing theories about the action of the small calibre, high-velocity bullet. On the way up the road, he was struck in the left thigh and was knocked down. Finding no wound and his leg not being disabled, he thought a spent ball had hit him, and he paid no more attention to it. The next day, after returning to camp, about twelve hours after the incident, his leg felt a little stiff, so he looked to see if it had been bruised. A bullet had passed completely through the muscles back of the left femur, leaving only a very slight mark on the skin on either side of the leg.

It is often asserted that a really brave man can have no imagination, but this theory had no confirmation at Camp Dewey. Several volunteer officers assured me that they had seen the Spaniards crawling about in the undergrowth within fifty yards of our lines, and one related, in all seriousness, how he went over the ground immediately in front of the breastworks in the early morning, and there he found great pools of fresh blood in the grass. The fight, as I have said, took place in a heavy rain which lasted for hours and half flooded the country. Another tale, still more extraordinary,

SPANISH SOLDIERS IN BAMBOO AMBUSH

was repeated for several weeks after and confirmed by at least two alleged witnesses. An officer and two friends went out along the Camino Real beyond the earthworks two days after the first affair and they counted fifty-odd dead Spaniards and actually brought back a skull in proof of the story. White ants, they asserted, had in forty-eight hours cleaned one skeleton entirely. This heap of slain was not more than fifty or sixty yards from the breastworks but no sign of the presence of the corpses was noticed in the lines. Imagination or no imagination there is no doubt that the men, both volunteers and regulars, had the most important qualities which distinguish good soldiers. They were cool, determined, obedient and intelligent, brave even to recklessness, and took to fighting as naturally as barbarians. The troops at Manila exemplified in a most striking manner a military paradox, for they were undisciplined and yet with the best possible discipline. By this I mean that they had not at that time ac-quired the training which is usually considered of prime ne-cessity to the soldier, but they understood the importance of perfect obedience to orders, knew when to take independent action and when to sink their individuality in the interests of the mass.

All preparations were made that day for a repetition of the affair of the night before, and the First Colorado Volunteers under Colonel Hale occupied the trenches. Shortly after nine in the evening the firing began and went on increasing and diminishing in volume at intervals for an hour or more and then stopped. Although the men were kept fairly well in hand, it was absolutely impossible to prevent them, in their state of nervous tension, from returning the enemy's fire, but they were able after a little flutter to sit and take it calmly. The electric lights on the water-front, which had given the city such a festive appearance went out that even-ing, a circumstance which stimulated the belief that an important movement was projected by the enemy. The Colorado men lost that night one killed and three wounded.

It rained in torrents pretty much all night and when the three battalions, two from the First Nebraska Volunteers and one from the Eighteenth Regulars, went out to the front the next morning to relieve the Colorado men they had to wade all the way, through ankle deep mud, and found the trenches in a most discouraging state of miry discomfort. The misery of a long day of waiting with only the diversion of hard labor with pick-axe and shovel or the preoccupation of trying to keep comfortable, was not the best preparation for the night. When the darkness settled down so dense that treetops could scarcely be distinguished against the sky, the men naturally became hypersensitive to impressions, and every bush and clump of grass stirred by the wind gave a little start to the nerves. When the firing began that night, what with the darkness, the storm, and the peculiar cracking of the bullets, these men, too, were convinced that the enemy was advancing and they returned the fire actively for a half hour or more, expending much ammunition, particularly the Regulars. The losses, one killed and seven wounded, fell all upon the Nebraska men.

Having experienced by daylight what a so-called attack was like, I naturally held the opinion from the first that these night affairs were quite the same as the insurgent "attack," we had watched a day or two before, a continuance in fact, of the tactics which had been practised by both sides during their entire campaign. There had been almost no fighting in the open, and the Spaniards had gradually been driven out of their advanced posts in the rough country, unable to oppose with disciplined troops the insurgents' methods. The natives were familiar with every inch of the territory, were perhaps superior in numbers, certainly more active and enterprising, and, hiding in ambush everywhere, so worried the Spaniards by constant peppering by day and by fusillades

COLORADO REGIMENT KNEELING ON THE BEACH TO FIRE

FIRST ADVANCE OF COMPANY I OF THE COLORADO REGIMENT THROUGH
THE GRASS

at night that they were forced at last to establish themselves in a line where the annoyances of this system of fighting were reduced to a minimum and where communications were easy. When the Spaniards saw the new entrenchments at Maytubig growing stronger day by day they believed, of course, that we were preparing to attack their works near the fort, and, knowing that this was scarcely to be undertaken in the daytime, at least without the co-operation of the fleet, they were in constant anticipation of an assault by night.

It is always safe to presume that the enemy is quite as much afraid of you as you are of him, and the belief that he is much more so is a powerful moral support. This does not often occur to green troops and probably was not a prevalent notion among our men.

One strong argument against the general idea that the enemy attempted to assault our positions at Maytubig was the knowledge that if they really made an effort to drive us out, their only chance of success was by an advance from the strong salient at Blockhouse Fourteen where they had opposed to them only a scattered force of insurgents with slight defences. Protected on both flanks by impassable morasses and streams and well under cover of a thick growth of trees, it was possible for the Spaniards to advance without meeting with any serious obstacle in the way of an earthwork into the village of Pasay, and thus threaten our rear at Maytubig and the unfortified camp, so that a general action would be brought on at a place where the fleet could give no effective aid to our resistance and from which our troops could not retreat, for there was no place for them to go. A sortie would have been only a dramatic flourish, to be sure, and would have had no effect on the ultimate result of the campaign. But conspicuous drama is often played in war with no greater results than the Spaniards might have expected reasonably from this move. The sortie of Osman Pasha at Plevna is an example of this.

Now the officers of the Third held tenaciously to their opinion that the Spaniards had never left their works in these night affairs, forming their judgment largely on their experience in the trenches on the night of the 31st. When the battalion went up to the front again on the 3rd of August, the day of the disastrous landing on the beach, Lieutenant Krayenbuhl said to me as we were paddling through the mud of the Camino Real:

"You can sleep to-night, for there won't be any firing."

I was amused a few moments later at the speech of a sergeant, the same one who had instructed his men how to behave at Honolulu. Transmitting the orders from the officers, he said:

"Now you fellows, look a-here! You're not to load your guns unless I order you to, and if we begin to fire I don't want to see you sittin' down on your hunkers in the mud and shooting into the wide, wide world, but I want you to prance right up on top of the breastwork and give them dagos hell!"

Not observing any entrenching tools carried by the men I asked Lieutenant Krayenbuhl, who was very keen about the construction of the breastworks, how many implements they had.

"We have two spades, one shovel and one pickaxe," he replied, "but we hope to borrow some more from the Nebraska boys!"

"How are you going to cut bamboo?" I asked.

"We'll have to bite it off if we can't get any axes," he said.

I hurried back to camp and, luckily, was able to send a note to the *Newport* in which I urged a friend to notify the proper officer that the men were sent up to the front to dig trenches, practically unprovided with implements, calling his attention at the same time to the fact that ten thousand entrenching tools were rusting in the hold of the *Morgan City* and from the character of the packages in which such articles are shipped would probably be found on the top of the cargo. In the postscript I suggested that perhaps the bales of coffee sacks which were greatly needed for sand bags might possibly have been used to stow the entrenching tools with.

The Third came back to camp the next morning without having fired a shot.

Neither the weather, nor the discomforts of the trenches nor the trying experience of sitting still under the enemy's fire which was more and more impressed on the men as their duty, acted in the slightest degree as a deterrent to the great zeal of the troops to take an active part in the business, and the different organizations received their orders to go to the front with an enthusiasm as inspiriting as it was genuine. Considerable annoyance and no little jealousy were felt by those who, for some good reason, were not called upon in what they thought to be their turn. The men of the Astor battery, particularly, felt left out of it all and were much humiliated by their enforced idleness. They carried no rifles and therefore could not act as infantry, and there was absolutely no room in the trenches for the emplacement of their guns. So they were obliged to eat their hearts out in camp. They ceased to sing in their old way, and the chorus—"Zum! We are natural-born soldiers," etc., was no longer heard, and a new version, "For they're a lot of tin soldiers!" was once ventured upon by a mischievous fellow of another organization. If he had been caught he would have been flayed alive.

They were encouraged somewhat by the belief that, sooner or later they would have a chance to christen their pet Hotchkiss guns, and busied themselves in putting their fixed ammunition in order. A quantity of brown prismatic powder was obtained from the admiral and this they broke up into the proper size with ordinary carpenters' tools. The brass cases had to be cleaned out, carefully dried and re-charged, for they were filled with a black pasty mass of wet gunpowder. So great was their eagerness to be prepared for emergencies, that they refilled all their spoiled cartridge cases in twelve hours after they got the powder.

While the explosive was forthcoming one of the men who was prowling about restlessly brought word that there was a considerably quantity of powder abandoned by the insurgents at the bronze gun. A detail was at once sent up to secure it and a dozen or more large well filled flannel bags were brought back and safely deposited in the ammunition tent. Before they could use it, a squad of insurgents with an officer came hurrying into camp in search of the ammunition of their bronze gun which they asserted had been stolen by our men. The property was traced easily, of course, and Captain March was obliged to let them carry it away, for they explained with great volubility that the gun crew had only gone away to breakfast and when they returned to their post they found every charge of powder had disappeared.

In these first days of what might be called active operations, the sobering effect of the casualties was felt strongly. There was no sunshine to cheer up the camp; the skies were dull, gray, and lowering; the ground was soaked and half flooded, and violent winds unceasingly drove the rain into the open shelter, pitilessly drenching the men and all their possessions.

The plot first used for a burial ground was in a walled enclosure around a large building in the hamlet of Malabay quite near the camp, just beyond the Camino Real and across the Parañaque river. The natives objected to this site, and a few days later a small piece of waste land on the west bank of the stream was enclosed by a bamboo fence and the bodies first buried were then taken to the new burial ground. No more depressing and dismal sight have I ever seen than these funeral ceremonies. Services were held by the chaplain over the body in a tent in camp and then a long line of soldiers, four of them bearing a stretcher with the body wrapped in a gray army blanket and draped with the Stars and Stripes, moved slowly across the camp-ground and wound its way through the muddy lane to the burial place. Here, in a grave already dug in the sodden, water-soaked earth, the limp form was deposited. No funeral mutes ever looked so grewsome as the soldiers draped in the rigid folds of black ponchos with the campaign hats beaten over their faces by the pouring rain. A short, earnest prayer and a few appreciative words by the chaplain at the grave, the three sharp volleys and the long mournful notes of the bugle which haunted the memory ever after, made up the final episode of each tragedy. The surroundings so out of harmony with all our experiences and traditions made it all seem uncanny and unreal. The sense of our wide separation of distance and time from home and home friends; the uncertainties of the future; the ever-present sense of responsibility and, above all and stronger than all the overwhelming and unwelcome consciousness that these lives were wasted, filled our minds with vague apprehensions and our hearts with oppressive sadness. Never can I forget the wail of that bugle as it broke the dull murmur of the storm and, with ruffled echo, carried the mournful accents of this final tribute to a comrade's heroism far into the depths of the jungle and across the great encampment to the tossing waters of the bay where it was lost in the deep roar of the waves.

CHAPTER VIII

CAMP rumor, for once quite correct, had it that, soon after
the arrival of the *Monterey*, there would be a change in the
situation, and eager watchers on the beach let no sign of
smoke escape their notice. About ten o'clock in the morning of the 4th of August the unmistakable outlines of the
monitor were seen in the distance and half the camp flocked
to the shore and cheered and shouted with joy as she rounded
to and dropped anchor near the flagship.

Up to this time we had lost twelve killed and fifty-two
wounded.

Would the navy ever wake up and act? Would the thirteen-inch guns of the *Monterey* knock the sand out of those
embrasures which so impudently stand across the marsh at
Maytubig? Would we be allowed to fight instead of sitting
like so many bumps on a log to be shot at by the Spaniards?
Would this pottering and useless waste of life now stop and
we be allowed to make one clean job of it? A thousand
questions, which nobody could answer, flew around the
camp, many and ingenious were the speculations and wild
beyond every belief were the reports of peace negotiations
in progress and of the imminent unconditional surrender of
the Spanish forces. Smoke from some insignificant conflagration in the native quarter of the suburbs started the rumor that the Spaniards were burning the walled town and a
white-cross flag discovered flying somewhere in Malate
started the report of a threatened bombardment by the fleet.
The extinction of the electric lights along the Luneta which
proved to be final, was considered full proof that in a few
hours something decisive would soon occur. The camp was

SPANISH SOLDIERS ON BALCONY OF BARRICADED HOUSE

in a fever of expectation, but the soldiers had not yet learned
their whole lesson. The Pennsylvanians were in the trenches
that night.

The next day the field telegraph came along through the
camp at a pace which indicated that this branch of the service was well up to its work. I caught sight of the men as
they passed with a *carromato* loaded with coils of insulated
wire, and as soon as I could shed my clogs and get into my
boots I ran after them. They were out of sight beyond the
camp before I could catch them and I had to follow the wire
to find out where they were. They simply unrolled the
thickly coated wire along the ground, fastening it to trees
beyond reach when they came to a path or to the entrance of
an enclosure, and then went on at a fast walk straight along
between the Camino Real and the trees near the beach and
up to the trenches where they established their headquarters
in the rear of the Capuchin house and constructed there a
partially bomb-proof shelter.

General Greene went off in the forenoon towards Parañaque, and rumor had it that he had gone on board the *Olympia*
to arrange with the admiral for a combined attack on the
Spaniards without delay. The news had leaked out that the
general had a box of blue lights in his quarters and the theory was advanced that these were to be used to signal to the
Raleigh, which vessel had replaced the *Boston* as a guard
ship off the landing, whenever the army was prepared to
make a night assault under cover of the guns of the fleet,
thus paying the enemy back in its own coin but at a larger
ratio of value than that which existed between the Mexican
and the United States dollar. It was remarkable what a
strain of truth ran through the common gossip of the camp,
particularly at this time when everybody was on the watch
for any indication, however slight, of what was going on.

The fact was that the general had gone aboard the *Olympia,* but not by any means to arrange for a combined attack

of the army and navy. He was very much distressed at the loss of life in the trenches which, although apparently unavoidable, was quite useless, and he was very anxious to put a stop to it. He accordingly wrote General Merritt urging him to request the admiral to send the *Monterey* to batter down the stone fort opposite our lines in order to teach the enemy a lesson which would probably put an end to their picket firing and fusillades. General Merritt handed the letter over to Admiral Dewey and sent for General Greene to come to Parañaque, where he met him with his steam launch and carried him on board the *Newport*. It was then decided that General Greene should explain the situation in person to Admiral Dewey and accordingly he had an interview with him on the flagship. The admiral was not willing to entertain the proposition submitted, for various reasons. First, the monitor was not in good working condition after her long voyage; second, because he thought it injudicious to wake up the twenty-four centimetre Krupp guns on the water front at Manila until both the floating batteries of thirteen-inch guns had joined the squadron, and lastly, because he was sure that the army was not ready for a forward movement, because a large part of General MacArthur's brigade had not yet landed on account of the storm. At the same time he deplored the loss of life and expressed his willingness, in case of any move of the enemy which seriously threatened the force in camp, to order the *Boston*, the *Raleigh*, the *Charleston*, and the *Monterey*, all of which vessels were under steam day and night, to bombard the Spanish works. Notice could be given the camp by flag signal by day and by a blue light at night.

I have since learned that he also suggested that the trenches be evacuated or, if held at all, to be occupied with a very small force, but this General Greene was by no means willing to do for such a movement would have had the worst possible effect on the men.

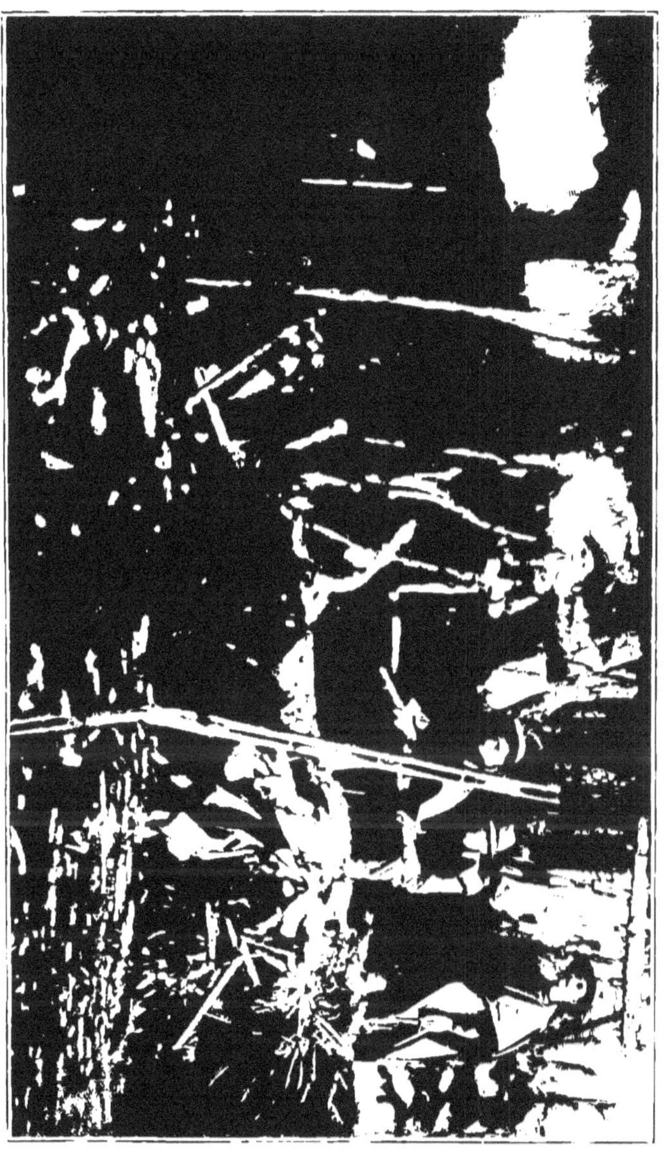

IN THE TRENCHES

General Greene came back to camp before dinner time rather tired after his excursion, uncommunicative and depressed, as I thought.

The arrival of the *Monterey* and the comparative quiet of the past two nights had made it more hopeful that the ineffective and annoying disturbances at the front had now ceased. We were quietly chatting in the mess tent after dinner when a steady rattle of small arms, punctuated by an occasional deeper report, suddenly began. The field telegraph had been established in an adjoining tent and here the officers of the brigade staff and of the signal corps assembled. The news came quickly that an attack of the enemy was in progress.

One battalion of the First Nebraska Volunteers and one from the Twenty-third and one from the Fourteenth Regulars were in the trenches.

The little tent interior made a most dramatic picture. General Greene was busy writing at a camp desk or dictating orders to Captain Bates, chief of staff. The telegraph operators were preoccupied with the instrument near a small petroleum lamp. Now and then an orderly entered, saluted and delivered a letter or a brief verbal report. The triangle of ruddy light with its ever-changing group in a strong Rembrandtesque effect of light and shade and framed by the impenetrable darkness, was occasionally veiled by a screen of drifting rain like the gauze curtain in front of a *tableau vivant*. The tent was the focus of intense human interest, for there was serious work at the front and the pulse of the action was immediately felt in the tent through the agency of the slender wire. The rattle and splutter continued without cessation. Messengers arrived for ammunition which was speedily loaded into *carromatos* and sent to the front. The native drivers were reluctant to face the danger and often had to be threatened before they would move. One young fellow cried bitterly as he drove away.

Written orders were sent here and there into the darkness of the camp where all was quiet and calm.

I endeavored to persuade two of the men from the front to take something to eat, as they seemed pretty well worn out.

"We haven't any time to eat," they replied. "We've got to get back to help out."

They had run a mile and a half in the mud, a good third of the way under a hot fire, and were only too eager to face the danger again and to rejoin their comrades.

In the height of the excitement the telegraph instrument suddenly ceased to work. The current was undoubtedly broken.

"I'll go up and see what the matter is," quietly remarked young Corporal Brazier of the Signal Corps, and off he started in the gloom. A half hour passed, perhaps more—it seemed hours, indeed—and then the cheery "tick, tick" began again. The corporal had followed up the wire, groping his way along until he came to a place where it had been cut by a bursting shell and here, in the storm and the darkness and under a rain of bullets, he had repaired the break. He presently returned and quickly resumed his work. He was made sergeant, for he had well earned a promotion.

A single visit to the trenches at night satisfied my curiosity and I never repeated the experience. There was little to see, a good deal to hear at times, and nothing to do but to sit in the rain and try to be cheerful, an effort which palled considerably as the hours wore on. Once in the lines, the high earthworks gave ample protection so the element of danger was scarcely to be considered by a non-combatant. The darkness was so intense that all sorts of incidents of a serious nature might go on without being known except to those near the spot. I was surprised at the number of men crowded into the limited space, often as many, indeed, as three to the running yard, far too many, it seemed to me, for

WHITE HOUSE IN THE AMERICAN LINES, NEAR MAYTUBIG, USED BY GENERAL
GREENE AS HEADQUARTERS ON THE DAY OF THE CAPTURE OF MANILA

convenience or for effective action. They literally fell over one another at times. I remembered on the occasion of my visit, an evening in the trenches before Plevna, when one of Skobeleff's fights was in progress. Lieutenant Greene and I were then astonished at the small number of Russians who were expected to hold the earthworks, certainly not more than one soldier to ten yards. Every few minutes an officer came along to see that his men were all attentive and once he ran along breathlessly crying:

"Here they come! Here they come! Look out children! Look out!"

We almost felt lonesome in those trenches.

At Maytubig there was, if anything, an excess of company. The white house and the hut had plenty of lodgers, and there was no space to let.

Although Manila was invested by land and blockaded by sea there was a certain amount of recognized communication with the town through the agency of the foreign fleet. Occasionally, too, foreigners had permission to enter or to leave the town and twice or three times several Englishmen in business in Manila came aboard the *Newport*. They were very reticent about the situation in the town, evidently considering themselves bound in honor not to impart any information at all, but they did not deny that they had a full larder themselves or contradict the statement that the inhabitants were reduced to eat horseflesh. The Belgian consul, M. André, was apparently the recognized official messenger between the belligerents and it was reported that he was earnestly trying to persuade the Spanish authorities to surrender the place and avoid further loss of life. He afterwards told me that this was so and that the governor-general refused to consider the proposition, declaring that Spanish honor was at stake and this would be compromised in the eyes of the world if he surrendered the place without a fight. M. André aptly remarked to me that this was a *façon de parler* and that he knew at the time they would continue to make that assertion as long as they found any one to believe it. His negotiations to this end came to nothing, because they were always blocked by the high sounding phrase: "Spanish honor," and the drama went on.

It was to be expected that this general situation should create distrust and suspicion on the part of those who were carefully observing events with various means of obtaining information not always within the cognizance of the authorities. It is the business of a correspondent to get information, not always, of necessity for publication, be it remarked. I have noticed that when the chief actors themselves put pen to paper after the event, as they are almost always tempted to do nowadays, they disclose by far more of the inside workings of the machinery than a correspondent would ever be justified in doing. Some of us at Manila felt very strongly that there was a great deal going on *sub rosa* which would never be made public, not for the reason that the integrity of any person would be compromised thereby but the drama which was evidently being planned for public entertainment on this stage of the world would lose most of its effective incidents if the skeleton of the plot were exposed. This idea arose in great part from the knowledge of the fact, patent to all, that Admiral Dewey could, now that there was a sufficient army of occupation on the spot, force the surrender of Manila at any time he chose. The impression that the gallery was being played to, so to speak, was confirmed by various scraps of information more or less authentic of which one was suggestive at least. This was the statement that the governor-general in Manila had written in his own hand a suggestion of the manner in which the town should be occupied by the American troops. There was nothing particularly startling in this report for such a proceeding is by no means unusual on the eve of inevitable surrender of a place where every effort must be made to protect the interests of private individuals and to spare innocent lives. Still, after all, it scarcely seemed worth while to keep up the fiction that we were engaged in a serious campaign on the land, at least. If General Merritt had taken the field or even if he established his headquarters at Cavité, the deception would have been less apparent. All this made the business on the land, which was, as I have shown, deadly serious to those engaged in it, seem an almost bombastic display which was greatly to be deplored because it was costing valuable lives and much treasure.

Newspapers were frequently brought out of Manila and in the one of August 5 we read that the Madrid government, by a telegram dated July 24, had removed his excellency, the Lieutenant-General Basilo Augustin Davila, from his position as governor-general and captain-general of the archipelago and general in command of the troops, and had appointed to succeed him his excellency General of Division Don Fermin Jaudenes Alvarez the second in command. Further, that the latter had, by virtue of his new authority, appointed his excellency General of Division Francesco Rizzo second in command, and General Monet to succeed the latter in his position as general of division. The same paper also contained the information that the King of Spain, in a telegram dated July 21 thanked the soldiers at Manila for their heroic services, and promised handsome rewards to those who might perform deeds of valor in the cause of the country. An army order was also quoted which instructed the sick and wounded to recover as soon as possible so that the ranks of the soldiers in the trenches might be filled. No such order was needed at Camp Dewey, it is needless to add.

The character of the gentleman just supplanted in his important office was chiefly known to the public by a remarkable proclamation which he had issued only a week before the destruction of the Spanish fleet. It read in translation, as follows:

"Extraordinary Proclamation by the Governor-General of the Philippines.

"Spaniards: Between the United States and Spain hostilities have broken out. The moment has arrived to prove to the world that we possess the spirit to conquer those who, pretending to be loyal friends, take advantage of our misfortunes and abuse our hospitality, using means which civilized nations count unworthy and disreputable.

"The North American people, constituted of all the social excrescences, have exhausted our patience and provoked war, with their perfidious machinations, with their acts of treachery, with their outrages against the law of nations and international conventions.

"The struggle will be short and decisive. The God of victories will give us one as brilliant and complete as the righteousness and justice of our cause demand. Spain, which will count upon the sympathies of all the nations, will emerge triumphantly from this new test, humiliating and blasting the adventurers from those states that, without cohesion and without a history, offer to humanity only infamous traditions and the ungrateful spectacle of chambers in which appear united insolence and defamation, cowardice and cynicism.

"A squadron manned by foreigners, possessing neither instruction nor discipline, is preparing to come to this archipelago with the ruffianly intention of robbing us of all that means life, honor and liberty. Pretending to be inspired by a courage of which they are incapable, the North American seamen undertake as an enterprise capable of realization, the substitution of Protestantism for the Catholic religion you profess, to treat you as tribes refractory to civilization, to take possession of your riches as if they were unacquainted with the rights of property, and to kidnap those persons whom they consider useful to man their ships or to be exploited in agricultural or industrial labor.

"Vain designs! Ridiculous boastings!

"Your indomitable bravery will suffice to frustrate the attempt to carry them into realization. You will not allow the faith you profess to be made a mock of; impious hands to be placed on the temple of the true God, the images you adore to be thrown down by unbelief. The aggressors shall not profane the tombs of your fathers, they shall not gratify their lustful passions at the cost of your wives and daughters' honor, or appropriate the property your industry has accumulated as a provision for old age. No! They shall not perpetrate any of the crimes inspired by their wickedness and covetousness, because your valor and patriotism will suffice to punish and abase the people that, claiming to be civilized and cultivated, have exterminated the natives of North America instead of bringing to them the life of civilization and progress.

"Filipinos, prepare for the struggle, and, united under the glorious Spanish flag, which is ever covered with laurels, let us fight with the conviction that victory will crown our efforts, and to the calls of our enemies let us oppose with the decision of the Christian and the patriotic cry of 'Viva España.'

"Manila, 23d April, 1898.

"Your General,
"BASILO AUGUSTIN DAVILA."

Captain Chichester in command of the British first-class cruiser the *Immortalité* stationed at Manila since the opening of hostilities there was in very cordial relations with Admiral Dewey and was the authoritative medium of commucation with the Spanish officials. All ordinary messages to or from them were supposed to be sent through him. We never learned by what agency the Madrid telegrams above quoted were delivered in Manila but it was the current belief that it was through the Germans, because they had frequently shown a strong bias towards the Spanish cause and were known to have sent provisions into the town on more than one occasion. An interesting rumor was also circulated, the substance of which has since been confirmed in print by Mr. Stickney, the *Herald* correspondent, and others, that Admiral Dewey had warned Admiral von Diederichs that a continuance of his unfriendly actions would be construed as open hostility. We were naturally prejudiced against the Germans by these reports and by what we could all see of their actions. Their warships did not enter or leave the harbor by the same route which the vessels of other nationalities took, but for some reason or other steamed away across the bay near the western shore, whither the launch from the *Olympia* which always ran alongside incoming or outgoing vessels, was obliged to go to perform this duty. The Germans alone of the different nationalities represented in the bay protested against the simple regulations which Admiral Dewey enforced as the commander of the blockading squadron.

At the end of the first week of August things were evidently coming to a head, as I have suggested, and it was in the air that something was soon to happen. Everybody felt this. A hint at such a time is worth a great deal and late on the afternoon of the 6th something of that nature lurked in a verbal message left at my tent by a friend from Cavité. There was a very heavy blow on, and the *Albany* which had been lying off the breakers all day at last steamed away for I was unable to signal to her and no boat would venture to run the surf. Parañaque was the nearest place where I could hope to get a boat to go to Cavité and it was already half past five when I started for that village. In a *casco* near the bridge I found Colonel McClure and his son and Major Kilbourne all from the *Newport*, who were trying to get back to the steamer. We joined forces and sent for a native boatman. After some argument and a great deal of bargaining, we hired a large dugout without outriggers, paddled by four men besides the steersman. It was nearly dark before we crossed the bar and the crew seemed nearly used up before we fetched clear of the line of breakers, for it was very rough and they had to paddle with all their strength to make any headway in the tumbling sea. She was a stanch craft and we did not ship much water. What little we took on board we knew about because we were obliged to sit flat in the bottom of the canoe to give her stability. The crew needed a good deal of encouragement and the steersman chaunted a barbaric refrain at intervals which woke them up and they paddled like mad for a few strokes and then settled down again to the slow and wearisome pace. The wind was dead ahead and "blowing half a gale" as the Atlantic captains say when the worst weather is met. Darkness came on rapidly, almost without the warning of twilight, and the feeble glimmer at Cavité alone gave us a true direction for presently we could not see the fleet at all.

Suddenly, a number of colored lights flashed and blinked first on one vessel and then on another and the great beam of a powerful searchlight swept over the water, nervously waving up and down, now bringing into gleaming prominence the white buildings of Cavité, now throwing into strong relief the black hulls of the transports and now spreading all along the line of trees on the shore. One by one the vessels of the fleet all turned on their searchlights, and then we observed them all directed at one point, the open ground between the lines at Maytubig. Almost simultaneously a strong beam from the foreign fleet settled on the same mark, as nearly as we could judge. We were told afterwards by the men who were in the trenches at the time, that this single beam was from the *Kaiserin Augusta*, and was directed upon the white house and the full front of our earthworks, causing the enemy to open fire at once.

We paddled steadily on as fast as we could, knowing the orders about circulation on the water at night and anxious to make a good distance before the searchlights began wandering again, and we succeeded in getting quite close to a transport without being observed by any one on the squadron. We hailed the silent, dark mass and a voice sounding very distant and high above our heads answered us and gave us elaborate directions in fractions of points of the compass which we tried at once to follow before we should forget them. We felt comparatively at home in the company of the transports and went on cheerfully and hailed the next great towering mass we came to. From this and from the next one we got plenty of advice but none which we managed to follow, try as hard as we could. All ships look alike in the dark when you cannot even see to count their masts. We began to think we were in for a night in Cavité.

The searchlights started to roam again. How restless and fidgety they were that night! Soon one caught us full in the face. The natives stopped paddling at once. A voice rang out, "Halt! who goes there? Who are you? Keep off or I'll fire!" and we saw we were nearly aboard the *Monterey*. We hurriedly explained our position and asked for the direction of the *Newport*. The men on deck had never heard of her, but we knew she was somewhere between the monitor and Cavité and we made the boatmen paddle the canoe in that direction, the searchlight which nearly frightened the natives silly, glaring at us now and then in a most confusing and irritating manner. All at once, by great good luck, we ran fairly under the stern of the steamer we were looking for, and then the great beam of light, for the first time friendly to us, showed us the faces of our comrades sitting on the deck.

The next day was Sunday and everybody had a very quiet manner on, which I at first thought might be the day and then concluded it was induced by the possession of some important secret. The evening before I had vainly tried to wheedle some unconsidered trifle of information out of Colonel Whittier but he was too discreet for me and turned on sumptuous hospitality with generosity enough to excuse parsimony of confidences and made me for the time almost forget the camp. He was a little preoccupied in the morning and guarded in his conversation, like the others.

A strange launch, said to belong to the Belgian consul, came steaming across from the direction of the foreign vessels and ran alongside the *Olympia*. The *Cañacao* was waiting at the companion ladder of our steamer. General

Merritt and one or two other officers came on deck in full uniform or dressed, at least, with unusual care and the *Cañacao* took them to the *Olympia*. Shortly after they went aboard, a launch from the flagship steamed rapidly away in the direction of Manila and then the officers came back and everybody tried to look as if nothing was going on.

I had only to put two and two together and I was at the threshold of an open door. A decisive message of some kind had evidently been sent to the Spanish authorities in Manila, probably a demand for immediate surrender under penalty of bombardment and assault. Special information on this point was of no use to me, I was sure to get it all before there was an opportunity of sending it away and I therefore decided to leave the party of Sphinxes on the *Newport* and go back to camp; so I signalled for the *Albany* and tried to land at Parañaque with Major Thompson and his men as before described.

CHAPTER IX

CAMP rumor, which spread more rapidly than scandal in
a village street, was, in the main, correct. A joint note signed
by General Merritt and Admiral Dewey, had been sent on
Sunday forenoon to the commander-in-chief of the Spanish
forces in Manila warning him that operations against the
defences of the town by the land and naval forces of the
United States might begin at any time after the expiration
of forty-eight hours from the time the notice was received,
or sooner if an attack was made on our lines by the Spanish troops. The British vice-consul, Mr. H. A. Ramsden, who
was in charge of the American consular interests in the besieged city, delivered the note to the Spanish, received a reply to it and sent this at once to Admiral Dewey. The reply
was signed by Governor-General and Captain-General Fermin Jaudenes and stated that he had received the joint note
at half past twelve o'clock. Without giving any definite indication of his intentions he returned his grateful acknowl-
edgments of the humane sentiments expressed in the note
and simply added that, as he was surrounded by insurrectionary forces, he was unable to remove the sick and
wounded and other non-combatants to a place of safety. By
the tone of his reply it was evident that he did not expect
the threat of bombardment would be carried out. Indeed,
the ultimatum was not put in such strong terms as to suggest that such a deplorable step would be taken except as a
last resort. The words "may begin at any time," etc., used
instead of the words "will begin at once," etc., have a perfunctory sound and the qualifying clause at the end of the

document in regard to the attack on our lines did not strengthen the demand implied in the note.

A joint letter was at once sent back calling the attention of General Jaudenes in rather verbose and empty-sounding phrases to the sufferings of the non-combatants in case a bombardment should occur and ending with a demand for the surrender of the town and the Spanish forces. On the next day General Jaudenes replied that he desired time to consult with the Madrid government before deciding this important question, not asking, meanwhile, that the non-combatants be permitted to pass through the investing lines nor, indeed, that any facilities should be afforded him for the removal of the sick and wounded and the women and children to places of refuge. The limit of time set by the ultimatum had expired within a few hours when this letter was written. On the 10th, the day after the expiration of the notices, a joint reply was sent to the last letter from the Spanish general stating that his request for more time was not granted. Here, as far as I know, the recorded correspondence ended. It is not easy to explain the tone of the letters which passed between the parties except on the theory that the documents were edited for home consumption particularly for Spain.

It is as well, perhaps, to append the text of the letters relating to this important event.

No. 679—M.

"UNITED STATES NAVAL FORCE ON ASIATIC STATION.
"FLAGSHIP OLYMPIA,

'CAVITE, P. I., *August* 6, 1898.

"SIR:—I have the honor to acknowledge the receipt of your communication in reference to our ultimatum to the Spanish authorities in Manila.

"I agree with you that it would be well to send at once a joint letter to the captain-general notifying him that he should remove from the city all non-combatants within forty-eight hours, and that operations against the defences of Manila may begin at any time after the expiration of the said forty-eight hours.

"In my judgment the ultimatum would be stronger without any qualification.

"If you will cause such a letter to be prepared I will sign it.   Very respectfully,
"GEORGE DEWEY,
"*Rear Admiral U. S. Navy,*
"Commanding U. S. Naval Force on Asiatic Station.

"Major-General WESLEY MERRITT, U. S. Army,
"Commanding U. S. Forces."

"HEADQUARTERS UNITED STATES LAND AND NAVAL FORCES,
"MANILA BAY, PHILIPPINE ISLANDS,

"*August 7,* 1898.

"To *The General-in-Chief, Commanding Spanish Forces in Manila:*

"SIR:—We have the honor to notify Your Excellency that operations of the land and naval forces of the United States against the defences of Manila may begin at any time after the expiration of forty-eight hours from the hour of receipt by you of this communication, or sooner if made necessary by an attack on your part.

"This notice is given in order to afford you an opportunity to remove all non-combatants from the city.
"Very respectfully,
"WESLEY MERRITT,
"*Major-General U. S. Army,*
"Commanding Land Forces of the United States.

"GEORGE DEWEY,
"*Rear-Admiral, U. S. Navy,*
"Commanding United States Naval Forces on Asiatic Station."

"BRITISH CONSULATE, MANILA,

"*August 7,* 1898.

"MOST EXCELLENT SIR:—I beg to acknowledge the receipt of Your Excellency's communication under to-day's date which was delivered to me on the wharf.

"I immediately drove to see His Excellency the Governor and Captain-General and handed personally the communication addressed to His Excellency, by Your Excellency and Major-General Merritt.

"It was half-past twelve P..M. when the communication was handed to His Excellency, and I begged of His Excellency to cause the time to be stated in His Excellency's reply, when the communication was received.

"I have now the honor to transmit herewith enclosed to Your Excellency the answer from His Excellency the Governor-General.

"I have the honor to be,
"Your Excellency's Most obedient Humble Servant,
"(Signed)   H. A. RAMSDEN,
                    "British Vice-Consul,
"In charge of U. S. Consular Interests.

"His Excellency Rear-Admiral DEWEY,
"Commanding the United States Naval Forces on Asiatic Station.
"U. S. Flagship *Olympia.*"

[Translation.]

"MANILA, *August 7,* 1898.

"THE GOVERNOR-GENERAL AND CAPTAIN-GENERAL OF THE PHILIPPINES,

To *The Major-General of the Army and the Rear-Admiral of the Navy, Commanding respectively the Military and Naval Forces of the United States:*

"GENTLEMEN:—I have the honor to inform Your Excellencies that at half past twelve to-day I received the notice with which you favor me, that after forty-eight hours have elapsed you may begin operations against this fortified city or at an earlier hour if the forces under your command are attacked by mine.

"As your notice is sent for the purpose of providing for the safety of non-combatants, I give thanks to Your Excellencies for the humane sentiments you have shown, and state that, finding myself surrounded by insurrectionary forces,

I am without places of refuge for the increased numbers of wounded, sick, women and children who are now lodged within the walls.

"Very respectfully and kissing the hands of
"Your Excellencies,
"(Signed)   FERMIN JAUDENES,
"Governor-General and Captain-General of the Philippines."

"HEADQUARTERS UNITED STATES LAND AND NAVAL FORCES, MANILA BAY, PHILIPPINE ISLANDS,

"August 7, 1898.

"To *The Governor-General and Captain-General of the Philippines:*

"SIR:—The inevitable suffering in store for the wounded, sick, women and children, in the event that it becomes our duty to reduce the defences of the walled town in which they are gathered, will, we feel assured, appeal successfully to the sympathies of a General capable of making the determined and prolonged resistance which Your Excellency has exhibited after the loss of your Naval forces and without hope of succor.

"We therefore submit, without prejudice to the high sentiments of honor and duty which Your Excellency entertains, that surrounded on every side as you are by a constantly increasing force, with a powerful fleet in your front and deprived of all prospect of reinforcement and assistance, a most useless sacrifice of life would result in the event of an attack, and therefore every consideration of humanity makes it imperative that you should not subject your city to the horrors of a bombardment. Accordingly we demand the surrender of the city of Manila and the Spanish forces under your command.

"Very respectfully,
"WESLEY MERRITT,
"Major-General U. S. Army,
"Commanding Land Forces of the United States.

"GEORGE DEWEY,
"Rear-Admiral, U. S. Navy,
"Commanding United States Naval Forces on Asiatic Station."

[Translation.]

"August 8, 1898.

"THE GOVERNOR-GENERAL AND CAPTAIN-GENERAL OF THE
  PHILIPPINES,

To *The Major-General of the Army and the Rear-Admiral
  of the Navy, commanding respectively the Military and
  Naval Forces of the United States:*

"GENTLEMEN :—Having received an intimation from Your
Excellencies that, in obedience to sentiments of humanity to
which you appeal and which I share, I should surrender this
city and the forces under my orders, I have assembled the
Council of Defence, which declares that your request cannot
be granted, but taking account of the most exceptional circumstances existing in this city which Your Excellencies
recite and which I unfortunately have to admit, I would consult my government if Your Excellencies will grant the
time strictly necessary for this communication by way of
Hong Kong.   Very respectfully,

"FERMIN JAUDENES,
"*Governor-General and Captain-General of the Philippines.*"

"HEADQUARTERS UNITED STATES LAND AND
NAVAL FORCES, MANILA BAY,

"August 10, 1898.

"To *The Governor-General and Captain-General of the Philippine Islands:*

"SIR:—We have the honor to acknowledge the communication of Your Excellency of the 8th inst., in which you suggest your desire to consult your government in regard to the
exceptional circumstances in your city, provided the time to
do so can be granted by us.

"In reply we respectfully inform Your Excellency that we
decline to grant the time requested.   Very respectfully,

"WESLEY MERRITT,
"*Major-General U. S. Army,*
"Commanding United States Land Forces.

"GEORGE DEWEY,
  "*Rear-Admiral, U. S. Navy,*

"Commanding United States Naval Forces, Asiatic Station."

The watchers on the seashore saw in the early morning of the day after the ultimatum was sent a number of launches with lighters in tow steaming out from the breakwater to the foreign warships, and as the hours passed this unusual movement in the harbor increased. The watchers in the trenches saw the sandbags begin to pile higher and higher on the enemy's breastworks and noticed that the irritating compliments from the Spanish Mausers were omitted for the first time in some days. Gradually the men gained confidence that the enemy had concluded to stop their picket firing, and they began to wander freely up and down the beach, and the work of strengthening and enlarging the earthworks was carried on with increased zeal and in much greater comfort without the spasmodic accompaniment of whistling bullets. We in camp were surprised to flush quite a covey of generals in the vicinity of headquarters. General MacArthur and General Greene went off to inspect the lines and, in their absence, General Merritt and General Anderson came into camp. All four, later in the day, spent some time under the shelter of our canvas portico. General MacArthur's brigade was busily landing at Parañaque, and now that he was established on shore he assumed temporary command of both brigades by virtue of his seniority in rank until General Anderson should establish his headquarters at Tambo, which he did two days later. General Greene continued in active command of the force at the front.

Nobody knew whether General Merritt intended to take the field or not. The men were all talking about it and having the greatest admiration for their veteran commander, although few knew him by sight, they were anxious to see him established in camp. I was asked a hundred times if he was going to take active command of his troops. It was my impression that he would, although I did not say so, for I had heard him ask Captain Mott where the saddles were and

ARTHUR MacARTHUR

I had received an urgent request from a member of his staff to secure at once a good weight-carrying pony.

A contagious fever of expectation ran through the camp, and the men were seen gathered in knots earnestly discussing the meaning of the activity in the harbor and the unusual quiet of the enemy. The rain continued, and although the monsoon ceased its vicious lashing, the discomfort in camp and at the front increased every hour. The mud trenches, as we used to call them, were almost untenable now from the deep mud in all the footways and from the water which flooded all the surrounding territory. It was impossible to move from one part of the works to another without plunging almost up to the knees in black, fetid mud, and the smell of the festering marshes was almost unendurable. About eighty yards in front of the general line of entrenchments first built, a long, straight breastwork was thrown up at the north end of the morass east of the Camino Real, where the Pennsylvanians had passed such a bad hour on the night of July 31. Through the tangle of bamboo beyond this and a little to the rear, a line of short defences had been constructed, first along a bamboo hedge, then across a marsh, then around a native hut and so on in the dense growth of the swamp. Compared to these the earthworks in Virginia in the sixties in the rainy weather were as palaces to hovels. The line ended at a group of huts, one of them with a stone foundation, near the swale and not over two hundred yards from the dam. Three roads led up to the works from the rear, the Camino Real and two narrow lanes from the Pasay cross road, on one of which, the most easterly of the two, the insurgents had their bronze gun. General Greene had played the juggling game so well that he had ousted the insurgents from all their territory, covering a front of about half a mile, without exciting any noticeable animosity or calling out any official protest. Both our flanks were now protected by impassable natural barriers, the left by the bay and the right by the swale. Hitherto the right had been covered by the insurgents, whose effectiveness and loyalty were unknown quantities.

Next to Maytubig, the most important position along the whole line south of the Pasig was that opposite Blockhouse Fourteen. This position the insurgents were resolved to cling to, and their actions plainly indicated that they did not propose to be shouldered out of it, for they would not let any one pass their guards without written permission from Aguinaldo, and rather looked with suspicion on any visitors. They built a number of small defences in the bamboo and covered with a line of rifle pits the narrow neck between the swale and the river, which muddy stream, after winding through the broad marsh north of the road from Pasay to San Pedro de Macati, then under the bamboo bridge and through the thicket past Malabay, flowed into the bay at Parañaque.

From their point of view the insurgents were perfectly right in holding this front on the Pasay road. It was quite as good a route from Bacoor to Manila as the Camino Real, and it was perhaps even a little shorter distance by this road to the main bridges across the Pasig near the walled town. If they gave up this front they would be completely shut out from an approach to Manila on the south, and the only route open to them would be by the circuitous and almost impassable one viâ San Pedro Macati. They proposed to have a hand in the occupation of the town, naturally considering it their full right by virtue of their long service in besieging the place from the land side. Not being advised in any way of our plans or of our intentions, but having the same means of observation of external signs which our men in camp possessed, they drew their own conclusions, sat tight, said nothing, and waited for their chance.

The first important visible result of the ultimatum was the movement of the foreign fleet on the morning of Tuesday the 9th. The forty-eight hours' notice elapsed at half-past

A KITCHEN IN AN INSURGENT CAMP

twelve on that day. About ten o'clock we saw from the beach the English and Japanese vessels leave their anchorage and slowly steam across the bay to Cavité, where they took up a position near our squadron. The two German ships and the two French cruisers remained, as far as we could see, at their moorings off the breakwater. This circumstance was interpreted at once as a full confirmation of the reported trouble brewing between the Germans and ourselves, and full proof of the French sympathy with the Spaniards which had been more or less plainly observable since the beginning of the war. Interesting complications were now confidently expected, in fact, it did not seem possible to avoid them.

With the exception of the constant traffic between the shore and the German and French ships, the bay was now quiet. Red Cross flags began to flutter everywhere in the town, and this day and the next half the day on Friday wore away with no visible change in the situation.

What were we waiting for? Those of us who were fortunate to know the exact terms of the ultimatum were as much in the dark about the cause of the delay as the privates in the ranks. General MacArthur's brigade was all landed with its ammunition and stores. General Greene's brigade had been prepared for a move for a week or more. A single balky mule has been known to have stopped the advance of a whole army corps. Could it be, reasoned the camp oracles, that everything hung on the completion of the bamboo trestles which Captain Connor and his engineers were building on the beach to use to cross the stream near the stone fort in case the bridge was blown up. This could not be the balky mule, argued the more knowing ones, for the spidery frames were all finished by Thursday night, and still we did not go ahead. This delay was worse than standing the enemy's fire without returning it.

Meanwhile the Spaniards did not fire a shot from their

trenches, and the study of the ground between the lines was carried on day and night without any interruption by sharpshooting. Major Bell with Lieutenant Means of the First Colorado Regiment, made a daring reconnaissance on Thursday to within a revolver shot of the water battery under the stone fort, the former wading and swimming until he had satisfied himself of the fordable depth of the inlet or mouth of the stream, and knew its approximate width. The Spanish soldiers watched these operations without opening fire. On the same day Father McKinnon, chaplain of the First California Regiment, walked calmly up to the Spanish lines, without a flag of truce or anything but his costume to announce his peaceful intentions, was allowed to enter the lines and was taken at his request to the Archbishop, with whom he had a long conference on the reported dangers threatening the brethren of the priesthood and on kindred subjects. He then came back to the stone fort, was passed through the lines and reached camp in the afternoon safe and sound.

With the information gained by the restless enterprise of the scouts, both at this time and earlier in the campaign, maps were drawn by the engineers and copies were distributed to the proper officers of the troops. The details of these maps were accurate enough for all purposes except, as it happened, in the vicinity of Blockhouse Fourteen, where there were one or two important defences the existence of which was unknown until they were discovered on the day of the advance.

General Merritt with Colonel Whittier and Major Bement came to camp on the 11th, and after a few hours there in the drenching rain, returned to the *Newport* and, as nothing was said about the general's taking the field we reluctantly concluded that he did not propose to take an active part in the land operations. This confirmed the impression which was rapidly gaining ground, that the enemy was expected to

ASTOR BATTERY GOING TO THE FRONT

make no resistance, but would yield at once on the proper display of force on our side.

In the afternoon of the 12th, the Astors received their long desired orders to move up to the front. Never did school-boys welcome an unexpected holiday more joyfully than did the battery receive the news that it was to march. Every-thing was soon in readiness, and off they started about four o'clock, dragging their guns as if they were as light as per-ambulators, followed by buffalo carts full of ammunition. The remaining guns of the two Utah batteries were also sent forward. Orders were issued by the division general and by the brigade commanders for the troops to prepare for an ad-vance against the enemy's works on the following morning at ten o'clock, and detailed instructions were sent out as to the disposition of the force at the front and in reserve. I quote from General Greene's order a paragraph in full which will show how the men were to be uniformed and equipped for this action: ·

"All troops that have been furnished with brown canvas uniforms will wear them, and officers may at their discretion wear the same or blue shirts, provided they wear shoulder straps. Other troops will wear blue shirts and trousers, and all will wear campaign hats. The men will carry their ponchos or rubber blankets, folded and hung at the belt. Each man will carry his rifle, bayonet belt, haversack, canteen and 200 rounds of ammunition, the belt being full and the rest in his haversack. In his haversack will be car-ried two days' rations of meat and hardbread, and the mess kit; front rank men will fill their canteens with coffee, and rear rank men with water. In firing, the ammunition in the haversacks will be used first, and that in the belts reserved until the last. All spades, shovels, axes and hatchets in the possession of the regiments will be taken forward and dis-tributed uniformly through the companies so as to give, if possible, at least one entrenching tool for each set of fours,

one hatchet or axe in each section and one pick in each platoon. Regimental commanders will designate definitely the
men in each squad, section or platoon, by whom these tools
are to be carried."

It only remains to add that all this made a very heavy load,
particularly for the volunteers with their .45 calibre Spring-
field rifles. The amount of ammunition carried was doubled
after the first orders were issued by General Anderson, who
thought that one hundred rounds would be sufficient. The
distance to be marched was very short, but the difficulties of
sending up supplies were almost insurmountable, and it was
decided to give the men this large number of cartridges with
the most stringent orders against waste. Four hundred
rounds per man was all that could be obtained in San Francisco, and a good part of this was already expended, so the
greatest care was necessary in the use of what remained.

In general terms, the forces were dispersed by General Anderson, under instructions from General Merritt as follows:

The First Brigade, commanded by General MacArthur,
was to move up to the narrow front held by the insurgents
opposite Blockhouse Fourteen, with one of the Utah guns
and the Astor Battery on the extreme right near the river.
Five battalions were to occupy the insurgent earthworks
there if it could be done without bringing on rupture with the
natives, and the remaining six were to be kept in reserve near
the village of Pasay.

The Second Brigade, under General Greene, was to advance to the front already occupied by part of this force,
seven battalions to be stationed in the trenches and eight to
be held in reserve between the Pasay cross road and the lines.
Seven guns of the Utah batteries were to be put in the best
positions found on the line of earthworks, and three landing
guns from the navy, manned by volunteer gunners from the
Third Artillery, were to be posted on the extreme right of
the brigade.

The instructions received from General Merritt in a memorandum sent to the general officers on the afternoon of the 12th, left the question still open whether the proposed attack would be made after all. A quotation from this memorandum will explain more fully than chapters of description, the actual state of affairs and will certainly give to the careful reader an excellent idea of the manner in which this important act of the drama was intended to be put on the stage. It read:

"The navy under Rear-Admiral Dewey is to sail at nine o'clock in the morning, August 13, moving up to the different positions assigned to the warships, and open fire about ten A. M. The troops are to hold themselves in readiness, as already agreed upon, to advance on the enemy in front, occupying the entrenchments after they are so shaken as to make the advance practicable without a serious disadvantage to our troops. In case the navy is delayed in disabling the enemy's guns and levelling the works, no advance is to be made by the army unless ordered from these headquarters. In the event of a white flag being displayed on the angle of the walled city, or prominently anywhere else in sight, coupled with a cessation of firing on our part, it will mean surrender, as the admiral proposes, after having fired a satisfactory number of shots, to move up toward the walled city and display the international signal '*Surrender.*' If a white flag is displayed, this will be an answer to his demand, and the troops will advance in good order and quietly."

"These headquarters will be on board the *Zafiro*, which has been placed at the disposition of the commanding general by the admiral. Six companies of the Second Oregon Regiment now quartered at Cavité will accompany these headquarters, to be used in occupying and keeping order in the walled city in the event of necessity. If the white flag is displayed, the admiral will send his flag-lieutenant ashore, accompanied by a staff officer from these headquarters, who will bring word as to the propositions made by the enemy.

"The troops in the meantime will advance and, entering the enemy's works by the left flank, move into such positions as may be assigned them by orders from these headquarters. This is not intended to interdict the entrance, if possible, by the First Brigade or part of the troops, over the enemy's works on the right.

"It is intended that these results shall be accomplished without loss of life, and while the firing continues from the enemy with their heavy guns, or if there is an important fire from their entrenchments, the troops will not attempt an advance unless ordered from these headquarters.

"In the event of unfavorable weather for the service of guns on board ship, the action will be delayed until further orders."

In addition to the instructions regarding the advance upon the works, careful directions were given for the disposition of the troops on the occupation of the town and its suburbs. Doubt was implied in these instructions as well as in the memorandum above quoted, as to the prompt advance of General MacArthur's force. This was probably because the Spaniards had confidence that the American troops who occupied the left without any leaven of natives among them would observe the laws of civilized belligerents regarding a capitulation, but from their experience with the insurgents they had no faith that the force of irresponsible natives which was concentrated opposite Blockhouse Fourteen would let them retreat to the town without attacking them after they had left the shelter of their works. This was a perfectly reasonable presumption, and what they feared actually happened, as will be recorded later.

General MacArthur was directed, in case he could enter the enemy's lines at Blockhouse Fourteen, to leave guards in the trenches there, with strict orders to allow no armed bodies, other than American troops, to pass, and to move up the road through the village of Singalong past Paco, leaving a guard on the bridge at this village and also on one further along, and finally to take possession of the Puentes de Ayala, which cross the river Pasig at the Isla de Convalecencia. After this was done he was to establish his headquarters in Ermita or Malate as might be thought best at the time, and dispose his brigade there according to circumstances, promptly raising the American flag as a sign of occupation.

In case General MacArthur did not succeed in carrying out this programme simultaneously with the advance on the left, General Greene was to send details to guard the various bridges against the insurgents. At the same time he was to carry out the movements assigned to his brigade, which were a rapid advance through Malate and Ermita and around the walled town on the outside, across the Puente de España, and the Puente Colgante, over the Pasig and into the business and residential quarters to the north of this river, establishing his headquarters in the centre of the commercial district of Binondo.

Both these brigade commanders were explicitly and definitely ordered to avoid all encounters with the natives, were ordered, in fact, to keep the armed insurgents from entering the suburbs, and were practically told not to use force in doing this. The Spanish defences were nowhere continuous except between the seashore and Blockhouse Fourteen, and nothing was to prevent the insurgents from skirting the small breastworks and swarming up to the very walls of the citadel, a procedure which, as I have before remarked, the Spaniards anticipated with terror.

CHAPTER X

Most of us in headquarters camp were late turning in on Friday night, for all our traps had to be securely packed up so they could be brought on after us when required, as we had no expectation of returning to the spot again. General Greene had invited me to accompany him, so my billet for the next day was settled. Some of the correspondents had arranged to follow their favorite regiments, others had accepted invitations to watch the bombardment from the squadron, and a goodly number had agreed to go on the *Albany*, which was to cruise along as near the scene of action as she could. The seashore was likely to be far the most interesting place, because at this point it was possible to observe both the land and naval operations. The Third Artillery and the Astor Battery, the organizations in which I felt the most interest on account of my intimate acquaintance with them, were both stationed so far from the shore that I had no hope of seeing them at all during the action. I could not join either one of them with advantage, because, as experience had taught me, in order to cover a broad horizon and to get an intelligent notion of the general operations, it was absolutely necessary to keep in touch with the head of active direction of affairs, putting aside all questions of personal sympathy with any particular organization. I knew that General Greene was sure to be in whatever interesting was going on.

At four o'clock the bugles sounded their harsh call, and this time there was no grumbling to be heard as we struggled into our wet clothes, at least near my tent, which I now occupied alone, as Colonel Potter had gone away ill. A slight

WATER BUFFALO DRAGGING GUNS OF THE UTAH BATTERY INTO POSITION

COLORADO TROOPS REPELLING SPANISH ATTACK FROM DESERTED SPANISH
TRENCHES

drizzle was falling, and the skies were lowering and the atmosphere was heavy and depressing. After a hasty breakfast at six o'clock, General Greene and his staff mounted their ponies, and, crossing the camp, already half deserted, plodded slowly through the mud up the Camino Real. Long lines of men, for all the world like Confederates in their slouch hats and ragged brown uniforms, silently followed a sinuous trail through the fields, and other detachments picked their way along the canal of black slime which now bore little resemblance to a highway. We had gone but a short distance beyond the camp when a violent tempest swept across the sea and land, and peal after peal of heavy thunder rumbled ominously all around us. The rain came down in streams, not in drops, and ponchos were little protection in the driving storm. In a pause of the echoing thunder we suddenly heard, just ahead of us, and a little to the right, the familiar dull and heavy boom of the insurgent cannon on the Pasay road. General Greene, who was leading our little cavalcade, turned around with a look of disgust as much as to say: "Those idiots of insurgents will spoil the whole game with their foolishness!"

We heard no reply from the Spaniards, and we moved along as fast as we could until we came to a little cross road a hundred and fifty yards or so in the rear of the trenches where we dismounted and tied our ponies, and wallowed up the road on foot and into the white house.

The Pennsylvanians had been at the front for twenty-four hours, and were preparing to join the reserves, the First Colorado Regiment having been ordered to relieve them. By eight o'clock this change had been made, and the Colorados and the Utah men were all in place and impatient for their work to begin. The quiet, recently so grateful, was now most irritating to the nerves. It was like waiting to see where the lightning from a rapidly approaching storm is going to strike, and the silence was as strange and foreboding as the hush of nature before the bursting of a tempest. We noticed that the embrasures on the water battery under the stone fort were no longer darkened by the muzzles of the field pieces which had so often annoyed us. This was significant, and did not look like business. The insurgent gun, which had sullenly pounded away for a time was now quiet, and not a shot was heard.

General Babcock came up about nine o'clock, bringing the last instructions which, as far as I can remember, were for General Greene to send a regiment forward as soon as the bombardment had inflicted any serious damage on the stone fort and on the neighboring works. Still we did not yet know for sure whether there would be any bombardment, as great masses of vapor and heavy showers of rain were drifting across the water, and we could not even see Cavité and the fleet there. We did not expect anything until ten o'clock, and were killing time as best we could, occasionally studying the water, now a horizonless expanse of gray, when out of the mist to the southwest emerged the ugly and aggressive shape of the *Monterey* silently steaming along, her two long forward guns pointing Manila-wards and projecting like the antennae of a huge beetle. First another and then a third and a fourth warship came in sight, as if following in the wake of the monitor at equal intervals apart, then the fifth, a little nearer inshore, which we at once recognized as the *Olympia*. It was then just a half hour before the time set for the bombardment to begin, and the nearest vessel was quite two miles from the stone fort.

Scarcely had we made out the flagship before there burst from her side a great whirling mass of smoke, gleaming white against the dull gray background of mist and rain, sweeping along the water and then rising high in the air in the shape of a great cumulus cloud, which completely hid the vessel from our sight. A second or two of suspense, and then came two loud reports in quick succession followed by the tearing sound of shells, startlingly close at hand. A great splash of water just abreast the fort and a fan-shaped mass of gray sand rising from the beach marked where the vicious messengers had fallen.

General Babcock hastened to the shore and I followed him. There Major Thompson had established his signal station, and had built out of sandbags quite a strong little shelter behind the old iron hulk, the top of which made an excellent post of observation. This station was connected by wire with the headquarters of the division and of each brigade, and here men and materials were assembled, ready to accompany the advance with the field telegraph.

Now other ships, which we could not recognize in the thick atmosphere, opened also on the fort, and at the same time there stole up behind us from her station near the camp landing, the little captured *Callao,* almost in the breakers, and she at once began to bang away with her machine guns, rattling out bullets with a noise like striking a piece of bamboo with a stick. The tiny launch *Barcelo* served her one small piece in comical emulation of her fellow-captive. There was a shower of projectiles from those two ambitious craft knocking against the strong walls of the fort, and above the confused din on the water near at hand, and the heavy crash of the eight and the five-inch guns on the *Olympia* and her consorts, came the loud staccato reports of the Utah guns, which were now steadily at work.

From the signal station, the effect of the large shells could be accurately marked, and as Major Thompson saw the projectiles strike too low, he said to the signalman in quiet but emphatic tones:

"Flag them 'Higher'! Flag them 'Higher'!" and the tall soldier frantically waved his flag in the strong wind.

For twenty minutes the great shells came tearing across the bay, sometimes a little too high, generally a few feet too low, throwing up the earth under the foot of the gray wall like the explosion of a mine. The signalman wig-wagged messages without intermission. The mist and rain made it impossible for the navy gunners to shoot with accuracy. One shell came screaming over our heads and flew away off into the distance. We did not hear it burst nor could we tell where it came from. The enemy made no sign.

The roar of the large calibre guns ceased for a while and the vessels all slowly approached nearer the fort. We went back into the white house, and from the windows watched the effect of the Utah guns, which were working with monotonous regularity. The practice was excellent, and nearly every shell struck into the parapet, throwing the little sand bags in all directions. Two of the guns were in position between the house and the Camino Real, the nearest only about ten yards from the building, and not in line with the front of it, because the earthwork ranged a few yards to the rear of the line, extending to the beach, and met the house midway along the west wall. When this piece went off bricks and plaster fell about us, and the few remaining squares of shell in the windows rattled down as if an earthquake were shaking the building to pieces. Captain Young, who was in command of these guns, walked slowly up and down, as if he were on his own veranda, and quietly ordered "Shell" or "Shrapnel" as he thought most effective. Captain Grant of B Battery was similarly occupied in another part of the line, and the range of all the guns was most accurate. Some of our shrapnel, I fancy, was sent a little high and wide, just to encourage the retreat. The *Callao* and the *Barcelo* were having, all the while, a little spree together. They were stripped for a fight and were bound to have it. Following the orders of the admiral to land all combustibles, Captain Tappan of the *Callao* had sent ashore a can of petroleum and it was reported that there was nothing on the *Barcelo* in the shape of liquids which would burn.

At ten o'clock the *Olympia* opened fire again, this time

about three thousand yards away, and she had fired but a few shots, when out of the fort rose first one and then another column of smoke, dust and rubbish. Two eight-inch shells had completely passed through the three-foot walls of solid masonry, and each of them had exploded in one of the buildings of the fort, completely shattering them and killing several men.

Back to the shore, then to the house again, and once more to the signal station—each point was too interesting to be left for an instant. Off in the distance the artillery of the First Brigade could be heard. The Astors were having their innings.

At precisely ten minutes past ten General Babcock, who had been for some minutes saying over and over again:— "They are not replying. It is time to advance!" received a message from General Greene, in these words: "My infantry is advancing. Navy should be notified." Almost before we could turn round the whole breastwork swarmed with leaping, scrambling figures, who crouched and ran forward in open order in the underbrush and tall grass. A second line followed not far behind, and soon both were well forward in the comparatively open space. A few scraggly trees, a strawstack, the thatch of small huts, and the great roof of the Malate church made the horizon as seen from the rough ground in front of the trenches. From some points the flag on the fort could be seen, and the parapet too, but the Spanish earthworks were hidden by the intervening growth and tangle of small bamboo reeds and bushes.

As soon as the trenches were vacated, the First California Regiment came swinging across the open meadow behind and piled themselves up two deep against the breastwork. It was most inspiriting to see the determined, eager expression in the faces of these great stalwart children of the Pacific slope as they were rushing up, inspired by that belligerent ardor so difficult to restrain. They were spoiling for a fight. It was written on their faces.

General Babcock, in whom these rapidly succeeding incidents had revived the long-forgotten emotions of his early soldier life in the Rebellion, carried away, as we all were, by the contagious enthusiasm of the moment, greeted them warmly, with a hearty, "Boys, you look as if you could eat those Spaniards up." "Give us a chance!" they all shouted. On the right the firing was still going on and was apparently increasing.

The first and second line were working their way through the underbrush, and when the advanced skirmishers reached a point whence they could see the enemy's breastworks, they knelt and began to fire. Why they were firing, it was by no means clear, for we could see no Spaniards in the trenches, and no shots were coming from that direction. A messenger was hurried off to put a stop to the fusillade.

The guns of the fleet still kept up their hammering at the stone fort, and we began to think that the admiral remembered the tale of Nelson's blind eye, for no attention was paid to our signals, nor to the advance of the Colorado battalion along the beach, which soon halted and began to turn back. Two signalmen ran along the sand, each waving a flag. Still the bombardment continued for a weary time and did not stop, indeed, until half past ten, full twenty minutes after the first line advanced.

The moment the shells ceased to batter the fort and to plough up the surrounding territory, the Colorado men streamed up the beach, waded the inlet and scattered all around the fort. It was evidently deserted. The signal men, who had kept along with the advance, left behind them a trail of insulated wire as they went.

Believing it was all over, as it had probably been prearranged, I ran back from the inlet where I had been watching the crossing, and to the Camino Real to get my pony,

IN THE AMERICAN TRENCHES—AWAITING THE WORD TO FIRE

AMERICAN FLAG RAISED BY LIEUTENANT-COLONEL McCOY, FIRST
COLORADO VOLUNTEERS

annoyed at having, in my excitement, ignored one of the elementary rules of the business of correspondent, which is: Never let your saddle leave your sight on your horse or off him. When I reached the road I found, to my dismay, the bullets splashing in the mud and cracking in the bamboo on all sides, evidently coming from the vicinity of Blockhouse Fourteen. It was no time to be particular about a little mud and I was already soaking wet to the waist so I floundered down the road in quick time, mounted the pony and hurried back. Just as I reached the beach again the ragged bunting on the staff of the fort which bore so little resemblance to a Spanish flag that we had quite forgotten its existence, fluttered down, and the Stars and Stripes floated in its place. Lieutenant-Colonel McCoy, of the Colorado battalion, had won the prize for his regiment. The exultant yell which swept along our whole line as the bright colors of the flag shone out vividly against the gray sky, drowned all other sounds with its strident, savage note of victory. By the time I had crossed the inlet the sound of music rose on the beach and the Colorado band came marching along at a rapid pace playing as if on parade and soon took up a position just under the fort, where in pauses of the music the bullets could be heard singing merrily over their heads. A rattling and cracking in the woods behind Blockhouse Fourteen showed where the shots were coming from which were now sweeping the whole beach, and a more confused medley of reports of small-arms and cannon indicated that the focus of interest was now along the Singalong road.

As General Greene did not come up I concluded he had gone to the right of the line and I galloped back again down the beach, pausing beyond the inlet to watch the manœuvres of the fleet. The whole squadron was closing in towards the town, and the *Callao* and her little sister, the *Barcelo,* were well up the shore opposite Malate, apparently watching for another opportunity to continue their target practice. The

Albany, too, was in the procession and was slowly steaming along just outside the line of breakers, as nearly as I could judge, just about in the outer edge of the line of fire. The men on board were preoccupied with something, for I could not get any reply to my signals, and, as it was none too healthy where I was standing, I gave up attempting to make connection with my own naval force and went in search of the general. He soon came along and said that General MacArthur was meeting with stubborn resistance and that the only thing for us to do was to push on and get up to the city as soon as possible. So we all rode rapidly up the beach and beyond the fort upon the high bank along shore which was honeycombed with rifle pits and zigzags.

Some two hundred yards north of the fort across an open space interrupted only by a small building where the shore end of the cable enters, the garden walls, barricaded houses and a high sand-bag breastwork made the second line of defences across the Camino Real, and, from this short distance, looked formidable enough, particularly as a party of Spanish sharpshooters caught sight of us and, opening on us at short range, obliged us to retire. One or two of us who were a little slow in going back were warned by the puffs of dust which rose uncomfortably near our feet that the Spaniards were getting the range pretty accurately, and so we hitched our horses in the rifle pits and waited for the storm to blow over. Two or three infantrymen dodged in with us and tried to pick off the sharpshooters, but they showed themselves too short a time to make a good mark and as no smoke disclosed their stations our men ceased to waste ammunition on them. Major Jones, the active quartermaster of Camp Dewey, who was as irrepressible as a school boy out on a holiday, tried in vain to locate our annoying neighbors from the elevated position of a stone sentry box at an angle of the fort and at last Captain Mott and I tired of the onesided game, and, irritated by the useless resistance, clambered over the parapet of the water battery and wandered around under the fort and across the small green meadow which was covered with the miscellaneous rubbish which is always found in the wake of a retreating enemy.

The base of the fort was piled high at places with a morraine of broken stone and mortar from the parapet above and from the ragged excavations which the great projectiles had made in the masonry. A huge, brightly polished shell, still warm, lay on the turf near the angle of the fort as if it had been carefully deposited there by hand.

Finding a convenient gap in the high sandbag breastwork where it met the fort on the east side, we clambered over it and found General Greene and two or three members of his staff already there. From this point we could look along the rear of the Spanish lines to the point where the strong sandbag breastwork turned off at an angle towards Blockhouse Fourteen. Beyond the bridge, the parapet of which had been roughly treated by the Utah guns, a few broken toys of the War-God lay in the trench and at our feet near the wall of the fort one still groaning from an ugly wound in the head was tossing about on the ground. Our ambulance men rolled the poor wretch upon a blanket and carried him to the rear.

A spattering fire continued from the houses of Malate and once in a while a heavier drift of bullets would come spasmodically from the woods to the right. Now our men began to stream along the Camino Real, across the bridge and up the road towards the houses, not at all as if they were advancing upon an enemy but as if on march, with their coffee coolers along and their rifles at right shoulder shift. In one of the showers of Mauser bullets a party of infantrymen made a break for the gap through which we had climbed, preparing, as they sought cover of the sandbags, to have a crack at the invisible enemy, but the general sternly ordered them back and they went off with rather a discouraged look as much as to say that it was poor fun to march up into fire and

not have the privilege of using a rifle. It was not the best of
fun standing there, either, without the excitement of seeing
the enemy who were hidden away almost within hailing distance, and it was not a little disconcerting to be unable to see
any smoke in front of us. Waiting until he was sure of the
direction of the most annoying fire, the general ordered it to
be returned by a few volleys and then turning to his staff,
said:

"Now get the horses!"

One of the staff, thinking aloud and remembering that the
horses were in rather a warm corner, said:

"I will if I can!"

Language followed and Captain Mott and I scurried off
to our rifle pits again. Major Jones had disappeared with
his pony and was probably half way up to the walled town.
The Spanish sharpshooters were still enjoying their sniping
and our appearance on the parapet of the water battery put
them on the alert again. We had to make a dash for it so
we unhitched the ponies and dragged them after us down
the steep bank to the beach so as to get behind the breastwork which ran to high water mark. I started first and
came in for only the first flight of the compliments but my
companion who was a half dozen yards behind me seemed
to give them the range and as we almost literally tumbled
around the end of the breastwork into a group of infantrymen in shelter there, we felt as if we had disturbed a hor-
net's nest in a hay field.

We met the general behind the fort and at that moment
the Californians came marching up the beach, dripping from
their wade through and their ardor only stimulated and increased by the sound of the whistling bullets. The Colorado
band which had been ringing the changes on patriotic airs
now struck up in lively measure "There'll Be a Hot Time in
the Old Town To-night," calling forth a chorus from the
Californians which made the old fort echo and drove all se-

rious thoughts from our minds. The picnic spirit was on us again and as we galloped up to the houses which a moment before we had been regarding almost with apprehension, we only thought of the old walled town and longed to be there without delay.

Leaving the beach under the garden wall of the first barricaded house which the enemy's sharpshooters had occupied we entered the Camino Real behind the high breastwork of the second line of defences. The broad, straight thoroughfare was now busy with our men dashing across by squads from one side to the other and peppering the retreating Spaniards whenever they caught sight of them. Now they climbed into the garden of a pleasant villa, now they dodged among the plantains and behind the wattled fences of the native huts, always advancing and firing. Deliberately and stubbornly the scattered enemy retired from corner to corner, from cover to cover, pausing only to pump out bullets as they went.

Across the road two or three hundred yards from the second line of defences a strong sandbag breastwork blocked the street, but the Californians and the Eighteenth Regulars in front, the Nebraska regiment wading in the shallow water along shore and the Colorado battalions which were rushing the parallel street to the east made it too uncomfortable in a few minutes for the defenders of the breastwork and they scuttled away every man for himself and left the way open to the square of Malate where stands the large church which for so many days had been to us a prominent landmark of the suburb.

Here General Greene halted his men and reformed the regiments which had been necessarily broken in formation during the advance. The small open space was soon packed with our men and then the forward move was begun again. A few insurgents suddenly appeared, their rifles still warm. They were promptly disarmed and sent to the rear. Natives began to emerge from their hiding places and to jabber unintelligible words of friendly welcome, offering glasses of water with bits of brown sugar and bunches of fresh bananas in sign of amicable intentions.

It was now exactly noon and although we were not yet in sight of the walled town we knew it was but a short mile to the gates. Pushing rapidly on up the street we met a civilian who shouted:

"The Spaniards have raised a white flag!"

Without waiting for more the general, followed by a half dozen of us who were mounted, galloped up the street past the squads who were busy clearing the houses of Ermita of the annoying sharpshooters and out into the great open Campo de Bagumabayan between Ermita and the walled town. The public promenade called the Luneta, a drive in the shape of an ancient hippodrome, occupies the larger part of the space between the Camino Real and the bay and is notable chiefly because during the period of the recent insurrection the usual daily entertainment of a band concert was occasionally varied by a public execution of the captured insurgents.

As we rode out of the shelter of the houses into this open space there was no one in sight in front of us. The dreary waste of the Luneta, with its shabby bandstand, its scrubby trees and ugly lampposts, was quite deserted and uninviting in its baldness. The gray walls of the citadel frowned ominously directly in front four hundred yards away and on a prominent corner a great white sheet, hastily tied by its corners to a swaying bamboo pole planted in the turf, fluttered lazily in the wind. To the left, as we galloped on, we glanced once at the great grassy mounds which concealed two of the famous twenty-four centimetre Krupp guns and to the right and further away we noticed, with an instinct of suspicion, a masonry demi-lune rising in threatening solidity above the marshy level of the meadow. Still further to the right and

THE LUNETA, MANILA

beyond this we could see, as we advanced, the parapet of the high walls covered with Spanish infantrymen, particularly opposite the houses which cluster along the Paco road where it meets the broad esplanade, the Calzada de Vidal.

The moment we came out into this open space, a familiar and annoying cracking began all around us and the gravel began to jump on every side. We urged our little ponies to their full speed but the poor beasts were unshod and they hobbled painfully over the rough hard ground and put no heart into their gait. The farther we went on the more we seemed to become the target of the enemy and we could not always tell where the shots came from, behind us or from the right or even from the walls of the town. Our little party had none of the outward signs of authority about it but resembled a group of irregular cavalry more than a general with his staff. Every one wore a rain coat or a poncho and all were splashed from head to foot with mud. I thought as we rode along that it was not altogether the fault of the enemy if they did not understand at once that our mission was the first move towards the cessation of hostilities.

In a few minutes we reached a heavy barricade of railway iron across the sea front promenade under the low battery at the southwest angle of the citadel. Here at a small embrasure, from which a Krupp field piece pushed out its shining muzzle, an officer and a private soldier appeared as we drew near. General Greene asked him if the town had surrendered, and he replied that he did not know, as he had simply been ordered to put up the white flag. In response to the general's request to be permitted to enter the town, now that the white flag indicated a suspension of hostilities, he directed us to go along the Calzada to the first bridge over the moat at the Puerta Real and there we would probably be met by an officer. The shooting in our direction had ceased when we halted at the barricade, but we could hear a confused firing still going on among the houses of Ermita and along the Paco road. Just before we turned away to gallop towards the bridge, we saw, to our relief, the brown uniforms of our men as they assembled in front of the houses of Ermita and heard their welcome volleys answering the fire of the scattered enemy. Then we saw a small brown mass of our men quietly march out of the Paco road and across the Calzada, and form under the large trees near the moat only a few yards away from the parapet crowded with Spanish soldiers. Hastening up to them we found it was H company of the Twenty-third Regulars under Captain O'Connor, a veteran of the civil war, which, in the confusion of the advance over a rough country, had become separated from its battalion. The gallant captain had led his men steadily on under the cross fire of the enemy until his progress was effectually stopped by the walls of the town and there he stood awaiting orders.

Looking down the Paco road we saw to our surprise that it was filled with Spanish infantry for a long distance. Captain O'Connor explained that this was the force retreating from Santa Ana and that he had halted them and had refused to let them enter the town until he had been ordered to do so. A California battalion now came up from across the campo and halted just beyond the bridge. The firing still went on near at hand. Loud calls for a surgeon came from the Californians and the men declared that they had received a volley from the city walls. This no one could verify because the smokeless powder gave no sign. It was easy to see, however, that the Spaniards on the walls, four or five thousand in number, were in a state of excitement and might start in to wipe out our small force at any moment. Besides this important force on our front there were several battalions quite as close at hand in the rear and a detachment of the veteran guard of Manila as well. Beyond and behind these troops there was a confusion of men, mostly in white, running across the road and a continuous sound of firing.

It was a critical moment and no one could foretell what might happen. A single careless shot might start an annihilating fire and bring about a terrible disaster.

General Greene looked anxiously down the road. "I can see our flag down there!" he exclaimed.

I wanted to see it very much and tried hard to make it out but could not do so and I told the general I thought he was mistaken. We looked again and again through our glasses and in a few minutes we saw the brown uniforms of our men far down the road and then the fluttering colors! The situation was saved. The general now ordered the Spanish officers to march their men into the town. Soon after they had disappeared in the covered way beyond the bridge, a carriage and pair with two men in livery came dashing out and a note was handed to the general. Taking with him Captain Bates, his chief of staff, he entered the carriage and drove into the town, leaving orders for the troops to remain where they were until his return and under no circumstances to open fire unless they were attacked.

CHAPTER XI

It was now shortly after two o'clock and the white flag
had been flying since midday and the firing had not yet
stopped. What was going on we could not understand. The
Spaniards on the parapet were eagerly watching something
off to the south, often gesticulating and pointing, but nothing
developed. Meanwhile the troops of the Second Brigade kept
coming up. The two batteries of the Third Heavy Artillery
marched down the Paco road as fresh as if they were coming
in from a guard mount in the rain and Captain O'Hara told
me with a humorous expression that they had been on a
coffee-coolers' parade and had not even loaded their rifles.
The Pennsylvanians followed, tired and bedraggled after
their twenty-four hours in the trenches, and soon the whole
brigade was massed in front of the Puerta Real. All had
heard the firing on the right which had been going on for
several hours but no one, not even the company of the
Twenty-third, knew anything of the advance of General
MacArthur's brigade.

What had actually happened on the right of our line was
this. The Astor Battery and a Utah gun had been sent up
to the front near Blockhouse Fourteen on Friday evening,
as I have before related. Finding the insurgents unwilling
to give up their positions, they had passed the night among
the native huts and waited for the developments of the morning. Their trouble began early enough, for the first insurgent gun which startled us on our way to the front awoke
the Spaniards to activity and they began a fusillade which
at that close range was very troublesome. As soon as possible after breakfast Captain March cut a path through the

THE GUN WHICH DESTROYED SPANISH BLOCK-HOUSE NO. 14

bamboo and dragged two of his guns up to a group of native huts directly opposite the Singalong road where it makes a sharp turn to the west to meet the Pasig road in front of Blockhouse Fourteen. He placed one of the guns in a hastily constructed embrasure and the other he was obliged to drag under one of the huts, almost directly in range of the first gun, because this was the only place where there was an opening through which he could fire.

When the bombardment by the fleet began the three pieces of artillery were set to work, the Utah men directing their attention chiefly on Blockhouse Fourteen, a short two hundred yards away, and the Astors throwing shell first into this and then into Blockhouse Thirteen, a large structure with thick stone walls on the west side of the Singalong road. The Spanish gunners had the range of the insurgent positions very accurately, for the first shell they fired struck one of the Astor guns and wounded three men, one of them, Private Dunn, mortally. Fortunately the shell did not explode or the story would be different. The Thirteenth Minnesota Regiment was supporting the artillery and when the converging fire from the three pieces made the blockhouse untenable they rushed across the narrow open space and took possession of this stronghold with its adjacent earthworks and captured a number of prisoners. The Twenty-third Regulars advanced across the open to the left and entered the line of the enemy's entrenchments, meeting with no very serious opposition.

Shortly after this incident which was attended by slight casualties, Blockhouse Thirteen was seen to be in flames and a general advance along the Singalong road was ordered. Abreast the flaming building a strong entrenchment with two embrasures was encountered, but the Astor men quickly broke down the parapet and, partly filling the ditch, dragged and lifted their guns over the obstruction into the road beyond. In the blockhouse were stored thousands of rounds of small-arms ammunition and this was exploding with the noise of a continuous fusillade, causing those who were not in the immediate vicinity to believe that a vigorous resistance was met at this point. The Minnesota regiment pushed steadily forward in open order through the gardens and swamps, and driving the enemy's rear guard before them, soon occupied the village of Singalong where General MacArthur immediately established his headquarters.

This village is an important one, containing a large number of houses and a large church standing in a broad open space partly surrounded by stone walls. Near the church on both sides of the roads are substantially built shops and residences and beyond these, toward the town, many native huts are hidden away among the bamboo along the road which makes a gentle turn to the northwest and disappears in the dense growth of trees. When the village was occupied, a sharp fire was met from the bamboo thicket beyond the village and it soon developed into such a serious obstacle that a decided check was put on the advance. There had been no report of another line of defences on this road, although it was known to have been the scene of several bloody conflicts between the Spaniards and the insurgents. From the firing it was certain, however, that there was a strong defence of some kind not far down the road. Two of the Astor guns had kept along with the firing line and, when the check came, Captain March and ten or twelve of the men drew their revolvers and dashed to the front. Scarcely had they left the village before Sergeant Sillman fell with a bullet in his knee, and First Sergeant Holmes, bending over to give him assistance, was shot in the mouth and instantly killed. Sergeant Crimmins, who went to the relief of Private Hayden, who was wounded, was also instantly killed, and, before the little band had covered fifty 'yards, they had lost two killed and five wounded, more than half their number. Nothing was to be accomplished by this movement, so

BARRICADED HOUSE BEYOND SINGALING, TOWARDS WHICH THE ASTOR BATTERY CHARGED

Captain March ordered the men to take cover and make their way back to the village.

There was plenty of shelter in the houses and behind the walls and as the retreat of the enemy was a foregone conclusion there was no necessity for reckless exposure. But the pent-up ardor was not readily cooled off and it was almost impossible to restrain the men even after the disastrous experience of the Astors. A line of Minnesota men lay across the open road so crowded together that they could scarcely handle their rifles and, exposed to the severe fire at close range, lost heavily and to no purpose.

The character of the obstacle remained a mystery until Captain Sawtelle of General MacArthur's staff and Captain March made a reconnoissance, and found it to be a heavily barricaded house with a sandbag breastwork across the road not over two hundred yards beyond the village. Responding to a call for volunteers, a party of Astor and Minnesota men, led by the above mentioned officers, made a dash up the road in a lull in the firing and found the stronghold deserted. The way was then open to the town, and the brigade advanced and took up its assigned position in Malate and Ermita raising the flag at half past three or fully three hours after the second brigade had occupied these suburbs.

During the check at Singalong, many large bands of insurgents pushed forward on the flanks and, avoiding the guards which had been left at the designated points, moved rapidly towards the town, sometimes crowding in with our troops in such a way that they had to be elbowed aside as they marched along. When the brigade was swung round to the left to take its position near the seashore, the insurgents, now increased to a force of several thousand, swarmed over the rice fields between Ermita and Paco and, finding themselves neck and neck with the retreating Spaniards, promptly opened fire on them and quite an active little battle took place near the Observatory, in the course of which both parties lost quite heavily and one of the insurgent leaders, Mariana de la Cruz, was killed. The Spaniards hurried on towards the town and escaped further conflict by coming into our lines. It was the skirmishing between these troops and the insurgents which was visible from the walls of the town and caused the confusion down the Paco road which we were unable to account for.

General Greene was absent in town over an hour and the firing had gradually subsided until no more was heard. He returned in the same carriage and informing us that General Merritt was expected every moment at the Ayuntamiento or municipal building where the peace negotiations were in progress, General Babcock decided to go into the walled town and kindly asked me to accompany him. Leaving my pony in the care of a friendly correspondent who was unmounted, I entered the carriage with the general and we drove confidently over the bridge and through the covered way to the Puerta Real. The gate was shut and the sentinels on the parapet warned us off. In vain we argued and expostulated, nothing would move them even to send for an officer and we had to turn back. Believing there was some confusion of orders, since General Greene had been permitted to enter and to come out by this gate, we concluded to drive to the next one, and rattled off along the Calzada towards the botanical gardens, now a neglected waste covered with weeds and stumps of trees, meeting as we went several private carriages filled with Europeans waving their hats and cheering lustily.

Suddenly there appeared from a side street just in front of us a band of twenty or thirty armed natives carrying a large insurgent flag, and a short distance behind them was massed a large body of insurgents apparently just halted. As we approached a few of the natives knelt down and covered us with their rifles and the rest of the advanced guard began to spread out right and left. General Babcock

GENERAL FRANCIS V. GREENE AT BLOCKHOUSE 14 AFTER THE SURRENDER

alighted and shouted: "We are Americans!" and they held their fire but did not lower their pieces In a minute or two an officer came to the front and, recognizing the American uniform, held up his hand to indicate that it was all right and ordered the men to stand up. We started to drive on again but the officer waved us back and the men again took aim at us and the coachman, who was in Spanish livery, was only too ready to turn the carriage around and drive us back. Reporting the incident to General Greene, he immediately led the Nebraska regiment to the scene of our trouble and the giant volunteers crowded the insurgents off the Calzada much the same as a line of policemen clears a city street by sheer weight and show of authority. We then drove along without opposition to the Puerta Parian, one of the largest gates of the town, approached through a long covered way. Here we met with the same reception as at the first gate and the situation was only different because we were far away from any of our troops and quite out of sight among the high embankments. The sentries ordered us to keep off but we slowly advanced until we were within twenty-five or thirty yards of the gate trusting to the impressive appearance of our borrowed livery and the well known turn out. After some delay and much parleying, an officer was brought who insisted that he had the strictest orders to admit no one. Just at that moment a wounded Spaniard was brought into the covered way accompanied by an officer and several men. They were also refused admittance and we therefore turned around and followed them back. We began now to understand that the gates were shut for fear of the insurgents entering the walled town, a movement which, from the Spanish point of view, seemed likely enough, since the natives were seen advancing shoulder to shoulder with our own men.

While we were delayed at this gate the Second Brigade moved along the Calzada and over the Puente de España and the Puente Colgante into the business and residential quarters and strong guards were placed at every point. On the south side of the Pasig the barracks and hospital and engineers' offices were taken possession of, and as we drove again towards the Luneta it was a gratifying spectacle to see everywhere in the immediate vicinity masses of brown-clad men standing in formation awaiting orders while squads and files moved away in every direction.

Remembering that the railway iron barricade across the water-front promenade was apparently a movable affair, for I had noticed small iron wheels on a track underneath it, I suggested that we try to enter at that point as it was farthest away from where the insurgents were seen. When we reached it we found it had already been moved back a foot or two and Major Simpson and Major Wadsworth of General Merritt's staff, were just squeezing out as we drove up. We four, together with two or three natives and a friendly Spanish soldier, put our joint weight on the barricade and rolled it aside far enough to allow our carriage to enter and then blocked the wheels. Weeks after we noticed it still in the same position. The road was now open for traffic and a crowd of loaded *carramatos* and people on foot streamed out across the Luneta towards Ermita. Meeting with no further opposition, and, indeed anticipating none, we drove rapidly through the Puerta Santa Lucia which was wide open but guarded by Spanish sentinels and to the great shady square in front of the cathedral. The neighboring streets were packed full of Spanish soldiers looking as cool and neat and dry as possible, a notable contrast to our own men we had just left. They made way for the well-known turn-out of the governor-general and we alighted at the entrance of the Ayuntamiento or city hall, an imposing edifice on the east side of the cathedral square or Plaza de Palacio. One or two Oregon men were keeping informal guard at the staircase which was thronged with Spanish officials in uniform

PUERTA SANTA LUCIA

and civilians looking none the worse for the long siege. Following the current of people we soon came to the offices and in the corner one we found General Merritt, Colonel Whittier, and other members of headquarters staff, all in earnest conference with the Spanish officers.

It was by no means an impressive moment. The absence of formality, particularly on our side, made it impossible to realize that it was a historic incident. I had seen other capitulations and was a little disappointed that this one promised to be neither dramatic nor picturesque. Still it was exceedingly interesting because of the striking contrasts presented in the crowded office where everybody seemed to be talking at once and every one appeared to have as much to say as the next man. Then, elbowing one another like brokers in the stock exchange, were generals and colonels, aide-de-camps and civilians, types of two distinct races, the representative democrat and the born aristocrat, the easy mannered citizen of the great republic and the ostentatiously formal official of a monarchy. The differences were wide and suggestive, and the air of irrepressible youth and vigor about our officers, many of whom stood a full head above the Spaniards, made the others look worn out and decadent. None of our officers were in full dress uniform, most of them wearing the gray linen, although all had swords which they promptly threw aside as useless encumbrances. The Spanish were in their most formal attire, with broad red sashes, richly ornamented swords, a dazzling array of decorations and glittering insignia of rank. A casual observer would have come to the conclusion that we were suing for peace at the hands of these high and mighty officials. The most conspicuous figure among the Spaniards was the newly appointed Governor-General and Captain-General Jaudenes, whose uncongenial duty it was to surrender the town and his army, knowing all the time that he was being made a scapegoat for the failure of others. He is a man of unusually small stature, scarcely over five feet in height, and has rather the air of a professor than of a general who has commanded a division. The late governor-general, Augustin, Admiral Montojo, General Rizzo and many others were present at this preliminary conference and the discussion was prolonged and wearisome on the details of the rough draft of the capitulation articles, which, after all, were held to bind no one but were intended to be a guarantee of the cessation of hostilities.

For my own part I could not see the necessity of an elaborately phrased set of articles, for the town had long been at the mercy of our fleet and they could expect in reason nothing more than could be tersely expressed in a single sentence. But in this, as in most of our dealings with the Spaniards, we were far more generous and lenient than they expected or than was good for either party, probably because we felt that the enormous superiority of our strength obliged us to be magnanimous even to the point of weakness. The Spaniards in Manila had learned to appreciate this sentiment long before the surrender and they made the most of their opportunities. Countless individual acts after the capitulation proved that the general impression among them was that we were vastly inferior in every quality except physical strength and they bore themselves as if they had been conferring a great favor on us by condescending to surrender. A little more formality on our part, a proper assumption of authority and a rigid definition of the recognized rights of the conqueror would have saved a deal of trouble not only with the Spaniards but with the natives. Here as in many other parts of the world the man who allows himself to be got the better of is never respected and authority is largely based on outward display.

While we had been waiting outside the walls, quite a little drama had been going on in the town. Shortly after the white flag had been shown, Lieutenant-Colonel Whittier and

Flag-Lieutenant Brumby came ashore in the Belgian consul's launch and had been driven up to the Ayuntamiento where they met the Spanish officers and were shown a draft of the proposed terms of surrender. Lieutenant Brumby shortly returned to the fleet with a message to General Merritt leaving Colonel Whittier to hold and to occupy the walled town by himself. It was not a very agreeable situation for the plans of the day had apparently miscarried somehow and the contest was still going on a mile or so away, notwithstanding the fact that the white flag was flying. On the other hand the great Spanish ensign was still displayed on the water-front, and, although the result of all this was inevitable, no one was quite sure what was going to happen before the formal surrender actually took place. The firing approached nearer and nearer the walls, detachments of retreating troops assembled in the square bringing reports that the insurgents were advancing side by side with the Americans. The Spanish officers grew nervous and apprehensive, knowing all too well what would happen if the armed natives made their way inside the citadel. At last it was suggested that a note should be sent to the general commanding the American forces near the walled town asking him to order a cessation of hostilities. Colonel Whittier wrote a brief letter to this effect and it was sent out and handed to General Greene, as before mentioned, who decided to come in and report the situation and also explain that he was unable to occupy the district north of the Pasig as long as the confusion brought about by the check to General MacArthur's advance was unsettled. It was fortunate, by the way, that General Greene's brigade remained before the walls of the town, for except for their presence the whole insurgent army from the province of Cavité would have been massed there.

General Merritt with his headquarters' staff and two companies of the Second Oregon regiment on the *Zafiro*, followed by the *Kwonghoi* with six more companies of the same organization, was off the mouth of the Pasig when Colonel Whittier's message reached him and he decided to land at once. Finding no carriage awaiting him, as his coming was not announced, and without waiting for an escort, he walked up from the river front, accompanied by a few staff officers. The Oregon men were soon landed in small boats and about half past four o'clock, while the discussion was still going on in the Ayuntamiento, we saw from the windows the main body of the detachment enter the square, make their way through the solid mass of Spanish troops and form a line around the square, facing outward. Shortly before this incident I learned, in conversation with some Spanish officers, that the German consul was going to send off a dispatch to his government that same afternoon and as I had been gradually building up a descriptive telegram during the day, I hastily closed it with a brief statement of existing conditions and, securing the services of one of the employees of the Ayuntamiento, sent him off with a letter to the German consul requesting him to forward the enclosure to Hong Kong. It is scarcely necessary to add that I never heard of the despatch again. The *Kaiserin Augusta* left her moorings and sailed away as soon as possible after the signing of the preliminary terms of capitulation, carrying the late governor-general, Augustin, and his family, Admiral von Diederichs omitting, in his hurry to depart, the usual courtesies to the commanding officers of the victorious forces. On arriving at Hong Kong a brief despatch to the *Daily Telegraph* and to Reuter's Agency was sent ashore, but the Germans were persistently reticent on the subject of the events occurring at Manila.

It was about five o'clock before an agreement was reached on the rough draft of the articles of capitulation, and all this time the large Spanish ensign was flying on the northwest bastion of the walled town, visible all over the bay and in full sight of our troops at Ermita and Malate. General Merritt had instructed Major Sturgis of his staff to put up the headquarters flag on the Ayuntamiento and the Stars and Stripes in the place of the Spanish flag as soon as the signatures were affixed to the much discussed document and the major had invited me to assist him. While we were standing there waiting, Lieutenant Brumby, who had brought ashore a very large new flag, went up to General Merritt and apparently asked a question. We heard the general reply: "All right! Go ahead!" and the lieutenant with his men hurriedly left the building. Major Sturgis who looked rather disconcerted asked if he should put up the headquarters flag.

"Certainly," replied the general, "and the other one too!"

"We are euchred out of the Spanish flag," said the major as we left the room. "The navy has got the better of us. But perhaps we can find another flagstaff."

Shouldering our way through the crowd of excited Spaniards, we found a pole fastened to a balcony overlooking the square, and Major Sturgis hoisted the blue flag which indicated that this was now the headquarters of the Eighth Army Corps. The crowd below gazed silently at the fluttering bunting and one officer at our elbow sadly remarked:

"This is a bitter moment for us!"

As we were hurrying down the staircase with the other flag, a messenger came to report that Lieutenant Brumby was likely to have trouble because the Spaniards were very much excited and were taking a menacing attitude. The major asked for a company of the Oregon men to be sent off to the bastion at once, and we hastened on, hearing the rapid tramp of the men behind us. When we arrived we found the Spanish ensign had disappeared and the bright new red, white and blue bravely flying in its place while Lieutenant Brumby and one or two others were quietly standing at the base of the flagstaff to have their photographs taken. At the bottom of the ramp leading up to the parapet there was a crowd of about a hundred men and women, some of them ostentatiously weeping and not a few gesticulating wildly. We went in among them and asked what the trouble was and a half dozen sobbing women ejaculated with spasmodic volubility that the Americans were going to turn them out of their houses. We assured them that this was not so and, after our earnest protestations that no one would be disturbed, they dried their tears and became so friendly as to offer us cigarettes. This incident, trifling as it was, was made much of in the newspapers at the time, the report being current that the citizens attempted to resist the hoisting of the flag and that a serious disturbance was only averted by the timely arrival of our troops.

On returning to the square, we had to push our way past crowds of Spanish infantry slowly moving towards the cathedral. Many of them were in a hysterical state of excitement, tearing off their red and yellow hat-bands and cockades and even their marks of rank and trampling them in the mud. They paid no attention to us, however, and we were soon back in the Ayuntamiento, where the soldiers, now prisoners of war, had already begun to pile their rifles and ammunition at the foot of the staircase. As fast as this was done they quietly marched away to the barracks and the churches, where they took up their quarters.

The Spanish officials had now departed, the crowd in the Ayuntamiento had dispersed, and the excitement naturally consequent on the event of the surrender was fast subsiding, when a great cloud of smoke was seen rising above the buildings in the direction of the river. Hastening to the landing place, I saw a large Spanish transport which was anchored in the river near the harbormaster's office burning so fiercely that she was sure to sink within a few minutes. This was the last notable incident of the capture of the town and one which is scarcely to the honor of the individuals who are responsible for it. It was an act of spite which, while charac-

OUR TROOPS MARCHING INTO MANILA

teristic of the spirit which was almost universal among the Spaniards in Manila, was probably committed without the knowledge, or at least without the orders, of the authorities. It was far too flagrant an outrage of the rules of civilized warfare to be commended openly by those whose duty it was to prevent the useless destruction of property, still it was evidently considered to be rather a smart trick and I was unable to elicit from a single Spanish officer one word of condemnation of this breach of good faith.

As night came on we naturally began to think a little of our own comforts. Early in the day I had divided my two days' rations with others who had a smaller chance of getting a meal in the near future than I had and none of the rest of the party had as much as a biscuit. Colonel Whittier was, however, equal to the occasion.

"We must get up a nice little dinner now," he said, "to celebrate the capture of the town!"

This seemed about as reasonable a proposition as to ask for a mint julep in the desert of Sahara, but the colonel's instinct was keener than ours and he ridiculed the argument that because Manila had been long besieged and there were no hotels in the walled town it would be impossible to provide a dinner for ten people at this short notice.

Our first move was to explore the large building. In addition to the court rooms and offices, many of which are spacious and are elaborately if not quite tastefully decorated, we found various smaller rooms fitted up with ornately carved bedsteads and other pieces of furniture and observed many indications of hasty vacancy by their recent occupants. In one of the suites facing a side street, we discovered a large and sumptuous bath room, without water, of course, because the insurgents held the water works, a small and well appointed dining room and a kitchen provided with all necessary articles. Further, we succeeded in finding the cook and several employees who had not yet left the building and were quite ready to serve the new comers. The cook informed us that poultry, rice and vegetables were readily obtained, that there was plenty of wine in the shops near by and that the only thing he could not promise to provide was bread and this because it was so late in the day and the bakeries had all sold out. This did not sound like starvation nor suggest a very harrowing picture of the sufferings of the besieged. Bread was somehow forthcoming after all and an hour or so later we sat down to a meal which, to those of us who had been living on commissary supplies in the camp, was a perfect triumph of gastronomy. There were ten at the table, General Merritt, Colonel Whittier, Captain Mott, Majors Simpson, Sturgis, Wadsworth, Bement, Surgeon-Major Woodruff and myself. When we were engaged in this very pleasant function General Greene appeared to report on the final disposition of his troops and did not require much urging to join us. It was not the time to prolong a celebration, for, although all was quiet enough in the walled town, there was still a good deal of trouble all along the Spanish lines from Caloocan to Santa Mesa. Reports kept coming in thick and fast that the insurgents were attacking the Spaniards with great vigor, and several urgent appeals for reinforcements were sent in. To these requests for assistance, General Merritt replied that he advised the Spaniards to evacuate their positions and retire to the town inside our lines, a proceeding which resulted, of course, in the occupancy by the armed natives of not only all the Spanish defences but of a very large part of the suburbs, for our lines at that time were only established in the vicinity of the business and residential quarters on the north side of the river and along the Calzada, the Paco road, and in Malate and Ermita on the south.

About ten o'clock Captain Mott and I, mounted on captured ponies, accompanied General Greene to his temporary headquarters in the Hotel Oriente in Binondo. The streets inside the walls were quiet and deserted except by an occasional Oregon soldier or one of the veteran guards who were still performing their duties as policemen. The Spanish sentries were still at their posts at the gate and presented arms as we passed. Crossing the Puente de España into Binondo we found the same quiet prevailing, the shops all shut and our soldiers asleep on the sidewalks and in the doorways and under what shelter they could find. The Hotel Oriente proved to be a hostelry only in name but there was in my room a cane-bottomed bedstead without pillows or sheets or mosquito netting which after the mud of the camp looked so inviting that I scarcely missed the luxury of undressing.

CHAPTER XII

In the penetrating light of that bright Sunday morning the few guests of the Hotel Oriente looked scandalously disreputable. Captain Harper, of the Quartermaster's Department, who had been acting as aid to General Greene the day before, was detailed to go to Camp Dewey and bring up the baggage and before he started we persuaded the landlady who had dried her tears of terror which were copiously flowing when we arrived, to share her coffee and rolls with us in the kitchen. She also gave me a needle and thread so I could repair the worst damages to my khaki. The general whose costume was not quite up to Piccadilly standard, was able, on his appearance in the streets to take refuge in the glamour of a smart turn-out with coachman and tiger in livery which he had annexed for temporary service, but the rest of us had to console ourselves that we were no worse off than the majority of those who had left Camp Dewey and "changed our boarding house," as the soldiers said. I must confess I was loath to present myself in a mud stained and ragged suit which had evidently dried on me, among the spick and span officers of headquarters and the elaborately groomed Spaniards but there was no help for it, as the commission to draw up final articles of capitulation met at nine o'clock and the *Zafiro* was to sail for Hong Kong as soon as the document was signed.

Our men in the streets had not passed a very comfortable night, for heavy showers had frequently swept over the town, but their cheerfulness and patience were wonderful to see. Everywhere the brawny and rough-looking but good natured soldier was in conspicuous evidence, not by his appearance

GROUP OF AMERICAN OFFICERS BEFORE THE PUERTA REAL ON THE DAY OF THE SURRENDER
OF MANILA

alone, but by his honest, manly bearing and his orderly behavior. The worn and dirty brown uniforms were seen in every house, their wearers speedily making friends with the occupants. The absence of any sign of disorder soon gave the inhabitants confidence, and in a few hours some small native shops were opened and began to drive a market-day trade. Sentinels on all sides showed how complete was the occupation of this part of the town, and the perfect quiet which prevailed proved that the troops were effectively performing their duties and at the same time were acting the part of good citizens and honorable men. As I entered the walled town, detachments of Spanish troops were marching into every gate on their way to lay down their arms in the vestibule of the Ayuntamiento. By midday between three and four thousand rifles were piled up there, almost blocking the entrance, and a more appropriate place of deposit had to be selected. The commission met in one of the side rooms adjoining the office of the governor-general, and for weary hours discussed the separate items of the rough draft which had been signed the day before.

The *Albany*, which was supposed to report somewhere on the Pasig below the first bridge, had been seen in the river, but had disappeared and I could find no trace of her, and I began to be anxious about my communications, as it was necessary to keep my despatch until the very last moment. There was nothing to be done, however, as no boats could be hired, except to wait and see what turned up. This anxiety did not make the day seem shorter, and the interminable discussion over the details of the surrender seemed as unnecessary as they were wearisome. It was the middle of the afternoon before the signatures were finally affixed to the document which I here give in full. It scarcely needs comment, but I cannot refrain from repeating the axiom that the safest contract is the simplest one.

"MANILA, *August* 14, 1898.

"The undersigned, having been appointed a commission to determine the details of the capitulation of the city and defences of Manila and its suburbs, and the Spanish forces stationed therein, in accordance with the agreement entered into the previous day by Major-General Wesley Merritt, United States army, American commander-in-chief in the Philippines, and his Excellency Don Fermin Jaudenes, acting general-in-chief of the Spanish army in the Philippines, have agreed upon the following:

"1. The Spanish troops, European and native, capitulate with the city and its defences, with all the honors of war, depositing their arms in places designated by the authorities of the United States, and remaining in the quarters designated and under the orders of their officers and subject to control of the aforesaid United States authorities, until the conclusion of a treaty of peace between the two belligerent nations.

"All persons included in the capitulation remain at liberty, the officers remaining in their respective homes, which shall be respected as long as they observe the regulations prescribed for their government and the laws in force.

"2. Officers shall retain their side-arms, horses, and private property.

"3. All public horses and public property of all kinds shall be turned over to staff officers designated by the United States.

"4. Complete returns in duplicate of men by organizations, and full lists of public property and stores, shall be rendered to the United States within ten days from this date.

"5. All questions relating to the repatriation of officers and men of the Spanish forces, and of their families, and of the expenses which said repatriation may occasion, shall be referred to the government of the United States at Washington. Spanish families may leave Manila at any time convenient to them.

"The return of the arms surrendered by the Spanish forces shall take place when they evacuate the city, or when the American army evacuates.

"6. Officers and men included in the capitulation shall be supplied by the United States, according to their rank, with rations and necessary aid as though they were prisoners of war, until the conclusion of a treaty of peace between the United States and Spain.

"All the funds in the Spanish treasury and all other public funds shall be turned over to the authorities of the United States.

"7. This city, its inhabitants, its churches and religious worship, its educational establishments and its private property of all descriptions, are placed under the special safeguard of the faith and honor of the American army.

"F. V. GREENE,
"Brigadier-General of Volunteers, U. S. Army.

"B. P. LAMBERTON,
"Captain, U. S. Navy.

"CHARLES A. WHITTIER,
"Lieutenant-Colonel and Inspector-General.

"E. A. CROWDER,
"Lieutenant-Colonel and Judge-Advocate.

"NICHOLAS DE LA PENA,
"Auditor-General.

"CARLOS REYES,
"Coronel de Ingenieros.

"JOSE MARIA OLAGUEA FELIN,
"Coronel de Estado-Mayor."

The last paragraph will be recognized by every student of military history as identical, except for the substitution of the word "city" for the words "splendid capital," with paragraph seventeen of the articles of General Scott's famous order issued in the City of Mexico on September 17, 1847.

By the terms of this agreement were surrendered between thirteen and fourteen thousand prisoners; twenty-three thousand rifles; ten million rounds of small-arms ammunition; two hundred and thirteen pieces of artillery, ancient and modern; immense quantities of powder and projectiles; public funds in the treasury, the mint and the public offices, amounting to over a million dollars. The losses among the

American troops engaged in the investment and capture of the town had been twenty killed and one hundred and five wounded; very few had succumbed to disease.

I succeeded in getting out to the *Zafiro* with my despatches on a captured tugboat, finishing my work as we bobbed up and down on the rough waters of the bay. To my surprise I found Mr. Reid on board starting for Hong Kong, having sent the *Albany* to Cavité to await my orders, and it was a relief to know at last that the news he carried was sure to reach its destination.

The first few days of the occupation were so full of interesting and noteworthy incidents that, in the perspective of time, they are remembered only as an uninterrupted period of activity and anxious endeavor to keep touch with every operation. On Sunday afternoon General Merritt and staff moved up to the palace of Malicañang, in the district of San Miguel, the late residence of the Spanish governor-general, a large but inconveniently arranged and uncomfortable edifice on the bank of the Pasig, surrounded by extensive and ill-kept grounds, and flanked by a large brewery on one side, and by temptingly pleasant private villas on the other. The general is constitutionally averse to any display, and the very name of palace was repugnant to his simple tastes, but it was undoubtedly advisable, as far as could be reasonably done, to keep up some of the glamour of the position in order to avoid shocking the sensibilities of a community which had for so long a period been accustomed to associate intimately high rank with ostentatious show. A bed had been offered me in one of the many rooms of the Ayuntamiento, and I concluded to sleep there for the present, as it was near the centre of operations, and to trust to luck for my subsistence. As it happened, luck was a little coy and shy, and the feast on Saturday evening was the last square meal which came in my way for several days.

On Monday some of the shops of the better class in the

popular business street, the Escolta, took down their shutters, the Manila Club at Malate, which although well within range of our projectiles at Maytubig, had only shut its doors for a few hours during the evacuation of the quarter by the Spaniards, began to attract our officers with its freely professed hospitality, and the English and American residents gathered here to fraternize with the welcome visitors. On the following day the horse cars made spasmodic trips, several newspapers were published and on Wednesday the banks, temporarily guarded by our troops, resumed business.

As soon as possible after the surrender, General Merritt issued the following proclamation, which was printed in English, Spanish and Tagalo, and distributed all over the city and the suburbs:

"HEADQUARTERS DEPARTMENT OF THE PACIFIC,
"*August* 14, 1898.

"*To the People of the Philippines:*

"1. War has existed between the United States and Spain since April 21st of this year. Since that date you have witnessed the destruction, by an American fleet, of the Spanish naval power in these islands, the fall of the principal city, Manila, and its defences, and the surrender of the Spanish army of occupation to the forces of the United States.

"2. The commander of the United States forces now in possession has instructions from his government to assure the people that he has not come to wage war upon them, nor upon any party or faction among them, but to protect them in their homes, in their employments, and in their personal and religious rights. All persons who by active aid or honest submission co-operate with the United States in its efforts to give effect to this beneficent purpose will receive the reward of its support and protection.

"3. The government established among you by the United States army is a government of military occupation; and for the present it is ordered that the municipal laws, such as affect private rights of persons and property, regulate local institutions, and provide for the punishment of crime, shall be considered as continuing in force, so far as compatible with the purposes of military government, and that they be administered through the ordinary tribunals substantially as before occupation, but by officials appointed by the government of occupation.

"4. A provost marshal-general will be appointed for the city of Manila and its outlying districts. This territory will be divided into sub-districts, and there will be assigned to each a deputy provost-marshal.

"The duties of the provost marshal-general and his deputies will be set forth in detail in future orders. In a general way they are charged with the duty of making arrests of military as well as civil offenders, sending such of the former class as are triable by court-martial to their proper commands with statements of their offences and names of witnesses,and detaining in custody all other offenders for trial by military commission, provost courts, or native criminal courts, in accordance with law and the instructions hereafter to be issued.

"5. The port of Manila, and all other ports and places in the Philippines which may be in the actual possession of our land and naval forces, will be open, while our military occupation may continue, to the commerce of all neutral nations, as well as our own, in articles not contraband of war, and upon payment of the prescribed rates of duty which may be in force at the time of the importation.

"6. All churches and places devoted to religious worship and to the arts and sciences, all educational institutions, libraries, scientific collections, museums, are, so far as possible, to be protected; and all destruction or intentional defacement of such places or property, of historical monuments, archives, or works of science is prohibited, save when required by urgent military necessity. Severe punishment will be meted out for all violations of this regulation.

"The custodians of all properties of the character mentioned in this section will make prompt returns thereof to these headquarters, stating character and location, and embodying such recommendations as they may think proper for the full protection of the properties under their care and custody, that proper orders may issue enjoining the co-operation of both military and civil authorities in securing such protection.

"7. The commanding general, in announcing the establishment of military government and in entering upon his duties as military governor, in pursuance of his appointment as such by the government of the United States, desires to assure the people that so long as they preserve the peace and perform their duties towards the representatives of the United States, they will not be disturbed in their persons and property, except in so far as may be found necessary for the good of the service of the United States and the benefit of the people of the Philippines.

"WESLEY MERRITT,
"Major-General U. S. Army, Commanding."

In this connection it may be as well to quote the congratulatory order of General Merritt and a telegram from President McKinley.

"HEADQUARTERS DEPARTMENT OF THE PACIFIC AND EIGHTH ARMY CORPS, MANILA, P. I.,

"August 17, 1898.

"General Orders No. 6.

"The major-general commanding desires to congratulate the troops of this command upon their brilliant success in the capture, by assault, of the defences of Manila on Saturday, August 13, a date hereafter to be memorable in the history of American victories.

"After a journey of seven thousand miles by sea, the soldiers of the Philippine expedition encountered most serious difficulties in landing, due to protracted storms raising high surf through which it was necessary to pass the small boats which afforded the only means of disembarking the army and its supplies. This great task and the privations and hardships of a campaign during the rainy season in tropical lowlands, were accomplished and endured by all the troops in a spirit of soldierly fortitude, which has at all times during these days of trial given the commanding general the most heartfelt pride and confidence in his men. Nothing could be finer than the patient, uncomplaining devotion to duty which all have shown.

"Now, it is his pleasure to announce that, within three weeks after the arrival in the Philippines of the greater portion of the forces, the capital city of the Spanish provinces in the East, held by Spanish veterans, has fallen into our

175

hands, and he feels assured that all officers and men of this command have reason to be proud of the success of the expedition.

"The commanding general will hereafter take occasion to mention to the home government the names of officers, men, and organizations to whom special credit is due.

"By command of Major-General Merritt,

"J. B. BABCOCK,
"*Adjutant-General.*

"Official.
"Bentley Mott,
"Aid."

The telegram referred to above was as follows:

"WASHINGTON, D. C., *August 22,* 1898.

" *Major-General Merritt, U. S. A., Manila, via Hong-Kong:*

"In my own behalf and for the nation, I extend to yourself and to the officers and men of your command sincere thanks and congratulations for the conspicuously gallant conduct displayed in your campaign.

"WILLIAM McKINLEY."

In his official report to the government at Washington, referring to the capture and the orderly occupation of the town, General Merritt says it was "an act which only the law-abiding, temperate, resolute American soldier, well and skilfully handled by his regimental and brigade commanders, could accomplish."

General Merritt's first act of administration was to appoint General MacArthur provost-marshal and military governor of the walled town, and a day or two later he turned over the administration of the finances to General Greene, who was to perform the duties of the officer known as Intendente-General de Hacienda, appointed Major C. H. Whipple to take charge of the public funds, and Lieutenant-Colonel Whittier to be collector of customs, with Lieutenant-Colonel Colton as deputy. Then the other important offices were filled as the necessities of the situation demanded, Major Bement taking the position of collector of internal revenue, Lieutenant-Colonel Jewett that of provost judge, and the duties of captain of the port were entrusted to Captain Glass, of the navy. Practically within a few hours after the signing of the terms of capitulation, the new machinery of administration was set in motion. The men appointed to office were all eminently fitted for their different positions, and were familiar with operations similar to those which they were to undertake. Hence there was little or no delay in dealing with the complicated and intricate problems which arose in the extraordinary situation, except that caused by the Spaniards themselves, who stubbornly refused to give up their offices, resorting to the most childish and undignified tricks to obstruct and hinder the newly appointed officers in the performance of their duties. Their attitude was partly due to their belief that we, in granting such liberal terms of surrender, were only half-hearted in this enterprise and also to the knowledge gained from a telegram which arrived on the 16th, that a protocol had been signed at Washington, some hours before the surrender of Manila. By the terms of the protocol the settlement of the Philippine question had been left to a joint commission to be appointed in the future, and meanwhile hostilities were to be suspended, the United States forces were to occupy the bay and the town of Manila, with its suburbs, and the *status quo* was to exist until the final disposition of the archipelago was settled upon by the commission. In Spanish logic this meant that the Spanish governor-general still remained in authority, as well as all those officials whose functions were in any way related to the administration of the colony. Therefore they argued that only those officials whose duties were purely local could be removed from office; further, that all funds controlled by the Spanish governor-general, outside those in the municipal treasury, were not to be given up to the United States authorities until after the decision of the joint commission.

There was, to be sure, a certain show of reason in all this, because it was not by any means sure how long the occupation of the islands would continue. Besides it was impossible to interpret the phraseology of the protocol to mean that the United States was to assume the temporary government of the archipelago, and therefore the Spanish governor-general was still responsible for the administration of the government of the colony outside the limits of the bay and town. Thus he was left without resources to suppress the insurrection which would undoubtedly continue with renewed vigor, and all the small outlying garrisons as well as the property of Spanish residents all over the islands was deliberately given over to the tender mercies of the implacable enemies of the dominating race. It was little wonder, then, that the Spanish officials found it difficult to accept the anomalies of their position, and were slow to realize the fact that the critical situation of the Spaniards in the archipelago had been utterly ignored by the authors of the protocol. Their methods of submission to the inevitable were not, as I have suggested, to be commended. They gave up the keys of the offices only when threatened with the employment of force, and each officer entered a formal written protest to the effect that he had yielded up his authority only under compulsion. When the books of the treasury were being examined in the presence of both parties, a shortage of over three hundred thousand dollars was noticed. This was promptly explained to be on account of the defalcation of a well-known Spanish official. One of out officers bluntly asked:

"How much did Weyler get away with?"

"Something over three millions," was the innocent reply.

There was found in the treasury $170,000 in bills, and certified cheques on the Españo-Filipino Bank, $130,000 in silver, and $295,000 in copper coins. The bank proved to the satisfaction of General Greene that the Spanish government owed it, for loans granted under compulsion, some $1,900,-

THE PRISON, MANILA

ooo, of which about one-third part was promised to be repaid on August 15th. Relying on the truth of this statement the bank advanced its claim for the recovery of the money found in the treasury. Of course the claim could not be allowed. The ·case of the bank, however bad it appeared, was not worse than that of thousands of private individuals who had loaned money to the government on promise of liberal interest, and instead of cash had been obliged to accept bonds which were in turn supposed to bear interest, which never materialized.

Besides the claims of the bank and of various individuals, which were based on some reasonable grounds, there were thousands of others of a most ridiculously innocent nature, which were brought forward with annoying persistence. Employees in public offices who had been absent for months in the ranks of the insurgents, applied for back pay due them, various officials in high standing expected the United States to continue their salaries, which they asserted, and probably with truth, to be their only means of support. A certain colonel who had bought up a great many tickets in the May lottery which was never drawn, insisted with obnoxious pertinacity that the United States government must refund him the money. In most of the offices it was found that the number of employees was far greater than was necessary, but that the salaries were very small, the recognized custom being for every man to "squeeze" all he could out of the public and in this way add considerably to his stipend. This was particularly true in the custom-house, where the system of bribery has long been notorious. The resistance to the occupancy of the municipal and other offices continued spasmodically for a long time, and a month after the capture of the town two safes in the provost-marshal's office were still without keys. The Spaniards delayed and prevaricated and in the end stoutly asserted that each safe required three keys to open it, and that one of the parties holding a key was in

Paris, and besides there was nothing but private papers in the safes, anyhow. General Hughes, who had taken the office over from General MacArthur, finally lost patience and threatened to blow open the locks, whereupon the keys were produced and the safes were opened. Several thousand dollars in coin were found inside. The honorable and high-minded gentlemen had been sparring for time.

It is a curious sequel to all these troubles that, by the decision of the Paris Commission, all the public funds captured at Manila, together with'an immense amount of material which, according to all precedent belonged to the United States, were returned to the Spanish government.

CHAPTER XIII

ALTHOUGH we were masters of the town by right of conquest, there was the feeling in the air that we were only there on sufferance.   For weeks the Spanish officers in gorgeous uniforms with revolver and dangling sword paraded with an irritating assumption of superiority which recalled the strut of the Prussian officer in the streets of Berlin. They captured all the best carriages, often to the discomfiture and inconvenience of our own officers, and generally continued to act the part of masters over the natives who, having no assurance that the domination would not continue, were afraid to deny them the homage which they had always been forced to pay.   It occurred to me more than once during the first week, to be refused a meal in a restaurant on the plea of dearth of supplies, while the Spanish officers would be served with an abundance of food.   On one occasion a colonel went so far as to stop a *carromato* in which another correspondent and myself were riding and, because we were not in uniform, attempted, to his ultimate discomfiture, to drag us forcibly from our seats.   This attitude of the Spaniards, as might be expected, had a bad effect on the native population, who naturally attributed our endurance of this false position to fear rather than to commendable forbearance, and they began to comport themselves accordingly.

The insurgents, meanwhile, exasperated at their failure to participate in the occupation of the town proper, busied themselves at once in turning the Spanish earthworks into offensive positions, dug many new trenches and made active preparations for renewing the siege of the town, always with the excuse that when the United States troops evacuated Manila they might be ready to complete their conquest of the hated race. At Tondo, the northwesterly district of the town, they established their line within revolver shot of our barracks, and in many quarters of the town there was constantly recurring dispute as to which force had the right to occupy certain streets. They took possession of all the blockhouses from Number One to Number Fourteen, held the filtering reservoirs and the pumping station of the water-works, the villages of Santa Ana, Paco and Singalong, our earthworks at Maytubig and all the territory between the Paco road and the street parallel with the Camino Real in Malate and Ermita, including the Observatory and the exhibition buildings, and even pushed forward to the water front at Malate square, cutting through our own area of occupation in such a way that the men relieving guard at the stone fort were obliged to pass two lines of insurgent sentinels. They therefore controlled at will the approach to the cable station, greatly interfering with the business of the office for the reason that after one or two Spaniards had been run off by the natives, including a baker, horse, cart and load of bread, no one who could be recognized as a Spaniard dared venture through the cordon of native guards. The employees of the cable company who lived at the cable station, found no little difficulty in procuring supplies, and those of us who had to make our way there, often in the darkness and rain, were not a little hindered at times by the raw Malays on guard.

One of the first orders issued was against the bearing of arms by the natives within our lines, and this regulation was strictly carried out, every one being obliged to surrender his arms before he could pass our sentries. On one occasion a body of over two hundred insurgents attempted to pass the lines of the Colorado regiment, but Colonel Hale surrounded them with a superior force and, much to their chagrin, took their rifles from them. The insurgent officers were very much irritated by this regulation, and asserted that they had

AN INDIAN RESIDENCE, BOHOL.

quite as much right to carry arms in the town as the Spanish officers had. This complaint was not considered, but it was soon found necessary, all the same, to issue an order forbidding the prisoners of war to carry side arms.

The walled town now had about fifteen thousand added to its normal population, and was pretty well crowded. It was found that during the siege there had been no attempt at removing the garbage, and in most houses large piles of fetid refuse were poisoning the air. Speedy measures were taken to suppress these nuisances, and earnest efforts were made to induce the prisoners to police their quarters properly, and to observe the common decencies of life, but with little effect until rigorous orders were issued to this end. The prisoners, who were provided with an abundance of good food and were well sheltered in the churches and other large buildings, had full liberty to wander pretty much wherever they liked, and were met with all over the town, but never, it was observed, anywhere near the insurgent guards. They congregated all day long on the seashore and along the *Pasco* between the walls of the town and the beach, and were as happy there as so many picnic parties. A painful little incident, illustrative of the bitter feeling between the races occurred on the beach a few days after the surrender. I was riding on the *Pasco* with a friend, when we saw a sudden commotion among the prisoners and heard a stifled yell. One or two of our men who happened to be not far off, pushed into the crowd, and soon came out with one of the Spanish prisoners whom they dragged off into the town. An insurgent officer had ventured to stroll in among the prisoners and had been attacked by them and pounded and kicked to death. A week or two later I happened to think of the incident and went to look up the prisoner. He had not been tried, nor had it been proved that he was the guilty party, although he looked villainous enough to commit any atrocity. He had been literally thrown into one of the mediaeval dungeon pits of the Maestranza or Armory, and there I found him crouching on the three-foot barred entrance to the pit, holding his head with both hands and groaning piteously. A day or two later his miserable plight came to the attention of some one in authority, and he was allowed the freedom of a small area of the courtyard during the day. This was the only instance which came under my observation in which the treatment of any prisoners of war was not characterized by the greatest kindness and consideration. The insurgents, however, continued their starvation methods as I shall presently describe.

Simultaneously with the establishment of strong detachments of his troops in the suburbs of Manila, Aguinaldo began to make extraordinary demands in terms none too polite, basing these claims on the efficiency of his assistance in the capture of the town, and making use of his occupation of the waterworks as an argument why he had equal rights with the American commander-in-chief. In one of these remarkable communications sent to General Merritt three or four days after the surrender, he made the following specific and pretentious claims:

The insurgent forces to continue to hold the waterworks, and to occupy Cavité.

The insurgents, without regard to rank, to be given free access to Manila, and the Spaniards prohibited from leaving the town.

All arms taken from the insurgents to be returned to them.

The river Pasig to be opened to the free use of the insurgent vessels.

A proper division to be made of the Spanish property surrendered to the United States army.

The palace of Malicañang and the archbishop's palaces in Malate to be turned over to him for his own use.

General Merritt of course refused to allow any of these claims, but continued to temporize, acting presumably under orders from Washington which were understood to be al-

ways most explicit on one point, namely: to avoid rupture
with the insurgents at almost any cost. He was therefore
much in the position of his own men, whom he had ordered
on the day of the capture of the town to prevent the insurgents from advancing, but to use no force to stop them.

The question of the water supply was a very important
one, not so much so during the rainy season, when plenty of
fairly pure water could be caught from the corrugated iron
roofs with which the houses of the town are usually covered,
but because the rain would soon cease and there would be a
genuine water famine. Further it was known that before
the establishment of the system of water supply, which, by
the way, was a gift to the municipality by a wealthy and pub-
lic-spirited citizen, the health of the town was constantly
threatened, and cholera, typhoid fever and kindred diseases
flourished to an alarming extent. It was of the first necessity, then, to deal with this matter promptly, and consequently, on Tuesday the 16th, a detachment of two companies of the Colorado regiment was ordered to proceed to the
pumping station, which is situated about six miles out of
town on the San Mateo river, a large branch of the Pasig.
Delay in the arrival of supplies for the men obliged the expedition to be postponed until the following morning, when
it started under command of Major Bement, a well-known
and expert hydraulic engineer. Proceeding without opposition past the settlement of Santa Mesa, and over the San
Juan river, they arrived near the filtering reservoirs on San
Juan hill, when their passage along the road was disputed by
a force of insurgents, who refused to let them pass without
written authority from Aguinaldo. In this quandary none
of the officers knew quite what was to be done, for it was
understood that they must not have an open rupture with the
natives, and yet they were ordered to take possession of the
pumping station. While they were discussing the situation,

an aid galloped up with an order from headquarters for the expedition to return to town.

Exaggerated reports of this incident spread rapidly through the insurgent camps, and crystallized the impression, which had been diligently and ingeniously cultivated by the circulation of ridiculous stories, that the American troops were cowards, and were more afraid of the natives than the Spaniards were. Negotiations between General Merritt and Aguinaldo were continued in spite of this incident, and finally, on the 23d, ten days after the surrender, the water began to run. It is quite possible that the wily leader of the insurgents found it quite to his own advantage to make this concession, because thousands of his men were quartered within the town limits. The pumps were run at the expense of the United States authorities, who appointed Captain Connor of the Engineers to take charge of the system.

Perhaps the next question of vital importance was the telegraphic communication with Washington, and this could only be accomplished by repairing the cut cable and having the seals removed which had been put on the Hong-Kong end by the Spanish consul there. To do this it was necessary to secure the authorization of the Spanish officials in Manila, and, through the intercession of M. André, the Belgian consul, these high personages at last consented to write an order in compliance with a general desire, not only of the military authorities, but of the leading business men, and, after the usual period of procrastination, the order was signed late on Friday afternoon. In anticipation of this authorization, the steamer *China*, the fastest of the fleet of transports, was ordered to be in readiness to sail at a moment's notice. At the same time it was important to splice the cable as soon as possible so no time should be lost.

Water transportation was very scarce at that period, and I turned the *Albany* over to Major Thompson of the Signal Corps, who with his famous expert operator Kelly, and two or three of the employees of the telegraph company, was to go out and repair the break. I stipulated only that I should be taken to the *China* on the way, so I could arrange for the delivery of a large package of letters and despatches at Hong Kong. Running alongside the *China* we learned that the sailing orders had been countermanded, and that the mails had been transferred to the *Oxus,* a much smaller and slower boat. Thither we steamed and I deposited my precious bundle of news and, as it was then too late to be set on shore, was obliged to take part in the expedition myself. I may remark, in passing, that this particular mail somehow got transferred into a gun smuggling vessel, and disappeared entirely, and the *China* did, after all, sail for Hong-Kong that same evening. Thus in spite of every precaution communication with the outside world seemed to be the football of fate.

Having secured from the admiral an order to use the side-wheeler *Kwonghoi* to grapple for the cable, we were out in the channel off Cavité before sunset, cruising about to find the buoys which marked the cable ends. We picked up one without much difficulty, as the captain of the *Kwonghoi* had the ranges, but the other had disappeared, having been, as we afterwards found out by the cut rope, stolen by the natives. Leaving the *Albany* moored at the buoy as a marker in the dark, we began the slow process of dragging a grappling hook backwards and forwards for an hour or more, without success. Finally the line became rigid, and on hauling it up, we found a steel rope about an inch in diameter, joining the ends of the cable which were separated two or three hundred yards. There were no proper appliances on board for under-running this rope, so it had to be hauled in with great labor by the use of a watch-tackle, the tail of which was refastened every few feet by natives in a small boat, who worked with admirable courage and skill in the heavy sea which was breaking against the steamer's counter. This toilsome and monotonous operation continued an hour or more, and at last the end of a great, slimy green rope almost as large as a claret bottle, came on board and was promptly made fast. On scraping away the mud and sea growth, five copper cores were disclosed, one of which was selected for splicing, and its insulating envelope removed. The copper, carefully fixed in a special vice, was filed to an accurate wedge point. An insulated copper wire of the same dimensions was treated in a similar manner and the two bevelled and brightly polished surfaces were skilfully soldered together, and a free wire fastened so as to make a connection beyond the splice. The whole was then covered with melted gutta percha, and carefully smoothed and caressed with warm irons until the joint was scarcely distinguishable. The small insulated wire was then lashed to the steel rope, which we began to overhaul in the same toilsome way, and after much tossing and hard work hauled inboard the shore end of the break. After tests of this part as well as six hundred mile length to Hong-Kong, which, however, had no result which I could observe, a similar splice was made and the cable dropped overboard again. By the dim light of a flickering lantern, in a tumbling and angry sea, and with only the rudest appliances, the delicate operation of splicing and insulating had been done with perfect success. The seals at Hong-Kong were removed on the 21st, the insulation of the cable was perfect, and for the first time in sixteen weeks Manila was in direct communication with the rest of the world.

Our task was not finished until long after midnight, and when Major Thompson and I wearily strolled back to the Ayuntamiento about three o'clock in the morning and remembered that, although we had taken nothing but a cup of coffee at daybreak, we had nothing to expect from the bare cupboards of the stately building, we were almost ready to envy the prisoners sleeping peacefully after a good supper, just inside the broad portals of the great cathedral.

By the end of the first week of the occupation, everybody

began to feel more or less at home in the town, and the officers began to look about for permanent quarters, and the pleasant villas in Malate and Ermita found tenants as soon as they were offered for lease. General Greene took possession of the late official residence of Admiral Montojo in San Miguel, on the Pasig, a short distance below the palace of Malicañang; General MacArthur established his headquarters at Malate, and General Anderson returned to his original quarters at Cavité. After a week of ultra-bohemian existence in the Ayuntamiento, I was only too glad to accept an oft-repeated invitation to join my shipmates from the *Newport* at the palace of Malicañang, and accordingly moved my scanty impedimenta up there and occupied the spacious and airy billiard room with Major Wadsworth. The billiard table was useless for the purpose for which it was constructed, for there were no balls to play with, but it made an excellent broad shelf to hold our spare clothing, and we used the few cues which remained unbroken to support the mosquito nets over our make-shift beds.

The palace is a wonderfully ugly structure of two stories, and is said to have been erected in the last part of the seventeenth century. It is built of a variety of materials, around two tiny court-yards, each scarcely larger than an ordinary box stall. It is too confused in plan to be easily described, and is arranged with an irritating disregard of the first principles of comfort and convenience. The ground floor is given up to kitchen and larders, to cellars and storerooms and to unwholesome and uninhabitable offices, and the salons, the reception rooms, the dining rooms and the sleeping apartments are all on the upper floor. A large veranda projects over the river and, under the platform of this, is moored the official steam launch. Most of the rooms have the usual open corridor or long balcony on the outside like the Japanese houses and these are fitted with shutters or sliding frames glazed with small squares of translucent *concha* shells which keep out the heat and the rain and admit a tempered, mellow light to the interior. A broad wooden staircase leads straight from the front door into a large reception room to the right of the landing opposite the billiard room, with columns and many empty pedestals, a multitude of silent French clocks and furniture of the most uncomfortable and formal character. This room is, fortunately, not brilliantly illuminated except at night for the decorations are crude to a tormenting degree and the portraits of former governors-general are constant reproaches to the skill of the artists who executed them. Beyond this is a large and well proportioned salon or state audience room with a full length portrait of the late King Alfonso XII. at one end and of Queen Maria Cristina and the prince at the other. The decoration of this room is, like the others, in the worst possible taste, although an attempt has been made by the free use of gold leaf and by florid hand painted ornament to give to the interior an appearance of sumptuous luxury and splendor. The glare of day and even the blaze of the electric light which has been installed with lavish freedom all over the palace inside and out, reveals this to be as artificial as stage scenery and as crude as property room articles. The floors are the only parts of the interior which deserve commendation and these are laid with enormous and highly polished planks of the beautifully rich and fine-grained *narra* wood *(Pterocarpus Santalinus)*, closely resembling the best quality of mahogany. The surrounding grounds which are enclosed by a stone parapet surmounted by a lofty iron fence contain, perhaps, twenty acres and were originally laid out with some care and taste. Near the palace there are traces of conventionally arranged flower beds with winding paths and a shabby fountain bearing marks of long neglect and disuse. At the main entrance are guardhouses and the halberdiers' quarters, near by the stables and coach houses and on the river below the palace the residence and offices of the secre-

WOMEN OF A CASCO WASHING CLOTHES IN THE BAY

tary with a separate garden and an entrance on the street. Various other buildings of more or less importance are scattered around the grounds, all more or less in a ruinous condition.

From the veranda, or loggia, there is a pleasant view embracing the river for a long distance and extending beyond the low elevation of Santa Mesa to the hill of San Juan, across the broad marshes on the south side of the Pasig where the tower of Santa Ana church rises above the trees and Blockhouse Ten makes a prominent landmark against the dark foliage beyond, and away to the south and west towards Paco and Ermita until it is interrupted by the ugly outlines of the brewery and ice-factory with its tall chimney. In the far distance, high volcanic peaks rising near the southern shores of the Laguna de Bay form a skyline of great beauty. The proximity of the brewery to the palace is often annoying because clouds of black smoke are blown by the prevaïling wind directly across the building and render the loggia, which opens out of the dining room, quite untenable at the very hour of the day it is most agreeable to sit there. It was some time before we solved the mystery why this nuisance should have been permitted to exist, but the secret was out when it was discovered that the parties who ran the brewery had special concessions for the free importation of material, a certain immunity from taxation and were guaranteed against competition. The inference was clear that some past governor-general or perhaps all the recent governors-general received a "consolation squeeze" out of the large profits of the establishment.

In the rainy season, the current of the Pasig, which stream is about as wide as the Harlem river at High Bridge, is very strong and rapid and the surface is always covered with a water plant somewhat resembling a tiny cabbage, called the *quiapo*, which floats down from the Laguna and out into the harbor often covering that broad expanse of water with scattered masses of bright green extending in every direction as far as the eye can reach. This plant grows with extraordinary rapidity in all pools and along the shores of the lake and, detached by the wind or waves, is set adrift and after being wafted about for a time, is caught by the prevailing current and carried by the stream into the bay where it disappears after a few days. Early in the morning and after the heat of the day is passed, the river is busy with dugouts and *cascos,* and there is a constant and lively traffic to and from the market. The chief articles brought down the river are firewood, building stone, cocoa-nut oil in jars, forage, crasse, unglazed pottery, fruit and vegetables and cocoanuts, the latter piled high on bamboo rafts. Native passenger boats do a good business, up and down river, and it is a common spectacle to see a large dugout with a low awning shading a dozen or more natives, poled and paddled up against the current with extraordinary speed. Everywhere along the river on the banks and on all the native craft the men and women are always bathing and washing their clothes. The bath is usually taken in the Malay fashion by pouring water from a cup or dipper over the head and body, and it is no uncommon sight to see a laborer deliberately walk into the water, take off his garments one by one, wash them, put them on and walk away, a perambulating clothes-drier. The women, dressed in the thinnest cotton jacket and *sarong,* wade into the water up to their waists and beat the soiled garment with stones and clubs much the same as the peasants of European countries do.

Neither of the so-called palaces of the officials is larger or more pretentious than many a suburban residence in the small towns of the United States and not half as comfortable withal. The dwellings of the religious dignitaries in the walled town, the archbishop's palace and many others, are stately and well appointed and far more luxurious than those of the military and civil officials, probably because the occupants have much longer terms of position, for it has always been the practice of the governors-general and the other high officials appointed by the Spanish government to manage a recall as soon as they had got all they could hope to make out of the colony. In all these palaces and in the public buildings generally there are great numbers of modern works of art and many pretentious efforts of the young Spanish painters who have exhibited in the Paris Salon of recent years have found a refuge in this far-off capital.

CHAPTER XIV

Manila, according to the census of February, 1898, has a population of 400,238 of whom 41,998 are Chinese. It is generally called a city of suburbs because the name Manila is locally applied to that part of the town alone which is enclosed by the walls and moat. This elaborate and well preserved fortification of the Vauban type constructed early last century, is not only most interesting as one of the most perfect examples of this famous system of defence which now exists, but is valuable as affording a safe and necessary protection for the most important offices of the government and for the security of public funds and military stores. In a country like the Philippines where the conquest has been incomplete and always so oppressive that racial antagonisms have never been greatly modified by civilization, a strong citadel like the walled town has not only been of the utmost importance as a stronghold but its traditional impregnability has served as a powerful deterrent to the natives in plotting the destruction of the town. Its usefulness is by no means over, for the moral effect of this monument to the supremacy of the dominant power of the European is now and will continue to be for a long time very powerful and salutary on the native mind. The broad moat around the wall need not, if properly flushed as it was planned to be, become a menace to the health of the town and, although from the first moment of the surrender there has been talk of razing the walls and filling up the ditch, it is to be hoped that such an expensive and unnecessary change will not be undertaken without proper deliberation and after ripe experience with the unusual conditions prevailing in this mixed colony. The moat, which is over two miles in extent, is crossed by six bridges, and an equal number of gates give entrance to the city, each of them approached through covered ways and strongly protected by characteristically ingenious defences on all sides. The gates are monumental in style and bear the Spanish coats-of-arms and other symbols in stone carved above the portal. Besides massive doors of mediaeval aspect each gate has a drawbridge still in use. The general shape of the walled town is that of a semi-circle or half an irregular polygon with the diameter parallel to the shore of the bay from which the moat is separated by a broad and pleasant driveway called the Paseo de Maria Cristina, extending from the river southward to the Luneta. The walls are faced with cut stone, probably obtained at the great quarries on the Pasig and, though weathered and moss-covered in places, are in excellent repair. The part overlooking the river at the north end of the town is the oldest construction and, although it has been several times altered and improved, much of the masonry built by Perez Gomez at the end of the sixteenth century is still intact. In the enormous thickness of the walls at this point are many underground passages and dungeons and pits suggestive of mediaeval methods of disposing of offenders. The dungeons are on the primitive and simple plan of an underground room about twenty feet square and fifteen high without any opening except at the top where there is a trap door at the end of a ladder or a tiny barred door approached from below by a narrow stone stairway or a slippery incline. The entrance admits all the light and air which find their way into the gloomy and damp interior and this opening is generally only just large enough to admit a man's body. It was in one of these dungeon pits that seventy-five or a hundred revolting Filipinos were confined two years ago. As it was a very rainy night the sentinel thoughtfully shut the trap door to keep the prisoners from getting wet.

He saved them from a drenching but a good many died from suffocation.

In this part of the fortification is the Maestranza, or Armory which is a very extensive establishment, containing, besides the enormous storehouses and shops, many pleasant quarters for the officers. All along the ramparts, particularly near the bay and the river, are quantities of bronze cannon and mortars of antiquated pattern, among them many interesting specimens of elaborate workmanship worthy of a place in a museum. The only open space of notable dimensions within the walls besides the enclosure of the arsenal grounds is the Plaza de Palacio about one hundred yards square on the eastern side of which stands the Ayuntamiento. The huge cathedral with its spacious platform occupies the southern side and is an edifice more remarkable for dimensions than for beauty. It was begun in 1578 and, having been several times partly destroyed by earthquakes, has been rebuilt over and over again until little of the original structure is visible. After the great shock of 1880 the tower had to be pulled down, an operation which was necessary for safety but which ruined the aspect of the building as an imposing mass. There are only twenty-one streets in the town exclusive of those which run along under the walls, and they cross each other at right angles dividing the area into blocks of various sizes but generally about three by five hundred feet. The buildings which are of the Spanish type with balconies, barred windows and pleasant courtyards, are usually two stories in height and have glass windows in place of the concha shell in common use elsewhere. The streets have very little variety of aspect and are quite as monotonous in their way as the brown-stone side streets of New York city. A large third of the area enclosed by the walls is occupied by religious institutions and perhaps a quarter of the remainder is devoted to the purposes of the civil and the military governments.

The Jesuit fathers conduct a large university called the Real y Pontificia Universidad de Santo Tomás, founded in 1616, with a branch at the observatory, which useful institution is entirely under their charge and is one of the best in the world. The students of the university are mostly natives or *mestizos,* and the training they receive compares well with that of any European educational institution. The natives have a particular fondness for the study of law and many of them practise this profession with great success.

The Jesuit church near the water front in the walled town is a modern edifice simple to a fault on the exterior but with most elaborately craved *narra* wood ceilings and wainscoting and pulpit all of native workmanship and of remarkable perfection of execution. There are no hotels inside the walls, a few restaurants and only a small proportion of shops, printing offices and manufactories. The walled town has therefore the air of a quiet, dignified official and residential district, entirely different from any other quarter and, indeed, resembling in no way any other city in the East.

South of the citadel extends for nearly two miles along the shore the narrow suburbs of Ermita and Malate, a district of pleasant villas and gardens which has the advantage of the cool breezes from the bay.

The territory north of the Pasig, which river is crossed by three bridges, is cut up into numerous small islands by winding and muddy estuaries and, although the different areas are laid out in blocks as far as practicable, the irregular shape of the islands and the multitude of bridges make this portion of the town seem confused in plan and casual in arrangement. From west to east the quarters of Binondo, Santa Cruz, Quiapo and San Miguel follow the river bank and back of these in the same order are the districts of Tondo, Trozo, Dulumbayan, San Sebastian, Tanduay and Sampaloe. Of these different quarters or wards, Binondo is the largest, and is the active centre of the business interests, with the custom house, the harbormaster's office, several of the consulates, the internal revenue office, the banks, the leading commercial houses, the best shops and the hotels and restaurants. The vessels all discharge their cargoes on the water front of this district and there are several streets—the Escolta, the Rosario, the Anloague and others which are lined with shops and offices and are as busy, particularly the first two named, as similar thoroughfares in any small European capital.

Binondo is connected with the walled town by a ferry of native boats and by a wide and solidly constructed bridge called the Puente de España, which at all times is alive with passers and crowded with vehicles. San Miguel is the fashionable residential quarter and occupies a narrow strip of land between a sinuous estuary and the river, directly opposite the island of Convalescencia where an iron bridge, or rather two bridges meeting at the lower end of the island, called the Puentes de Ayala cross the stream and make the principal connection between the eastern part of the town north of the Pasig and the villages and suburbs to the south. The island, as its name implies, is devoted to hospital purposes and there are spacious buildings there under the administration of the religious orders.

The business quarters of Binondo, Santa Cruz and Quiapo are very much like those of any Spanish provincial town and, but for traces of native architecture and particularly the concha shell windows, one might well imagine he was in Mexico or in Cuba. In San Miguel the streets are broader, Belgian pavement gives way to macadam and large shade trees line the avenues and fill the pleasant gardens. A great deal of stone is used in the construction, particularly of the lower stories of the houses and the garden walls and stucco is freely employed to give a surface of imitation marble to piers and archways. Green mold of vividly noxious color covers everything in the way of masonry and suggests an unpleasant and unhealthy condition of dampness, the effect of which is, however, in some degree avoided by the habit of living entirely in the upper story of the houses. The character of the architecture is modified somewhat by the attempt to minimize the destructive effects of the frequent earthquakes, but in the commercial districts there are many stone and brick buildings which do not seem to have been restricted in height by anticipations of damage from this cause, and, indeed, it is said that these solidly built houses resist the shocks of earthquakes better than those constructed of wood. One of the ugliest features of the town is the roofs which are commonly made of unpainted corrugated iron.

The system of horsecars consists of four lines: The Intramural, one thousand metres long; the Malate, three kilometres; the Sampaloe, two kilometres, eight hundred metres, and the Tondo, two kilometres, four hundred metres. The routes are divided into sections of one kilometre each and the passenger pays so much per section, the fares being regulated according to the place occupied in the car. Those who stand on the platform pay only half price. The vehicles are of American build, are very light and are drawn by small horses or mules. They are always crowded to overflowing for the natives are averse to walking if they can possibly ride and, moreover, they are of a restless disposition and fond of wandering about. A steam tramway connects Manila with Malabon, the distance of seven kilometres.

Running through the above mentioned districts at some distance back from the river is a line of wide boulevards reaching from the bay to Sampaloe where several streets meet at a concourse or circular plaza called the Rotondo. Along these boulevards are the stations of the Manila-Dagúpan railway, the large central market, several tobacco factories, a theatre, and the great prison called the Carcel de Bilibid. These boulevards are not what the name suggests, attractive promenades, but are arid wastes of ill-kept roadway bordered with houses of every variety, from the hut of the native and the hovel of the Chinaman to the villa of the prosperous European. In some places a central strip of ragged turf with a stone curb occupies the middle of the broad thoroughfare, and here and there a few stunted and miserable trees and an occasional bench give a sad imitation of a continental boulevard. Fringing all the European and the commercial quarters are thousands upon thousands of native huts crowding into every available space, no matter how swampy, and, seen from the height of some tower or tall building, look like masses of brown fungus spreading out from the green paddy fields and the dense thickets which surround the town, creeping up near to the very heart of the busy centre of commercial activity. These native huts are, as I have before described, always built on stilts and in some of the suburbs the ground around them is often flooded during the rainy season for weeks at a time. In certain parts of the outside districts there is nothing else seen but these huts crowded together as closely as they can stick and as populous as so many anthills. When a fire starts in one of these native quarters it rages without opposition, spreading rapidly until it is stopped by some wide street or open space. Thousands of houses are thus burned up in a few hours. There was a fire of this sort on the day the third expedition arrived, the 31st of July, and from the smoke which arose we thought the whole district of Binondo was in flames. The burned territory was half built over again a month later, and there were very few traces of the fire to be seen. For service at all fires and particularly those in the European quarters there is a very efficient volunteer fire brigade under control of the English and Scotch residents, but this is seldom able to cope with a conflagration among the *nipa* huts. The most conspicuous of the native buildings are the cockfighting theatres, which are sometimes of extraordinary dimensions. One of the largest stands near the river bank a short distance

above the palace of Malicañang, and is an ingeniously constructed shelter of bamboo and *nipa* with an enormous roof which is a landmark for miles around.

There are three theatres in Manila, each of them more shabby and uncomfortable than the other, and a goodly number of open air cafés and waterside restaurants. There is a general air of neglect about all these places and not one of them makes a tempting display of comfort or of cleanliness. Compared with any other colonial town in the East, Manila, with the exception of the walled town, is conspicuously uninteresting in aspect and indescribably ill kept and squalid. In Shanghai, Hong Kong, Singapore, Batavia and Rangoon the traveller is surprised at the evidences of luxury and prosperity and solid comfort, while Manila, except in the residences of some of the Englishmen and Scotchmen on the Pasig at San Miguel or Santa Ana, is depressingly neglected and shabby and worn out in appearance. There are signs of projected improvements here and there. Half-finished docks of vast extent behind the breakwater at the mouth of the Pasig show that a scheme for the extension of harbor facilities has been started with more or less energy. On the east side of the Plaza de Palacio opposite the Ayuntamiento there are the foundations of a huge public building completed to the height of a man's head and there are several half-finished little squares and parks which need only a little care to make them very attractive. There are several statues of indifferent merit, one of Anda near the river bank at the end of the Paseo de Maria Cristina, one of Charles IV., in the Plaza de Palacio not half as monumental as a curious old belfry hidden away among the trees in front of the cathedral, a pompous looking effigy of Magellan in a small park under the walls below the Puenta de España, a statue of Isabella II., in front of the Variedades theatre and various others of little artistic merit. Everywhere prevails a discouraging air of neglect testifying to the hopeless decadence of the spirit of enterprise which formerly distinguished the Spaniards in their establishment of this colony and in their construction of the public works which remain sad monuments to former glories.

We made our acquaintance with the town under conditions so peculiar and unusual that we probably gained little idea of the pleasures of life in the capital and of the relations between the different classes of the population. For a day or two very few Spanish residents of the upper class were seen on the street, but when the Chinese coolies had brought back the furniture, which had been removed for fear of a bombardment and the markets opened and the horsecars began running, the ordinary habits of life were taken up again and the usual recreations went on even to the afternoon parade of carriages around the desert of the Luneta. Except for the ubiquitous American soldiers the streets resumed their usual aspect. The Spanish ladies were a little slow in coming out, but they could not long resist the temptation to display their costumes to a largely increased number of spectators and promenaded with an air of conscious superiority of race and with most unbecoming expressions of scorn and discontent.

The stock attractions to the sightseer besides those already described are the tobacco factories, the cemetery and the observatory. The former establishments are scattered everywhere from the middle of the business quarter to the remote suburbs, and number a score or more, large and small, giving employment to over twenty thousand natives, men, women and children. Most of the tobacco used comes by water from the province of Cagayan. In the smaller manufactories everything is done by hand, but the larger ones have all the improved machines for making cigarettes, some of which turn out sixty thousand a day, and for shaping the fillers of cheap cigars. These factories are wonderfully busy hives of labor and the natives who have small, nervous and nimble hands and whose ability to master difficult mechanical processes is very extraordinary, are skilful and reliable work-men. The cheaper grades of cigars are rolled by women and the fine, Havana-shaped ones are intrusted to the hands of men only. A good workman can seldom turn out more than one hundred and fifty of the best quality, while three times that number of the less expensive brands is no unusual day's task.

The Cemeterio General is situated on the Calle de Nozaleda or the Paco road, at the junction of this broad avenue with the Calle del Observatorio and the Calle de San Marcelius, about three quarters of a mile from the walled town. It is a circular enclosure about one hundred and twenty-five yards in diameter, surrounded by two concentric walls or rows of vaults of solid masonry. Each of these vaults is just large enough to hold a coffin which is pushed in lengthwise and the opening sealed with a slab of stone. The plot of ground enclosed by the concentric walls is laid out like a garden with lawns, flowering shrubs and ornamental shade trees and at the end of a broad central path which leads from the imposing gateway in the street there stands a mortuary chapel which contains the tombs of several men prominent in the history of the colony. Behind the chapel, and approached by means of a narrow stairway which leads up to the promenade on the top of the walls, is a deep pit or open cellar which is half full of human bones many of them evidently exposed to the elements but a short time, for long tresses of hair still cling to the skulls and other repulsive indications prove that they have been recently thrown upon the mouldering heap. The system of burial in this cemetery is scarcely in accordance with our ideas of respect for the dead. The vaults are leased on yearly payments and if the survivors of the deceased fail to pay the rent the remains are, after a stipulated number of notices, removed from the vault and thrown into the pit. The grewsome symbols of death which are prominently displayed at the end of beautiful vistas through the overhanging shrubbery are but little less repulsive than the heap of bones and the visitor does not linger long in the enclosure although, apart from its suggestive horrors, it is by far the most finished and well-cared-for public garden in Manila.

The observatory stands on the south side of the street which bears its name, rather more than half way from the cemetery to Ermita and, adjoining it are the grounds and extensive buildings of the Exposition Company. The large structure which contains the libraries, various class rooms, the apartments of the fathers, and the instruments for observing the meteorological conditions of the atmosphere and the terrestrial disturbances, stands back a little from the road and is surrounded by immense shade trees. The telescope house is a little apart and a third building, devoted mainly to the department of magnetic observation, is situated behind the large one in a pleasant flower garden full of rare and beautiful tropical plants.

Father Frederico Faura is the present director of the observatory, Father Miguel Saderra Masó has charge of the department of seismography and Father John Doyle is the head of the department of magnetism. There are a number of native students in the institution pursuing special branches of study. All the elaborate drawing and engraving connected with the publication of the scientific works which are continually issued are done by natives, who show an exceptional aptitude for these operations. The Jesuits all over the archipelago have always been on good terms with the natives, and while the Roman Catholic priests have, by their well known methods, excited the enmity of the Filipinos to such an extent that in many parishes the priests have been brutally murdered since the beginning of the insurrection, the Jesuit fathers have always been treated with great consideration and respect.

I was not surprised, then, to find, on the occasion of my

first visit to the observatory, the courtyard and the passages of the observatory crowded with women and children cooking and eating and carrying on all sorts of domestic operations. Some fifteen hundred refugees sought an asylum there during the siege of the town and were cared for by the fathers as well as their resources would permit. It was not altogether a place of safety because the bullets frequently rattled against the walls and perforated the iron roof and shells sometimes burst in the garden, but the natives did not lose confidence in the ability of the fathers to protect them, and they remained there until all was quiet after the surrender.

Father Faura kindly conducted me all over the institution and patiently explained the mysteries of the intricate and elaborate machines for recording earthquake shocks and the subterranean disturbances. These instruments together with the great pendulum and various other appliances are attached to an immense pier of solid masonry, which extends from a deep foundation to the roof without anywhere coming in contact with the building itself. Around the walls of the room especially devoted to seismography, megaphones, telephones and phonographs are adjusted so as to transmit and record the noises which occur in the bowels of the earth. The large new telescope which, as I understood, had been imported from the United States, was not yet set up for the elaborate joinery of the interior of the building was not finished, the work having been delayed by the siege. The iron dome of the house is as full of bullet holes as a colander.

Father John Doyle was not at home when I first visited the place but I met him on a subsequent occasion and found him to be just what his name suggested, an Irishman. He is enthusiastically devoted to science and is a man of great intelligence, wide experience and remarkable general knowledge. I asked him how long he had been in Ireland. "Only just long enough to be born there!" was his characteristic reply, in a delicious brogue.

The work accomplished by the Jesuit fathers in the observatory is by no means confined to the study of earthquakes and magnetic phenomena, for their most important function is the study of typhoons and the preparation of the weather reports which are of inestimable value to the navigators of the China sea and the adjacent waters. Fourteen substations have been established at different points in the archipelago and from these come daily and sometimes hourly reports by wire describing the meteorological conditions of the different localities. From these reports the approach and probable force and direction of the dreaded typhoons, which have their origin among the islands or near at hand, is immediately anticipated and a warning telegram is sent at once to Hong-Kong and thence transmitted to all important shipping ports in the China and Yellow seas. The danger from these devastating cyclones is thus minimized and there have been of late years very few disasters from them at sea, although great havoc has been wrought in their path across the land. In general terms the average direction of the typhoons is from the island of Luzon towards the coast of China near Hong-Kong, but they often take capricious routes which can be more or less accurately prognosticated by careful study of their behavior at the start.

It was gratifying beyond expression to find these men devoted to their endeavors to save life and property, and absorbed in their scientific pursuits apparently unconscious of the abnormal conditions around them. The awe-inspiring and terrifying phenomena of nature with which their studies and observations have familiarized them made the conflict and bitter strife around them seem insignificant, puny and futile and they talked of the siege and of the recent battle at their very gates with a refreshing calmness and placidity almost suggestive of indifference but really born of the habits of thought which belong to their profession and to their chosen occupation.

In that small room where every tremor of the earth is written down, one feels remote indeed from all the turmoil of the town and the wrangling and struggle of races and parties. The sensitive needle might record the shock of an exploding shell or the jar of a cannon, but it would be only a tiny, almost imperceptible waver on the line that marks the spasmodic throbbing of the earth which is constantly shaken by the restless forces which struggle to escape from the embrace of the solid crust. The thunders of the bombardment were music compared to the ominous and awful rumblings that precede and accompany an earthquake or a volcanic eruption, and the fathers smiled at the suggestion that they had ever been in danger at the hands of man.

CHAPTER XV

TIIE troops were quartered in the town in the barracks vacated by the Spanish soldiers and in various buildings in those districts where it was considered necessary to keep a strong guard. It was evident from the first that garrison duty was not to the taste of the volunteers for they performed the dull routine of the day with an indifferent air and little enthusiasm. Now that the active part of the campaign was over they began to think of home, and soon grew to loathe the life they were leading in Manila. This was perhaps not the universal feeling, but it was noticeably the common one, and was mostly due without doubt to their inexperience in military life. Discipline, as far as outside indications went, became discouragingly slack for a certain period. I accompanied General Greene on a tour of inspection around his lines a day or two after the surrender and nearly every man we saw on duty along the boulevards where the guards were not directly under the eye of an officer was keeping his post in a way which proved that he no longer took an interest in his vocation. One sentinel had deposited his rifle on the grass and was seated with his back against a tree smoking a cigar; another was sprawled out half asleep on a stone bench; others were familiarly hobnobbing with the natives and exhibiting the action of their rifles, and along the whole line there was a lamentable absence of martial spirit and pride. It was not their fault, perhaps, that their uniforms were ragged and dirty but they were careless in their dress even to ostentation. A common sight was a sentinel on guard at a bridge or some other public place dressed in ragged trousers without gaiters, in a blue shirt which had the sleeves cut off high up on the shoulders and a hat full of fantastic holes cut for the fun of the thing.

There is always a reaction after the exciting period and climax of an active campaign and then is the time to keep the men up to the highest standard of appearance and discipline possible and to divert their minds by constant occupation. The crew of an ocean steamer would become demoralized in a single short voyage unless they were always kept busy.

The men were given freedom in place of occupation and the crowds in the streets made it appear that when off guard duty they were free to roam wherever they pleased. I do not remember to have seen any general orders, for the first week or two at least, which touched on the points above mentioned and, besides, it is a well known fact that the regimental commanders often acted independently in their designated areas of occupation. One battalion which on the day of the surrender posted guards in the neighborhood wherever the major thought necessary never received a single order from headquarters for more than a month. It may be imagined that all this indifference to the conventionalities of military duty made a great impression on the Filipinos and excited the ridicule and scorn of the fastidious Spaniards. The native is a keen observer and is very sensitive to impressions and his preoccupation at that time was, for evident reasons, the study of the new type of man who had come to rule the country. He was not slow to make up his mind that the stranger was a good-natured, tender-hearted giant who had neither pluck nor military ardor and would be an easy victim to the superior fighting qualities of the native race.

The fourth expedition under command of General E. S. Otis arrived on the 21st, the day the cable was opened, bringing a notable addition to the forces not only in new organizations but in recruits for those already in the field. Two days later General Merritt, under instructions from Washington, assumed the duties of military governor of the Philippines —a title not quite expressive of the limited scope of the position—and transferred the command of the Eighth Army Corps to General Otis and there was an extensive movement of the pieces on the board with the exception of those officers who filled civil positions in the administration of the government. The office of the military governor was established near the palace of Malicañang, in the house which had been occupied by the Spanish secretary to the governor-general and where Colonel Smith of the California regiment which guarded the palace and the neighborhood now had his headquarters.

Up to this time the Guardia Civil Veterana, an organization largely composed of natives who had served in the Spanish ranks, had continued to perform their duties as guardians of the peace of the town, but they had never been very efficient, and, after the surrender, being no longer responsible to a rigidly autocratic head lost their interest and were rapidly becoming demoralized. The Thirteenth Minnesota regiment was selected to act as police with Colonel Reeve as chief, and four companies were detailed to take the places of the Spanish organization. The Minnesota men turned out in captured white uniforms with straw sombreros and made quite a stir on their first appearance. It is scarcely necessary to add that they performed their duties with intelligence and zeal and that the effect of the change was very gratifying, although it was doubtless somewhat handicapped by the fact that they did not wear the recognized uniform of the United States troops. I quote an order issued a week later because it contains an allusion to certain practices which were becoming notorious and indicated a growing spirit of arrogant independence among the insurgents which had to be met with vigorous measures:

GENERAL MACARTHUR AND GENERAL HALE IN CARRIAGES CONSULTING WITH INSURGENT CHIEFS

INSURGENTS DRAWN UP IN COMPANY FORMATION

"HEADQUARTERS OF THE PROVOST-MARSHAL-GENERAL AND
MILITARY COMMANDANT,

"MANILA, P. I., *September 2, 1898.*

General Order No. 9.

"The Thirteenth Minnesota U. S. Volunteers has been assigned to police duty and ordered to preserve the peace and decorum of the city; and also to afford protection to all well disposed citizens who make application therefor at any of the stations formerly occupied by the Guardia Civil Veterana.

"All disorders and crimes, reported as above, will be promptly investigated, especially attempts to impose taxes in public places, or to make collections for licenses for any purpose whatever, as no one is at present authorized to make such collections.

"The soldiers of this regiment may be known by a distinctive straw hat and a brass insignia, indicating the regiment and state to which they belong, worn upon the left breast.

"By command of Brigadier-General MACARTHUR,
"Provost Marshal-General.

"JOHN S. MALLORY,
"Inspector-General U. S. Vols.,
Adjutant-General.

"Official.
"P. Whiteworth
"2nd Lieut., 18th U. S. Inf.,
"Aid."

Almost immediately after the surrender the insurgent leaders, notably Pio del Pilar, a young man of considerable influence among the natives, an open advocate of the independence of the Filipinos and an avowed enemy of the Americans, began to assert their authority over the inhabitants and their right to govern the country by imposing taxes on all articles brought into the city. Often these taxes were prohibitive, and they were always so high that ordinary farm produce was, if obtainable at all, exceedingly dear. Meat rose to a dollar a pound, and eggs reached the high figure of seven dollars a hundred, while milk was ten times its usual price, and fruit and vegetables were at a great premium. Further, there were constant disturbances inside our lines, caused by natives of the insurgent force. Spaniards were often seized and dragged away, only to be released by our guards; houses were looted, highway robberies and many other acts of violence were committed, most of which were traced to Pilar's men, some of whom carried written authority from him to carry arms within our lines. Several men were arrested who had warrants signed by the same officer appointing them as tax collectors and as head men in certain districts inside our area of occupation, and there was constant trouble in the markets on account of the forcible collection of taxes and license fees by the insurgent agents. These latter were the practices which the newly appointed police were especially instructed to suppress, but there was no means of putting an end to the tax collecting at the insurgent lines around the suburbs. Prices gradually came down to the war level as the insurgents found best to deal more or less gently with their own people and let them make all they could out of the Americans.

Our legal minded methods, which had proved so expensive and cumbersome in the camp, were continued in the town, and the results of the system were felt all too soon. The natives held out for the high scale of wages established during the brief campaign, and it was impossible to employ labor for less than three times the ordinary compensation. Strikes on the horse car lines and in the manufactories became very frequent, and these together with the active recruiting which Aguinaldo was carrying on among the laborers and mechanics, seriously affected all branches of industry and disorganized trade just as it was beginning to flourish again. The additional burden of severe manual labor was put on our men, who should have been spared this, not only for reasons of their health, but for the dignity of their calling, for in a country where coolie labor is cheap and efficient, no white man is ever expected to perform the tasks undertaken by this useful class of the population. Clumsy buffalo carts heavily laden with commissary stores were dragged through the blistering heat of midday by fatigue parties of stalwart Westerners, and all sorts of menial tasks were performed with great cheerfulness, to be sure, but with a wasteful expenditure of strength and energy. I overheard one day a conversation between two privates which perfectly illustrated the spirit of the men. One said to the other:

"Hello, Bill! how're you getting on?"

"Bully!" was the reply. "Got a soft detail!"

"Where at?"

"In the Commissary Department!"

"Pushing a buffalo cart, I guess."

"Right you are, the first time!"

The Spanish and the insurgent officers were very careful to protect their men from the sun as well as from the rain by excellent shelters of *nipa* thatch, but it never seemed to occur to our officers that this was necessary, and the guard kept their posts in the blazing sun and in the terrible downpours, apparently unconscious that protection from the elements was as necessary to good health as proper food and pure water. It was marvellous that so few fell ill under this regime, but their vigorous constitutions and temperate habits pulled the men through and the general health continued to be remarkably good considering the life they led. Still, about ten per cent. of the force was on sick report within a month after the surrender.

Most of the members and European employees of the important business houses, chiefly Englishmen and Scotchmen, remained in the town during the siege, but as far as I could learn, only one American, Mr. W. A. Daland, had undergone the trials of this period of anxiety. All these gentlemen were most hospitable and friendly and, apart from the pleasure of their society, which did much to reconcile us to our casual mode of life, they were of the greatest service to us in our first days of bachelor housekeeping. Several of them had been in the country for many years, and at least one was connected by marriage with a leading Filipino family, and all had an accurate knowledge of the character of the natives which was acquired by long experience and intelligent observation. Two of the leading firms with which we were brought most in contact, Smith, Bell & Company, and Warner, Barnes & Company, were mines of valuable information to those of us who were seeking to learn something about the country and the people, because through their mills and agencies and other ramifications of their business all over the archipelago, they were in close touch with the natives and from long dealings with them appreciated their virtues and understood their faults.

Never did a military expedition land on a foreign soil less well equipped with useful data about the country they were to occupy, or with such a small proportion of men who were qualified from previous experience or from investigation of the problems of colonization to direct the policy of the proposed administration. We were practically without accurate information on most of the important points which concerned our occupation of the country and our assumption of the functions of government. Even with the sources of information indicated above, there was little effort made to study the intricate questions which multiplied as the work of the different departments of the temporary government began, and it seemed to be, rather, the determination of those in authority to introduce purely American methods, with little regard for the previous conditions or for the existing traditions. It was not to be expected, of course, that this first attempt at conquest and colonization would be more than experimental and tentative, because there were no precedents in the history of the United States to serve as guides of action, and it was all the more important that a hint should be taken from the successful colonizers in the Far East, notably the English in the Malay peninsula and the Dutch in Java, both of which colonies have a native population similar in character to that of the Philippines.

One great lesson taught by these colonies is that the only way to preserve amicable relations with the suspicious and hypersensitive Malay is to interfere as little as possible with the existing institutions of the country, trusting to time and to the gradual development of the influence of civilization to bring about desirable changes, and also to make it definitely understood in the beginning that the authority of the European is absolutely unquestioned and supreme.

Our position at Manila was unusual and peculiar, inasmuch as the *status quo*, the continuance of which was imposed by the terms of the protocol, gave us no authority outside the town and the bay, although we had a military governor of the Philippines at the head of the land forces. Moreover, no one knew whether we were to go or to stay, nor was any one able to prophesy whether our administration of the public affairs of Manila would last long enough for order to be brought out of the confusion which existed in every department. No more disheartening state of things could be imagined, and its moral effect on officers and men was almost as bad as the depression which would have followed a defeat. Further, while President McKinley's instructions to General Merritt as commander of the army of occupation of the Philippines were broad and comprehensive, and based almost entirely on the famous General Order Number 100, they practically gave to the leader of the expedition a free hand to deal' with the situation as he chose. Nevertheless, the frequent explicit orders received from Washington, particularly after the cable was opened, quite nullified this independent authority, and the policy of the governor-general and military governor of the Philippines was dicated from Washington where, naturally enough, the conditions existing in the colony were but vaguely comprehended if not wholly misunderstood. A more uncomfortable situation or one more calculated to bring discredit on our first trial at colonization could not possibly be invented, and the demoralization resulting from it was far reaching and will undoubtedly last for years.

Although the archbishop and other high dignitaries of the church strenuously and categorically denied that those priests who still held the respect and confidence of the natives were influencing them against the Americans, the insurgents made no secret that the priests encouraged their aspirations for complete independence. If their word may be taken on this subject, they were also encouraged to make forcible resistance to American authority. One of the most convincing proofs of the hostile attitude of the priests was a widely circulated tract which was intended to ferment a spirit of antagonism, and I append a translation of this remarkable production, at the end of which was a rude illustration of a Filipino harnessed to a wagon and driven by a Yankee.

"To the Partisans of the Yankees:

"'The best Indian is a dead Indian.'—American proverb.

"Read the extract from an article published in *El Comercio* of May 27, 1898, written by Father Garrand, S. J., and you will see, oh, Filipinos! your future. Do not let yourselves be deceived by promises and appearances.

"Among the works to which the Society of Jesus dedicates its watchful care in the United States of America, is the conversion and civilization of what remains of the Indian tribes in the Rocky Mountains and the foot-hills.

"In the larger part of the territories colonized by the Protestants, especially by the Anglo-Saxons, the system followed with the natives when they refuse to work or to pay taxes, is extermination, pure and simple. They begin this with bullets, with or without declaring war, and continue it with whiskey or other adulterated spirits. This last method, less odious in appearance, has been certainly the most fatal. This is why in Tasmania and Australia scarcely a native remains, and why they are rapidly disappearing in New Zealand. In the United States the flourishing tribes formerly counted millions of people, and to-day only a few hundred thousand remain who still live in peace, confined in semi-sterile regions which the adventurous gold-seekers still continue to invade. To be sure, the government has, at certain times, done much for the Indians, but often the different officials have largely nullified the effect of this, because more than half of the sums destined for the Indians remains in the hands of the agents. Many revolts of the natives are known to be caused by the failure to distribute the rations which are intended to support these miserable beings in the winter season.

"It is commonly asserted in the United States that it is impossible to civilize the Indians, who are lazy, unwilling to do anything, and are evil-minded and destined to disappear. Honorable people, and even certain Roman Catholics are heard repeating the phrase which has now become a proverb: 'The best Indian is the dead Indian,' and we Jesuits of the Rocky Mountains are more tolerated than liked by the Catholic population on the pretext that we do too much for the Indians.

"Our Indians have defects—we are the first to acknowledge it, but it is very often forgotten in these days that the civilization of a people or of a race is not done by steam-power. The first conquest of Paraguay was accomplished only at the end of a quarter of a century of constant toil, and that of a small and rudimentary character. In Europe the Franks of Charlemagne's time 'were by chance entirely civilized and preserved nothing of their primitive barbarism, notwithstanding three centuries had rolled by since the baptism of Clovis.'

"'The Yankees laugh at us,' said the great chief Ignatius to me. 'We cannot pray from our hearts when they are near us!'

"About Christmas, in 1888, the grand council met and decided to build a church in the reservation. The most skilful carpenters took hold of the work, assisted by their fellow tribesmen, and in 1890 the edifice was completed, and it certainly is an elegant structure.

"I have mentioned Ignatius, the great chief of the Yakimas. He is certainly not beautiful to look upon, but he has energy and talent.   He is the last survivor of the three chiefs who made the treaty of peace with the Americans in the war of 1855-56.   Respected by the government and by all the tribe, he is a good Catholic.   His wife Augustina is not inferior in intelligence to most white women, and enjoys an extraordinary influence among the faithful.

"One day one of our fathers asked Ignatius:

" 'When you were a boy, Ignatius, were there many Indians in these mountains?'

" 'Yes, father, and they were happy and were different men.'

" 'What do you mean by that?'

" 'They had food in abundance, deer on the mountains, buffalo on the plains, salmon in the river, wild potatoes in the ground and fruit on the trees.   What a fine life! Always hunting, eating, sleeping, and travelling!'

" 'But now you are owner of a cottage like the Yankees, and you say you are more—'

"Ignatius interrupted, angry and indignant, and eloquently replied: 'The Yankees have done no good to the Indians, quite the contrary.   Without counting the land they have robbed us of, they have decimated our tribes whenever they could and soon they will have exterminated our race.   Before they came we did not know what illness was, and now scrofula and consumption are slowly destroying us.   The Yankee catches us and decapitates us.'

"Please God that these trifling notes which I have just written may attract to the last descendants of those native tribes the sympathy of those persons who are interested in the progress of distant missions.   My last word will be to beg those who read this to pray for those unhappy Indians, and to supplicate the Sacred Heart and the Immaculate Virgin for courage and perseverance of her humble missionaries.

"What do you think of this Filipinos?   Will you still preserve your illusions?

—"Extract from 'The Catholic Missions.'"

"Thus I have to run harnessed to a carriage, I, the Indian of British India, in order to earn my daily bread.   Filipinos, you have to fear this evil for yourselves, because if the American heretics triumph here you with all your brothers will be treated in like manner."

Some of the most prominent of the early indications of the aggressive spirit of the insurgents have already been spoken of, but there were others so openly and so frequently manifested that it was plain to see that a revolt against the authority of the United States might occur at any moment, and on several occasions it was considered necessary to double the guards and to keep the men in quarters. Ten days after the surrender, one of the volunteers was killed and another severely wounded in a street brawl with the armed natives at Cavité. From what was learned at the time, a general attack on the American forces in Manila and Cavité was planned to take place on the first occasion when there would be found a reasonable pretext for it. If the revolt succeeded to any extent it would be a great triumph to the cause of Filipino independence, and if it were a failure, the outbreak could readily be denounced by Aguinaldo as the unauthorized action of one of his leaders, all of whom were supposed to be more or less independent chiefs.

The relations between our troops and the insurgents at Cavité were, perhaps, even more strained than in Manila, because the territory under joint occupation was much smaller, and the two forces were in closer contact. The natives, besides, had a more obnoxious air of proprietorship, which came from long possession of the town and their assumption of superior authority increased the tension more and more as time passed. Many things tended to keep up an active state of irritation, but nothing was more provocative of dislike of the native character or indicated more plainly his cruel disposition and barbaric instincts, than the treatment of the Spanish prisoners who were confined in a military prison hospital a very short distance away from General Anderson's headquarters, and directly opposite our own hospital building. Most of these prisoners were suffering from fevers of one kind or another and all were in a terrible state of emaciation and weakness. The windows of the lower floor were heavily barred, and those prisoners who were able to crawl up to the opening, were piteously begging all day long for food and money. Our men continually crowded around these windows, some from curiosity, but more from a desire to help the wretches and often shared their rations with them, and gave them what money they could spare. Our men had not been paid for two months, else the prisoners would doubtless have fared better in respect of cash contributions. The inmates of this prison died at a frightful rate, and oftener than not corpses would be seen among the living, lying stark for many hours before they were removed and dumped upon the sidewalk outside until they were carried away in a buffalo cart. One of our chaplains who asked for permission to read the service of his church over the dead in one of the rooms, was roughly denied this privilege, and he stood outside and read it through the grated window, to the great satisfaction of the surviving prisoners, and with the sympathetic encouragement of our soldiers.

The insurgents in charge of the prison made little objection to visitors if they were officers or civilians, and I went over the institution several times, once in company with a surgeon who took occasion to examine several of the prisoners, and confirmed the truth of the common report that they were dying for lack of proper nourishment. We had a long conversation in French with three Spanish officers who were shut up in a little room on the second floor. This language was not understood by the insurgent officer who was present, and they spoke freely and in detail of their treatment. No argument was necessary to prove that they were not only suffering from hunger, but also from the lack of medical care, and it was evident that they would not long survive if their condition was not improved. The young insurgent remarked in Spanish, after we had left the room:

"Those fellows have been telling you a pack of lies, I know; they are just as well off as I am. Besides, they deserve to die, for they tried to escape not long ago, and are always bothering me to turn them over to you Americans."

It was incredible that such a state of affairs could exist within our lines, but the previous attempt to assist the Spanish prisoners had resulted disastrously for them and, moreover, it was an unanswerable argument against interference that there were strict orders to avoid rupture with the natives at any cost. This revolting spectacle of starving men was a strange commentary on our humane crusade, all the same.

The insurgent guards were everywhere very vigilant, and at times and in certain places it was impossible to pass their lines without a written authority from Aguinaldo. In the vicinity of the town, circulation in their zone of occupation was not prohibited in the daytime, and their sentinels seldom halted anyone. After dark it was a different story, as I frequently found when I was returning from the cable office to the palace. It was necessary, first, to pass their lines at Malate church, which was never difficult, because our men were constantly going to and from the stone fort. Then after about a mile within our lines I came upon the insurgent guards again in the Observatory road, where they had very strong detachments of men quartered in the exhibition buildings and in the neighboring houses. In the darkness and pouring rain it was never pleasant to hear the rattle of the breech block of a Mauser and a sudden challenge, delivered in an excited tone. Many of the guards were boys of sixteen or seventeen years or perhaps younger, and were quite unaccustomed to handle a rifle. Without any training as soldiers to speak of, they only understood that part of their duties which consisted in halting anyone who approached, and keeping him at a safe distance and well covered with the rifle until an officer was called. Accidents might happen on any of these occasions and, indeed, the report of a rifle was no unusual sound at night, and ceased to excite remark. The half mile of this unlighted road was the part of the journey I never anticipated with pleasure, and always performed with a feeling of intense annoyance and irritation. We were thus, it will be understood, practically besieged by the insurgents, and unable to leave our own lines without acknowledging, tacitly at least, their authority everywhere the revolutionary flag was flying.

The field of this symbol of Filipino independence is a white triangle bearing a representation of the Malay sun and three stars, which occupies the entire width of the staff end of the flag, the rest of it being divided into two stripes, the upper one blue and the lower one red. For nearly a month after the surrender this aggressive emblem was flying on all the Spanish defences in the suburbs except the stone fort, was impudently fluttering within a few yards of our sentinels, even in the heart of the European quarters, and was prominently displayed in Paco, Santa Ana, Caloocan, and other neighboring towns, and even in Cavité. It was recognized as the banner of freedom up the Pasig, all over the Laguna de Bay and in the harbor, where every native boat of any size whatever carried it at the mast-head. The insurgents even planted it on the island of Corregidor, and took formal possession of this commanding position, but Admiral Dewey promptly ordered them off and threatened their fleet with extermination if they trespassed on his preserves.

Many wild reports constantly flew about the town regarding imminent hostilities, but these were usually traced to brief disturbances at the outposts. They had the effect, however, of exciting the suspicion of both parties, and of keeping alive the irritation. A letter from one of the soldiers to General Merritt shows the tenor of the gossip among the men, and has a grain of humor about it which is worthy of the situation. I suppress for obvious reasons the name of the soldier and of his regiment. It read as follows:

EXPEDITION TO THE PHILIPPINES

"MANILA, 22.

"HEADQUARTERS —— —— VOLUNTEERS.

"GENERAL WESLEY MERRITT:

"*My dear gen.:*—A rumer comes to me of a price on the head of insurgent leader, if its true and you want his head I can serve it up in any style.

"Yours respectfully,

"——— ——— ———."

Although the military organization of the insurgents was chaotic, and the leaders of the different forces around the town did not, at first, always acknowledge the authority of Aguinaldo, they all worked very diligently to bring the army up to a reasonable standard of discipline, and to increase the number of men under arms. Within a few days after the surrender, large bodies of recruits could be seen drilling on all sides, imitating the manœuvres of our troops and constantly practising volley firing. It is only just to state that wherever the insurgents went they preserved order among their own people, and that Aguinaldo, in his character of Father of his Country, exercised a paternal care over the morals of the natives which is much to be commended. Among other reforms, he put a stop to cockfighting and gambling, issued a strict order against the carrying of arms by civilians, forbade the exposure of corpses on the street, which was always part of the funeral ceremonies, and punished severely any infraction of these regulations. Only one case illustrating his methods of discipline came under my notice. I was visiting a tobacco factory in the suburbs in company with two or three friends, when there appeared a group of insurgent officers with a man under guard. He was identified by the manager of the factory as an individual who had, on the day of the surrender, invaded the establishment with a following of two or three hundred armed natives and, professing to be an insurgent colonel, had forcibly taken possession of the safe and carried away several hundred dol-

223

lars in cash and the manager's revolver. As soon as the identity of the man was proved beyond dispute, the officers remarked that, inasmuch as he had never been an officer and had committed robbery under arms, they should have him shot at once. By the expression on the victim's face it was apparent that he had no hope of reprieve or escape, and they led him away and promptly shot him without further trial.

From various sources of information we were able to estimate the number of rifles in the hands of the insurgents to be in the neighborhood of thirty-five thousand. They were allowed to take two thousand five hundred from the Cavité arsenal; imported two thousand through Jackson & Evans; received about nine thousand through the revolt of the militia who, after the amnesty, only returned about one quarter of the weapons which the Spanish government provided them with; and, according to the most reliable accounts, were supposed to have about fifteen thousand rifles which had been acquired in previous insurrections. It was impossible, of course, to verify this last estimate. At any rate the number of men in the army which Aguinaldo commanded could not now be far from the above estimated total of rifles, but these troops were by no means all in the vicinity of Manila. Many small expeditions were sent to besiege the Spanish garrisons in the outlying provinces, a large force was prepared for a dash into the island of Panay to occupy Iloilo, and take possession of Cebu and other neighboring islands.

On the 27th of August the news came that Aguinaldo was about to move his headquarters from Bacoor to Malolos, a large town on one of the numerous inlets of the north shore of the bay, thirty-seven kilometres or a little over twenty-three miles from Manila. At the same time it was announced that a call had been issued for delegates chosen by universal suffrage in the different provinces to assemble at Malolos at an early date, there to hold a congress and to establish a revolutionary government in the name of the Filipino Republic. Almost simultaneously with these interesting items of news came a well confirmed report that several thousand rifles and four Maxim guns had been landed at Batangas, the capital of the province of that name in the south of Luzon, whence they could be transported overland to the Laguna de Bay, or in native boats by sea to Malolos, without fear of hinderance.

The change of insurgent headquarters and the proposed establishment of a formal government, as well as the concentration of the bulk of the native troops north of Manila, were plain enough indications that, whatever might be the decision of the Paris Commission, the Filipinos did not propose to submit to any outside authority without a struggle, and were making a large bid for recognition as a nation by the powers interested in the colonization of the East. It also encouraged the suspicion that Aguinaldo would delay his open resistance to American authority only to such a time as he was able to organize his army and prepare it for a campaign. The official organ of the insurgents, the *Independencia,* began publication about this time, and its sentiments were unmistakable, for no attempt was made to conceal the feeling that the Americans were interlopers and that their reign would soon be over. This newspaper was edited by a coterie of young men, among whom Antonio Luna, who afterwards held an important command in the insurgent army, was a prominent figure.

This new move was of considerable strategic importance, and significance, because it involved the possession of the railway line and the advantages of a position controlling a number of rich and flourishing provinces inhabited largely by the Tagalo race, from which districts it was easy to draw large supplies and many recruits. The province of Cavité had been much exhausted by the campaign there, and was, from its position, its shape and its topography, little suited for aggressive or for defensive operations. A similar move had been made during the insurrection, which began just one year before, and with the mountains at their back, the insurgents had successfully resisted the Spaniards and so harassed them that they finally sued for peace, and at Biacnabató an impregnable stronghold in the mountains north of Manila, Aguinaldo had sold out his cause for a certain amount of cash, a notable sum in promises to pay and the assurances of desired reforms.

What might have been the action of General Merritt after this unmistakable declaration of the intentions of the insurgents, it is difficult to say, for he had no opportunity of initiating a new policy nor indeed of continuing his old one, because, on the very day after we learned of the proposed change of Aguinaldo's headquarters, a telegram came from Washington ordering the general to proceed at once to Paris to appear before the commission there. General Greene and General Babcock were ordered home a few hours later, and in two days these three generals embarked for Hong-Kong on the *China* with their aids and a number of other passengers including a native of the name of Agoncillo, who was permitted, at the instance of Aguinaldo, to take passage on his way to Washington as a special envoy to place the claims of the insurgents before the United States government.

With the departure of General Merritt and his party, a fever of unrest possessed nearly all the officers except those who had recently arrived, and who had not suffered from the depressing effects of the anti-climax of the campaign. The wires were kept hot with requests for recall and for leaves of absence, and those who were ordered home were looked upon as specially favored individuals. This feeling among the officers soon spread to the ranks, and gained strength there every day until even those who had been unaffected by the reaction from the excitement of life in the trenches, began to get the contagion of homesickness, together with the impression induced by the departure of the

military governor of the Philippines and two of his most
active and efficient generals, that after all the talk about
trouble with the insurgents the game was finished. The
regimental commanders, finding that their men were in a fair
way to be demoralized by this fever of homesickness, now
encouraged among them all sorts of diversions and recreations compatible with their duties. The base ball was flying
in the streets in the suburbs, and evening concerts and variety performances were given with great success, particularly
by the California Regiment, in the court yard, or *patio,* of a
residence in San Miguel, said to belong to a wealthy Chinaman, which was admirably adapted for such performances.
Nearly every afternoon a full regiment was marched over to
the Campo de Bagumbayan, and went through a dress parade there in the presence of many hundreds of spectators.
Guard mounts were held on the avenues and became more
and more important functions, and the battalion parades at
night always assembled a crowd of natives, who gazed with
wondering eyes on the evolutions of the giant strangers.

General Otis and his personal staff, together with General
Hughes, who assumed the duties of provost-marshal, in
place of General MacArthur, who returned to the command
of his brigade, moved into the palace of Malicañang a day or
two after General Merritt went away, and of the original
mess on the *Newport* there soon remained only Major Simpson, Major Wadsworth and myself, who were courteously
invited to retain our quarters there. The inevitable confusion resulting from the changes in the administration, and
the reassignment of many of the important positions made
the burden thrown upon the shoulders of General Otis no
light one to carry, and, although he had been overwhelmed
with work from the moment he arrived, he assumed the
added responsibilities and undertook his new functions with
wonderful zeal and energy. He did not deceive himself with
any theories about evacuation or the recognition of the Fili-

pino Republic, but preoccupied himself with the serious endeavor to bring order out of almost hopeless confusion, and to provide for every emergency which was suggested by the anomalous conditions of the occupation and the increasing complications of the insurgent question. With an exceptional capacity for work, and an eminent ability to master the details of every operation, he made the result of his labors felt in a very few days. Every possible encouragement was given to the resumption of trade with the other ports of the archipelago; the cable to Iloilo was opened and amicable relations were established with the Spanish military governor there, and the public began to gain confidence in the permanency of the American occupation. Colonel Whittier continued to carry on the affairs of the custom-house with great success, and the total receipts for duties during the first two weeks of his administration were $255,395.55 (Mexican money), of which $81,171.46 was paid in one day.

Possibly encouraged by the license which was permitted the natives in their newspaper the *Independencia,* the Spanish press began to publish articles not only aggressive in tone, but full of inventions, to call them by no stronger term. The editors who published the most flagrant of these screeds were warned by General Hughes that their newspapers would be suppressed unless the attacks on the good faith of the United States government and the honor of its army were discontinued.

Whenever there was an alarm, which was not an infrequent occurrence, the alacrity with which the troops turned out, and the immediate occupation of strategic points by important detachments was a welcome guarantee to the peaceful inhabitants that the order of the town would be preserved, and their lives and property would be adequately protected. The terror of the insurgents, which was an inheritance from the previous outbreak excited by the Catipunan society, as well as from the recent investment of the town, gradually

ELWELL S. OTIS

subsided in presence of the proofs of constant vigilance which were frequently displayed by the action of the troops, and a sense of comparative security was felt in all quarters.

The first step taken by General Otis to show that he proposed to be master of the situation, was the issue of an order to Aguinaldo to evacuate the suburbs of the town. The terms of the ultimatum had the approval of the government at Washington, and it was sent to Malolos on Friday, August 9. It was a carefully worded document, and stated in concise and plain language the reason why the various demands of the insurgents could not be allowed, and why they were ordered to withdraw from the immediate vicinity of the town. I am able to quote from memory with tolerable accuracy the text of the most important paragraph of the ultimatum, which will give a fair idea of its general tenor:

"It only remains for me, therefore, to notify you that my instructions compel me to demand that your armed forces evacuate the entire city of Manila and its suburbs, and that I shall be obliged to take action to that end within a very short time if you refuse to comply with my government's demands, and I hereby serve notice upon you that, unless you remove your troops from the city of Manila and the line of its suburbs before the 15th of September, I shall take forcible action, and my government will hold you responsible for any unfortunate consequences which may ensue."

The ultimatum, as we learned from many sources, was an unpleasant surprise to Aguinaldo and his officers. They had hitherto been undisturbed in their possession of the suburbs and as far as headquarters was concerned their presence had been absolutely ignored from the beginning. Many were in favor of immediate resistance and all were in a state of excitement which did not promise for peace. In this emergency there were brought into the councils at Malolos certain Filipinos of some eminence in the legal profession who argued that General Otis had taken a logical position and that it was best, for the present at least, to submit to the authority of the United States government, particularly because, as was stated in the ultimatum, Admiral Dewey was in accord with the commander-in-chief. Their sober advice prevailed and a delegation was sent to General Otis. They explained in terms which had now become stale from much repetition that Aguinaldo desired above all to be friends with the Americans; that he could not control his men if it became known that he was ordered to evacuate the town by General Otis; that he had all he could do to restrain their belligerent ardor and he was sure they would never submit to his humiliation at the hands of the Americans. Therefore, the delegates asserted that if the terms of the ultimatum were changed so as to suggest the idea of a friendly request instead of a demand, Aguinaldo would willingly order his troops to evacuate the suburbs. The general refused to change the phraseology or to write a new order, and only consented, after much argument, to send a letter to Aguinaldo stating that he had carefully discussed the matter with the delegates and explained to them his views which they thoroughly understood and agreed with. This interview was quite a characteristic exposition of Filipino methods which are quaintly tinged with puerility and are seldom based on a solid foundation of sincerity or truth.

CHAPTER XVI

THE Manila-Dagúpan railway, which was finished a few years ago, was built by English capital, is controlled by an English company and is under the management of Mr. Horace L. Higgins. It connects the bay of Manila with the gulf of Lingayen, passing through the provinces of Manila, Bulacán, Pampanga, Tárlac and Pangasinán and terminating at the town of Dagúpan, the capital of the province of Pangasinán, one hundred and twenty-two miles and a fraction from Manila. It is a single track of three-foot-six gauge and there are twenty-seven stations, all told, including the termini. Until the railway was built all the land traffic of any importance on the island of Luzon was carried on over three great post routes with their secondary branches. The first leads through the provinces now crossed by the railway and then in a northerly direction near the coast through La Union, South Ilocos and to the town of Laoag, the capital of the province of North Ilocos, situated near the mouth of the Rio Grande de Laoag, a short distance south of Cape Bojaedor, the northwesterly point of the island. The second, three hundred and fifty-three miles in length, traverses the provinces of Manila, Bulacán, Pampanga and Neuva Ecija, crosses the south Caraballo range into Neuva Vizcaya and follows the valley of the great Rio Grande de Cagayan through La Isabela and Cagayan to Aparri, a small port on the China sea at the mouth of the river. The third highway, three hundred and four miles in length, takes a general easterly direction through the province of Manila, across Laguna, Batangas, Tayabas, north and south Camarines and Albay to the capital of this province which bears the same name.

There is no richer territory in the tropics than that traversed by these three routes and the most populous and fertile portion of the island is found in the provinces directly to the north of Manila. The railway was projected to connect the centres of population in this region with the capital and to form a trunk line of a system which could be extended as circumstances might dictate. The physical difficulties in the way of construction were not great; there are few long bridges, no tunnels, and only one cutting of any importance. Nevertheless it was no small undertaking, for the climate was exceedingly trying to the Europeans who were not seasoned by long residence and the Spaniards, with their dictatorial and obstructionist methods, handicapped the enterprise with wearisome and annoying delays. It was only finished after a long period of energetic and continuous labor through all of which Mr. Higgins was a most efficient and stimulating chief, untiring in energy, irrepressibly cheerful in disposition, tactful in his dealings with both Spaniards and natives and full of resources in every emergency. There is probably no European on the island who understands better how to harmonize the constantly recurring antagonisms between the races or who more thoroughly understands the nature of the half civilized tribes which occupy this part of the island. Of the numerous dialects spoken in the archipelago at least six are heard along the railway, Tagalo being the first in importance and Ilocan the next.*

---

*In the official guide to the Philippines for 1898, compiled and published by the late secretary to Governor-General Augustin, is found a list of the various dialects and *patois* spoken in the archipelago, which gives an excellent idea of the wonderful variety of races and tribes among the population and of the extent of their isolation which is indicated by this remarkable diversity of speech. The list is, probably, not fully complete, because certain regions of the interior of several islands are yet to be explored. Arranged in alphabetical order the names of these dialects are as follows: Apayao, Agutaino, Atá, Batae, Banao, Bilan, Bilan-sanguil, Buquitnon, Cancanay, Cataoan, Coynoo, Calamiano, Calaganmanobo, Catalangan, Carolano, Dadaya, Dulagan, Engongote, Guinaan, Gaddan, Guianga,

During the siege, Mr. Higgins with his wife and children continued to live at Caloocan in his comfortable villa alongside the railway near the repair shops and storehouses and, although they were compelled by the Spanish bullets which entered the house to seek other quarters on several occasions, they suffered no great material loss. The insurgents cut the line in various places early in May and posted two large smoothbore cannon near Manila, and, as the Spaniards were scattered along the railway in considerable numbers, there were frequent small engagements between Manila and Dagúpan, always with the same result and in a few weeks the insurgents occupied the whole territory. Then, not satisfied with the great amount of money and valuables they had captured in the numerous religious establishments, they began to levy taxes on the inhabitants. In the course of this campaign a number of stations were severely damaged, the contents of some of them completely destroyed or stolen and the terminal at Dagúpan entirely consumed by fire. Two or three station-masters were killed or kidnapped, and the service was disorganized generally. The rolling-stock which was carefully watched by Mr. Higgins and protected to the best of his ability, was not much injured and only a few repairs to the line were needed to put the road in running order after the surrender.

Up to the time Aguinaldo decided to move his headquarters to Malolos he successfully practised the Spanish *mañana* method as regards the operation of the railway until he found it would be to his own interests to make use of this convenient means of communication and then he gave to Mr. Higgins the desired permission to open the line for traffic in

Ilocan, Ibanag, Inabaloy, Ibilao, Itetepan, Itaves, Idayan, Iliano, Iraya, Ifuga, Joloano, Manobo, Mamanua, Mandaya, Malanag, Maguindano, Pampanga, Pangasinan, Samal-laut, Subanao, Samalés, Tiruray, Tagabanua, Tagacaolo, Tagabeli, Tagalo, Tinguian, Tinguian-apayao, Tinguian-cancanay, Tandolano, Tino, Vicol, Visaya, Visaya-boholano, Visaya-panayano, Visaya-cebuano, Visaya-halagueina and halayo, Yacan, Yogat, and Zamboangan Spanish.

a general order "To the military commanders of the Fourth Zone of Manila and the other provinces traversed by the railway," signed by his brother in his capacity of Secretary of War. The order reads, in translation, as follows:

"REVOLUTIONARY GOVERNMENT OF THE PHILIPPINES,
"Military Department.

"SECRETARY OF WAR: At the request of the director of the Manila-Dagúpan Railway Company, he is authorized to continue the line into the station of Manila under the condition that no foreign troops, including the Spanish, shall be conveyed to points in possession of this government and that our forces shall be permitted to hold under guard the station at Caloocan and to inspect the trains there. By virtue of this permission you will give proper orders to the forces under your command that they shall place no impediment in the way of repairing the line and shall abstain, under severe penalties, from interfering with it for any reason except in the case of transportation of foreign troops.
"The Secretary of War,
"BALDORNERO AGUINALDO."
BACOOR, *August* 31, 1898."

There was no mistaking the meaning of the condition imposed on running the trains and Mr. Higgins consulted with General Otis before deciding to open the line. The general, probably having in mind the interests of the commercial houses who had great quantities of rice and other products at their mills along the railway, took no notice of the order except to assure Mr. Higgins that he would be unable to protect the property of the railway company outside the lines occupied by the American troops.

All the repairs were completed on Friday, September 2, and Mr. Higgins invited a few friends to accompany him on the following day on a trip over the entire line. The party consisted of Colonel Whittier, Major Bement, Mr. Robert H. Wood, of the firm of Smith, Bell & Company, Mr. H. W. Price, Mr. Higgins and myself. Although this was the first train out of Manila for nearly three months, the event had not been advertised in any way and, besides the station guard from the Third Artillery, there were no spectators on the platform except a few employees. The train was made up of an engine, a box-car, and Mr. Higgins's private car. The latter is very ingeniously arranged with an observation room at either end and a comfortable dining room in the middle. The kitchen paraphernalia—ice box, petroleum stove and provision safe—is portable and is transferred to the observation room at either end according to the direction in which the train is running. The roof of the car, like all the passenger coaches of the line, is double, with an overhanging dust and rain shield extending the whole length of the eaves, permitting the free circulation of air between the two coverings.

The Manila station, which is rather an imposing structure with a spacious yard and various adjoining buildings, stands on the boulevard not far from the water front and, beyond it to the north, are few or no habitations except scattered native huts and an occasional two-storied house of the usual type with corrugated iron roof and concha-shell windows. About a mile from the station, the line enters a tract of country identically the same in general character as that which was occupied by the opposing forces south of the town, small swamps lying between bamboo thickets and hedges and surrounded by impassable tangles of undergrowth. Here, close alongside the railway stands Blockhouse One, a plank structure of the regular type surrounded by admirably constructed earthworks with traverses and covered ways, and not over two hundred yards away, across an open swamp, the insurgents had a large smooth-bore ship's gun in position on the railway near a native house. They confessed to having fired this piece over two hundred times without once hitting the blockhouse opposite.

At this point their earthworks extend right and left through the bamboo thickets, well masked by the dense vegetation and the positions marked only by the bamboo clumps which have been fairly mown off by Mauser bullets a dozen feet or so above the ground. The white-clad insurgents were out in full force along their old lines and in the Spanish works, swarming in the bushes on every side. On the approach of the train some of the men awkwardly presented arms and here and there a native armed with a Mauser rifle would pop out of the undergrowth near the track, hold his weapon in readiness and stare at us as we passed, with a puzzled look as if uncertain whether to fire or not. On slightly higher ground, a little over three miles from Manila, we came to the station of Caloocan, a busy and prosperous-looking place with large machine shops, great quantities of construction material, and sidings crowded with freight and passenger cars. A strong detachment of native soldiers occupied the station and long files of them could be seen moving away in various directions as if some important manœuvres were in progress. Beyond Caloocan the country opens out into a succession of low uplands followed by a tract covered with immense rice fields broken by innumerable inlets whence the view extends far to the north into a broad valley bounded on the west by the Mariveles or west-coast range which form a jagged barrier not unlike the Dolomites in outline, and on the east by the succession of grand peaks of the Caraballo range, the back-bone of the island. In the early part of the day these summits stood out sharply against a clear sky, but, as the hour of noon approached, small wreaths of vapor began to settle on their flanks and soon great cumulus clouds were formed and hid the highest peaks with dazzling sunlit masses. The day was perfect. A bright sun was shining and the sky was as soft and clear as in June on the Atlantic seaboard. The temperature, moreover, was no more oppressive than on an average July day in New England and a gentle breeze made the air seem vital and refreshingly cool. The landscape of the great valley gave, in the distance at least, little suggestion of the tropics. The immense rice fields with their carpet of bright green paddy shimmered like young wheat in the warm sunlight, and the rounded forms of manga trees, accentuating with their dense, dark foliage the lighter masses of the cultivated ground, gave all the appearance of a pleasant farming country in some fertile region of the temperate zone.

After we passed Malolos, now interesting to us as the chosen seat of the revolutionary government, but scarcely visible from the train except as to its church towers, and as we steamed on past Calampit to San Fernando, a large town in the province of Pampanga at the junction of two important post roads, the horizon to the northeast was broken by a grand and lofty peak of Mount Arayat, which rose out of the plain before us as prominent a landmark as Vesuvius from the bay of Naples and disturbed the impression of a home landscape with its perfect cone. This is one of the many extinct volcanoes which are seen everywhere in the Philippines, but from its isolated position, immense size and symmetrical form is regarded by the inhabitants with especial veneration and many legends are related of its origin and of its former activity. It is wooded to the very crest of its broken crater and all traces of fire have long since disappeared under the cloak of verdure which softens every rugged line of its flanks and conceals all its ancient scars. It was only at a moderate distance in the perspective, of course, that the peculiarities of the tropical vegetation did not strike the eyes. Near at hand, the unfamiliar foliage and the startling dimensions of the leaves, the uncouth shapes and grotesque character of many of the plants and trees, the rank growth of reeds and grass and moss, and, withal, the barbaric huts, the busy natives working in the paddy fields in the scantiest of garbs and the clumsy water buffaloes wallowing in the muddy pools, made a perfect tropical picture. Occasionally we saw in the shadeless open country immense congregations of small huts of the simplest bamboo and *nipa* construction, desolate in spite of their numbers, uninviting and bald. No familiar grove of friendly native trees, no clusters of broad-leaved plantains, no little gardens, gave to these villages the pleasant and hospitable air which distinguishes even the rudest habitation of the home-loving native. These were monuments to Spanish misrule, to the futile endeavor of the dominant race to crush the native's spirit by outraging his traditions, his sentiments and his most intimate desires. The Spanish instituted in this region, as they did in Cuba, a system of reconcentration and obliged the inhabitants to leave their houses, which were everywhere scattered among the trees, and to assemble in villages like the one I have described in the open country, away from the shelter of the trees, where they could be under easy inspection and control. This spectacle gave me a better idea of the extent and kind of Spanish oppression than anything I saw in Manila and left in my mind a feeling of repugnance for the Spanish methods of government which time does not mitigate nor the perspective of long dist nce soften in the least respect.

Broadly speaking, the first third of the railway line runs through a purely rice-producing district, the second third through a sugar-cane country and the last part through a more purely tropical region where cocoanut palms are abundant, coffee is grown and spices and other minor products of the soil are found. For the larger extent of the whole line, water courses are numerous and in one place alone, a short distance north of Tarlac, one of the most flourishing towns through which the railway passes, is there any high ground worthy to be so described. Here there are a few slight gradients and a single fairly deep cutting through a stratum of volcanic stone. Everywhere in the outskirts of the towns, at the rivers and often in the open fields we saw freshly-constructed trenches, apparently in quite recent use and, at nearly every station Spanish prisoners were lounging about apparently quite contented with their lot.

About four o'clock in the afternoon we reached the freight station at Baulista, a little village near the town of Bayambang in the province of Pangasinan. Here is situated one of the large rice mills of Smith, Bell & Company, and, in the house of Mr. Clarke, the manager, we were to pass the night. The huge, corrugated-iron mill with its ugly chimney and clustering go-downs where the paddy is stored, is the principal feature of the landscape and dominates with irritating ugliness the long straggling village of native huts which are huddled together near a rapidly flowing but muddy stream.

We found the residence of our host to be a commodious, newly-built house of the usual type, shell windows and all, standing well back in a large enclosure facing the village street and surrounded on three sides by groves of palm trees. We were soon established in rooms which seemed palatial in their appointments compared with any we had occupied since leaving Honolulu and, after an inspection of the interesting process of hulling and cleaning rice in the mill, we had time to make a tour of the village and to study, all too superficially, the type and the habits of life of the natives in this, the heart of the insurgent country, far away from the turmoil of the capital.

The peasants here bear all the marks of the tiller of the soil. The color of the skin resembles that of the peons of Mexico and the hair is black, coarse and abundant. The type is stronger, a trifle heavier and more brutal than is met with in the neighborhood of Manila, and there is a notable mixture of Chinese blood in many of the families. They are industrious, up to a certain point at least, and are remarkably frugal and temperate. The prominent characteristics of these natives make them excellent and capable workmen. They are quick to learn, are interested in mechanical operations for which they have distinct talents, and have the sensitive and nervous temperament of the pure Malay. In their love for music, their predilection to acquire what is not strictly their own and in their instinct for trading, they are not unlike the gypsies of Europe. The women, at least those of pure stock, are often decidedly comely. They have a wide oval face, rather a flat profile, a well-formed but rather broad nose, a finely-cut mouth with excellent teeth, well-set, dark and expressive eyes, a strong but small chin and a low forehead from which the sleek, black hair is drawn tightly back and twisted into a simple knot. Their dress is quite the same as that of the native women in the vicinity of Manila. On week days and when at work they wear a simple jacket and *sarong,* but on holidays they wear much more civilized attire, a bright-colored petticoat with a narrow *sarong* wrapped about the waist and tucked in as the towel is fastened in a Turkish bath, a white cotton chemise often richly embroidered, and a transparent piña-cloth jacket with broad sleeves and a kerchief of the same material. Very few ornaments are worn by them and we saw no personal decorations in the way of gold and silver except a few rings and simple bracelets. The men dress according to their work and their station, the field hands often wearing all day long in the hot sun nothing more than a breech cloth, and those in the village affecting loose jacket and trousers, always of white cotton. Both men and women habitually go barefooted, but, in wet weather, high wooden clogs, not unlike those in use in Japan, are worn by both sexes. Women are seldom seen with a head-covering of any kind, except, perhaps, a kerchief, but the men, like all half-civilized people, are very fond of European hats, particularly the stiff black ones which they wear with great pride. In the rice fields they often protect their heads with the umbrella-like palm leaf disks such as the Chinese and Japanese coolies wear.

The native house of the common type is built usually with a framework of bamboo poles and covered, both roof and

TYPE OF FILIPINO WOMAN

walls, with leaves of the *nipa* palm ingeniously folded over bits of stick and tied to the battens by rattan. The eaves are very broad and the window openings, which are innocent of glass or of the concha-shell casements in use in the better class of habitations, are provided with thatched shutters, hung at the top, which are propped open in the daytime to admit light and air and are tightly closed at night. There are generally two rooms in the house, and the furniture consists chiefly of sleeping mats, pillows and a few wicker stools. The simplest and most primitive utensils are in use in the kitchen. The stove is a rude earthen sort of brazier, with projecting knuckles to hold the cooking vessel. Frequently this dwelling is extended, according to the taste or the ingenuity of the owner, into quite an elaborate arrangement of shaded platforms, store rooms and shelters. The whole structure is built around tall posts which, as in all the country houses, even the best bungalows, are firmly fixed in the ground and extend to the wall plate. The living and sleeping rooms, as I have mentioned in speaking of the huts near Manila, are raised five or six feet from the ground and the space below is sometimes enclosed by mats but oftener left open and is used as a store-house for the large earthen jars in which rain-water is kept and the great, flat wash tubs hollowed out of large blocks of wood.

One thing always strikes even the casual observer in all sections of the country and in all conditions of life, and that is the cleanliness of the people. They are always bathing and washing and it is the rarest thing to see a native in soiled garments. Even the beggars are comparatively clean. It is in consequence of these commendable habits that so few annoying pests of insect life are met with. During my two months' stay in the country I slept in all sorts of places from the meanest hut to the governor-general's palace and never had my rest disturbed by anything more annoying than mosquitoes which are mild and inoffensive compared with the breed which infests most places in America and many resorts in Europe. The writers on the Philippines have almost unanimously declared that the archipelago is the home of all sorts of insects and reptiles which make life burdensome and I would by no means assert that they do not exist. Still, as far as my limited experience proves, they are at least no more common in this part of the world than elsewhere and are infinitely less to be dreaded than in many parts of Europe. Many of the reptiles and insects which have a most noxious appearance are found on acquaintance to be absolutely harmless. The lizards which abound everywhere, even under the eye of the most careful housekeeper, are destructive only to flies and mosquitoes, the huge beetles are as harmless as grasshoppers and even the repulsive spiders which are almost as large as ordinary crabs may be handled with impunity. The white ant which devours everything is the most annoying pest.

But to return to our excursion. There assembled at dinner that evening not only our party but a number of natives, men and women, residents of the village, whose perfect decorum and charming manners quite captivated us. They all spoke Spanish with ease and fluency and the ladies had all the grace of the Castilians. During the progress of the dinner an orchestra of ten native musicians who were stationed on the broad veranda, played classical music with great skill and taste and with a spirit and dash and an individuality of expression which recalled the performance of the Hungarian gypsy bands. A dance naturally followed, and our friends proved to be as expert and graceful in the waltz and other modern and civilized dances as if they had passed their lives in European society. When at last the lateness of the hour urged the mothers to lead home our fascinating partners, they all strolled away with the musicians across the lawn in the clear, soft, embracing moonlight, singing as they went this patriotic air, known to them as the "Malate Volunteers."

VOLUNTARIOS VIVA ESPAÑA!

HIMNO.

The effect was at the same time highly dramatic and enchanting and we hung over the balustrade and watched the white-robed figures disappear among the palms and listened to the vanishing strains of the song until the melody became so faint in the distance that it was drowned by the chirping of the crickets and the shrill call of the tree-frogs.

The next morning we ran over the remaining twenty-odd miles of the railway to the terminus, Dagúpan, in the gulf of Lingayen, a flourishing little town with the usual important religious institution, many large iron-roofed warehouses and broad streets crowded with Chinese shops. Native huts cluster everywhere in the outskirts of the town and there are not a few comfortable looking dwellings of the better class. The station, riddled by shell and bullets, had been burned and was a total ruin. The insurgents were in large force there and on the platform a detachment of two or three hundred were boarding a special train which was to convey them to Tarlac. We strolled into the town, but were soon stopped by a vigilant officer who politely but firmly refused to let us proceed. Arguments and explanations followed, and at last he was convinced that we meant no harm and we were not troubled again. The insurgents were in a great state of exultation over the news which had just reached them that the Spanish authorities had just evacuated the town of Vigan, an important port in the province of South Ilocos, and had put out to sea in local vessels with eight hundred Spanish soldiers and twelve hundred natives, presumably en route for the province of Cazayan, where they would join the Spanish forces in that province and probably all fall into the hands of the expedition which was preparing to invade that territory. Another cause of elation was the announcement that Aguinaldo's agents had succeeded in making an alliance with the ecclesiastical party in the provinces of Zambales and Pangasinan, popularly known as the Santa Iglesia, a large faction under control of the priests, and said to have an armed force of over five thousand men, which had hitherto remained independent and had refused to acknowledge the authority of the present leader of the insurrectionists.

It so happened that the day we were at Dagúpan, General Macabulos, the popular hero of this part of the island, who controls the provinces of Zambales, Pangasinan, Tarlac and Neuva Ecija, was expected to travel by rail to Tarlac, where he was to hold a conference with the generals commanding the forces near Manila. On our way back we found the stations all dressed out with flags and palm branches to do honor to the general, and at one place a native band was in attendance which, curiously enough, played the Spanish national air as we slowly drew away from the station. Macabulos is a man of about thirty years of age, and is undoubtedly the most influential officer in the north, where he is always spoken of as the real leader of the insurgents. We were confidently informed many times that no one outside of the provinces of Cavité and Manila had any respect for Aguinaldo, not only on account of his dictatorial attitude, but because he posed as a heaven-born ruler, who was not to be looked upon by common people. Indeed, in our whole excursion we scarcely heard a good word spoken for the young President, who had evidently not recovered from the stigma of the transaction at Biacnabató.

A few days after our agreeable and instructive journey into the interior, we secured a pass from Aguinaldo and, at the invitation of Smith, Bell & Company, took a private steam launch flying the Union Jack for a trip up the Pasig, and around the Laguna de Bay. It was one of those placid, balmy mornings which drive away all thoughts of strife and fill the soul with a sense of peace and the joy of life. As we made our way against the whirling current, there were many shocks to the grateful sense of repose which the calmness of nature induced, for the ugly lines of sandbag breastworks cut the meadows and disfigured the pleasant hillsides of

Santa Mesa, while a Spanish blockhouse near the river bank intruded itself aggressively into the rural landscape, and here and there the buildings bore unsightly scars of the recent siege.

Above the mouth of the San Juan river, near Santa Mesa, the Pasig takes a number of abrupt turns and then passes the village of Santa Ana, with an immense church and a number of fine residences on either bank of the stream. The long, straight reach beyond this village, with its grassy banks and here and there a clump of feathery bamboos, is as pleasant and suggestive of picnics and boating parties as any part of the Thames. The charm of the river is not disturbed but rather increased by the queer little habitations which are half-hidden by the trees and by the happy groups of natives rambling over the meadows and through the small jungles. At intervals there is a populous little hamlet, with thickly clustered huts and a busy landing-place, where friendly people came out to wave greetings to us as we passed, and to exchange shouts with our native skipper. Just above San Pedro de Macati there is a comparatively straight passage through the broad ridge of undulating, low hills which extend from the Caraballo range of mountains in the north through the province of Manila, near the western shore of the lake, and finally dies out into the wide, marshy plain of the province of Cavité. This ridge has every appearance of an ancient stream of lava which flowed from the great volcanic peaks in the north and, as is readily seen from the character of the stone in the quarries in the hillsides along the river, is of pure volcanic composition.

The succession of delightful glades and tiny meadows, of steep hillsides and rocky gorges, and the wonderfully rich vegetation, not too obviously tropical, but luxurious as only such growth can be, gives a rare and peculiar charm to the river at this point. The cool retreats under the shade of the cliffs and the remote little nooks among the rocks and trees, attract the native to build his hut in these secluded and quiet spots, for, even with his love of the company of his kind, he often seems to have almost the instinct of a wild animal for hiding his dwelling away from the sight of a white man.   In this part of the river, too, great potteries with long sheds climbing up the hillside like the buildings of a coal mine, give employment to many people in peace times, and the great quarries are diligently worked to provide building stone for the capital and for exportation. *Cascos* piled high with *nipa* thatch from Malolos, others with cargoes of general merchandise, were sailing and poling up the stream in picturesque rank of fluttering sails and rich colors as we steamed along, and scores of dugouts filled with tidily dressed men and women dodged along the bank to escape our wash, or ferried across the stream from village to village. Occasionally a Chinaman came down to haul his net, ingeniously arranged on a framework of bamboo poles, or a party of natives with guitars and mandolins strolled down into one of the curious little bamboo platforms overhanging the water, there to pass the hours of recreation in the deep shadow of the great manga trees, with the ever changing panorama of river life before them.   It was a rare and grateful picture of peace, prosperity and contentment.

Near the large, rambling village of Pasig, which occupies the western end of a large island, the river San Mateo, from which is drawn the water supply of Manila, flows in from the north, and here also is the junction of the other branches of the Pasig which spread out like a fan and drain the lake through four important outlets.   Beyond the groves which surround this village great open marshes stretch away on either side to the shore of the lake, and the monotonous level line is uninterrupted by any prominent objects, save the great bamboo fish weirs and one or two small, rude wooden light-stations perched high above the water on slender piles.

The lake, which is very irregular in shape, with a shoreline about one hundred and twenty-five miles in length and a diameter at the broadest part of not over twenty-five miles, lies between two great mountain ranges. The jagged spurs of the Caraballos jut out into the lake in two high and rugged promontories, the smallest of which is prolonged by the high and steeply escarped island of Talim, notable for a beautifully rounded peak called by the natives *Susung-Ialaga,* or the maiden's breast. To the south, the great chain of summits, the Sungay-Maquiling range, runs east and west between the Pacific ocean and the China sea. In this great barrier Mount Banajao, which rises over eight thousand feet above sea-level, is the most imposing peak, while the active volcano Taal, in the middle of the lake of the same name, a few miles south of the Laguna de Bay, attracts the eye by its peculiar broken contour, and by the cloud of smoke which constantly pours out of its immense crater. Directly east, beyond the two lofty promontories, the mountain flanks on either side trend away into a moderately elevated neck of land between the lake and the ocean, which, like the ridge near the opposite shore, is evidently an ancient bed of lava, and suggests that the lake was once an open gulf, dividing the present island of Luzon into two parts, and that this connection between the China sea and the Pacific was closed by the eruptions of the great volcanoes of the adjacent mountain ranges, which have been now extinct for ages. With the exception of Taal all the summits visible from the lake are covered with trees and we were told that a river rises in the bottom of the crater of Banajao, which vast and densely wooded chasm is more than three miles in diameter and nearly one thousand feet deep.

The objective point of our excursion was originally the town of Santa Cruz, which is a popular resort on the eastern shore of the lake and within easy reach of the most famous gorge in this part of the island. We started rather late, however, and found it would be impossible to visit Santa Cruz and reach the Pasig again before navigation was effectually stopped by the darkness. We determined, therefore, to visit Los Baños, a small village on the southern shore of the lake, at the foot of Mount Maquiling, where, as the name of the place implies, there are mineral springs. These have been taken possession of by the Spanish government, and a large hydropathic establishment has been erected, which has been in successful operation for several years. Besides its reputation for its waters, the place is known as the shipping point for kaolin, which is found in the vicinity.

The white buildings at the springs are visible for a long distance, contrasting against the deep green of the tree-covered elevations behind. As we steamed to the southward, a beautiful panorama unfolded itself to the east of our route, where tempting expanses of quiet water reflected the mountains, and the gentle slopes were agreeably varied by cultivated land and forest, with here and there a cluster of native huts, with a fringe of bright green plantains about them. The broad, low ridge to the west of the lake, sloping gently off into the plain, showed a rich pattern of different tones of green, where rice and sugar cane plantations extended for miles in either direction, and great churches and convents marked the position of villages in this fertile region. The water of the lake was occasionally almost mustard yellow in color, from the presence of a minute vegetable growth, and everywhere the floating *quiapo* drifted along the surface, the sport of every breeze. Under the west shore a small gray steamer flying the insurgent flag stole along as we crossed the lake, and seemed to be following us with suspicion of our right to travel on these waters, but when our destination became evident, the watchful cruiser stood away for Santa Cruz and left us.

Los Baños does not boast a wharf, nor at present any facilities for the landing of visitors, except a few small outrigger canoes, several of which came out to meet us as we dropped anchor. It was a very hot day, and the village, which is a small collection of huts straggling along dusty, winding pathways, did not look inviting, nor did the clouds of steam which arose from the mouth of a rivulet on the shore just below the great buildings tempt us to test the efficacy of the waters. We landed all the same, and were met on the beach by a group of friendly natives, led by the head-man of the village, who offered us his own services as guide and hospitably gave us the freedom of the place. Our first question was:

"Where is the priest?" thinking he would be our best informant on the attractions of the place.

"The insurgents have taken him away," was the reply.

"What is going to happen to him?"

"Nothing, nothing at all. He is a good man and we all like him, and he is coming back again in a few days."

The people were evidently keeping the Sabbath, for no one was at work, and the village belles were promenading in full dress, followed at respectful distances by timid lovers in immaculate white suits. The rambling, shabby buildings of the hydropathic establishment are quite the same in general plan as similar institutions the world over, and contain, besides a series of small bath rooms, a number of spacious lounging and reading rooms, and special apartments for the officials, all of which must have been quite comfortable and fairly attractive before the insurgents knocked the place about and carried off all the movable furniture. In a prominent position on the main building is an inscription which records that the construction was begun by Moriones in 1879, and finished in 1892 by Gutierrez de la Vega. This moderate-sized establishment must have been a bonanza for the contractors, if this naïve inscription means anything.

The waters of the springs are said to contain a number of carbonates and sulphates, and a considerable proportion of iron. The color of the rocks over which the waste water flows indicates that it is strongly impregnated with the latter element. It is quite clear, and is slightly acid and decidedly astringent to the taste, and its chemical composition as well as its temperature cause it to be much esteemed in the treatment of gout, rheumatism, scrofula and many other diseases. The temperature varies from sixty-eight degrees to one hundred and forty-four degrees Fahrenheit, and the air of the warm rooms in the bath houses is sometimes as high as one hundred and seventeen degrees.

About a mile west of the village a low wooded island rises near the shore. It is regarded by the natives as a half-sacred place, and has neither clearings nor habitations. The name given to it by the Spaniards, Los Caimans (The Alligators), is more prosaic than the native appellation, The Enchanted Isle, and suggests the presence of these reptiles. It is oval in shape, and perhaps three-quarters of a mile wide on its longest diameter. A lake occupies the middle of the island, leaving only a narrow ridge of volcanic rock around its perimeter without any cleft or visible opening in this ring of dense jungle to serve as an outlet for the enclosed waters. In this desolate and lonely pool there are said to be numerous alligators of enormous size and of great ferocity, who retire here from the lake through a subterranean passage. We stole quietly up through the tangled undergrowth, and looked over the crest of the ridge, but could see no signs of life in the water, not even the swirl of fish. The native who guided us had the air of one who was trespassing on forbidden ground, probably assumed to impress us with the terrors of the island, which, whatever may be the traditions attached to its origin or to its present condition, is evidently the crater of an extinct volcano.

The Union Jack, which has long been a familiar object in this neighborhood, probably gave us immunity from the troublesome questions and delays we had anticipated on this trip, and although we passed an insurgent steamer on the way back, and in our delightful run down the stream saw several insurgent outposts, we were not challenged, and we reached the palace just as the beautiful landscape was in the climax of its splendor in the glow of sunset, and when the sound of distant bugles alone broke the peaceful quiet of the evening.

CHAPTER XVII

AFTER the failure of the Filipino delegates to secure from General Otis a modification of the phraseology of the ultimatum, nothing more was heard of the matter except by rumor, which had it that Aguinaldo had been requested to move his men out of the suburbs in order to avoid the constant troubles between the sentinels of the two forces. On Tuesday, September 13, however, a large detachment of the insurgent troops quartered in houses in Tondo, some of them actually within our own lines, was quietly marched away. The following day, which was the limit fixed by the ultimatum, opened with an unusual movement among the natives, both soldiers and civilians, and it was evident that the evacuation was going to take place, as indeed it was expected to do.

In the afternoon I accompanied Captain O'Hara, who was in command of the Third Artillery, which was stationed in Tondo and vicinity, into the insurgent lines just beyond our own sentinels, and we found several hundred men drawn up in line waiting for a band to arrive. Mounted officers in fine new uniforms galloped hither and thither as if they were about to conduct a review. When the band came and the last man was straightened up by the watchful subalterns, the commanding officer, a young man of distinct Mongolian type, politely asked Captain O'Hara if he might march his men around through our lines to another part of the district, where he was to pick up another detachment of his troops. The captain had always been on amicable terms with the natives, and while guarding his line with vigilance and strictness, had succeeded in avoiding any disturbance of the comfortable relations which existed here in a more marked degree than anywhere else in the whole circuit of the town. He therefore did not see why he should not grant the officer this permission, particularly as it seemed to be an unpremeditated evolution. So, with music and flags and in full martial array, they marched around a block past our sentinels, who presented arms, and out into the native quarter in the direction of Caloocan. The march into our lines was not so innocent a performance as it appeared, for similar manœuvres were executed in other districts, always with some satisfactory excuse, and it was undoubtedly a little dramatic celebration of their change of front, intended to prove to the natives that the evacuation was at the will of their leaders, and not at the command of the American general.

Hastening across the town towards the southern suburbs, the strains of military music echoing among the houses, beyond the Campo de Bagumbayan, announced that the movement was in progress in Ermita, and, in a few minutes we saw, to our great surprise, the head of a column of Filipinos emerge from the Camino Real, and wheel into the Calle de San Luis, which leads along the southern border of the great open space into the Paco road. By the time we had reached this street, it was filled with troops, numbering three thousand or more, headed by a gallant display of officers, and with three large and excellent bands playing as vigorously as those on a street parade on Saint Patrick's day. The column halted, officers and aids galloped backward and forward, and consulted and gave orders and were full of business generally. After a delay of ten or fifteen minutes, the order was given to march, and the column moved around through the Paco road, past the barracks of the Sixth Regular Light Artillery, into the Calzada, at the point where they had been forced away on the day of the surrender, and along under the walls of the town, crowded with Spanish prisoners, and to the Luneta. Here they wheeled into the Camino Real and marched down this thoroughfare the whole length of Ermita and Malate, and out into the gathering darkness among the bamboo thickets at Maytubig. They certainly made a brave show, for they were neatly uniformed, had excellent rifles, marched well and looked very soldierly and intelligent. As for the bands, in the words of many an enthusiast among our soldiers, they were "out of sight," and played with great skill and taste. There was no little good feeling shown on both sides during this parade, and cheers and other friendly courtesies were exchanged all along the route, until the column passed the large barracks at Malate, where our men hung over the fences and out of the windows and stood in little knots on the sidewalks and preserved a silence which seemed almost ominous.

No definite limit had been fixed beyond which the insurgents should retire, and some confusion resulted from the omission of this important detail. The first move they made was, in most parts of the line, far beyond the boundaries of the proper suburbs, and then, after a day or two, they pushed forward again until they came in touch with our lines. The town and its immediate vicinity are divided into ten districts, and the final adjustment of the limits of occupation very nearly coincided with those divisions. After the evacuation there was a general feeling of relief among our troops, and all felt that, although the situation remained anomalous, the terms of the protocol had been carried out and there was nothing to do but to patiently await the result of the Paris conference.

The date of the assembly of the much talked of congress, was postponed several times, and was at last definitely fixed for September 15, the day after the event just described. A few days before Aguinaldo had made a triumphant entry into Malolos in a carriage drawn by white horses, and there had been a general celebration of his arrival, with speeches, a gala dinner, open air concerts and a military parade. Mr. Higgins, the manager of the railway, kindly, offered to take me up to Malolos to witness the ceremony of the inauguration of the new government, and I was to board his special train at the station in Manila at seven o'clock in the morning, and meet him at Caloocan. The only other passenger was to be Aguinaldo's secretary, and as it is a well known fault of the natives to be indifferent about keeping appointments, I was asked not to hold the train a moment longer than I thought best. Five, ten, fifteen minutes passed and then, just as I was giving the order to start, the secretary, a small, boyish-looking young man, came hurrying across the platform and into the car, apologizing volubly for his tardiness.

We had scarcely run out of sight of Caloocan and its swarms of insurgents, before Mr. Higgins calmly remarked to the secretary that, in his opinion, if the affairs of the Filipino government were managed in the future as they were at present, the proposed republic would be nothing but a cheap farce. The secretary timidly asked what there was to complain about.

"You see for yourself," was the reply. "Your irresponsible people have wantonly destroyed my stations and brutally murdered my employees, and have vented personal spite and taken revenge for real or fancied wrongs all on the plea of making war against the enemies of the Filipino race. You have freely used this railway, contributing nothing to its expenses except promises to pay which I know to be useless, and now, when my organization is hampered by strikes, you encourage your so-called soldiers to take the part of the strikers and to keep my new hands from their work at the point of the bayonet. I am going to lay this fact before Aguinaldo to-day, and shall expect you to arrange an interview for my friend and myself."

"It does these chaps good to be talked to straight from the shoulder," he said to me in English. "Since they came to Malolos the earth isn't big enough to hold them."

We reached the station in about an hour and a half, and the

secretary, who had recovered his spirits by that time with a change of conversation, bustled about to get us a *carromato,* climbed into another himself, and we dashed away with reckless speed, jolting over the rough highway with discomfort and no little danger. Even the secretary could not control his own driver, who was intoxicated like all the natives we saw around the station, by the excitement at the prospect of the great event soon to take place in the quiet little town, and we could see him arguing and gesticulating earnestly. His protests were unheeded, however, until the wheels made a tremendous jump, threw the officer against the framework of the cover, smashed his hat, damaged one eye, and generally disarranged his careful toilette. After that we went along at an unofficial pace, and could see something of the new capital as we entered it.

The town, which is chiefly noted for its large convent and churches, and also as the centre of the manufacture of *nipa* thatch, which is sent from this place by water all over the island, is a long straggling assemblage of huts and houses a mile or so from the railway, and, together with the adjoining large village of Barasoain, numbers perhaps thirty or forty thousand people. The long narrow road was very gay with natives, as we drove along with a score of other *carromatos,* almost as heavily loaded down with human freight as the *carricoli* in Naples. From the first humble *nipa* hut to the great square where the convent stands, thousands of insurgent flags fluttered from every window and every post. Many of them were of home manufacture, with printed blue and red calico stripes; many of them were lacking the Malay sun and the three stars in the white triangle, but the general symbol of red, white, and blue, was there all the same, and the proud occupants of the lowliest huts did their best with palm leaves and flowers to give a support of festive appearance to their cherished banner. On either side of the road, in true Filipino taste, was a line of bamboo posts with fringes whit-

17   257

tled out at each joint, with swags of bamboo and rattan connecting the uprights so as to form a continuous border of rude but effective decoration. In front of these bamboo structures, which gave room for people to pass between them and the wattled fences, was a line of infantrymen, all armed and well dressed, mostly in captured Spanish uniforms. Every man had an insurgent tricolor cockade on his Spanish hat, and all but a very few of them were barefooted. The bridge over the river between Barasoain and Malolos was packed with people, and the hundreds of *barcas* laden with *nipa* thatch, which completely hid the water of the small stream, were swarming with white-clad natives, all eagerly watching the road. We passed on rapidly between the lines of soldiers and under a great bamboo triumphal arch into the convent yard, where a fine military band was playing under the shade of immense manga-trees. Just as we were alighting there appeared a party of twenty or more Spanish priests under a strong guard of insurgents, who paraded them off in triumph through the crowd. The priests were all dressed in black and carried black umbrellas, with which some of them managed to conceal their faces, for they apparently did not relish the performance. Those we could see were unshaven and unkempt, and not very charitable-looking individuals, but they were all fat and well fed enough, and gave the lie to the report that the insurgents are maltreating the Spanish priests they have captured. One of the officers at Malolos told me there were sixty priests at work on the roads not far away, but they were just as well off as any other prisoners.

We were soon informed that Aguinaldo would receive us, so we followed the secretary up the broad stairs of the convent, through a long, wide corridor, always between lines of infantrymen, meeting on our way a score of generals and high officials, some of them in *khaki* uniforms, some of them in Spanish blue linen, and certain dignitaries in full evening dress. Ushered into a large salon, hideous with the usual Hispano-Filipino painted decoration and glittering with mirrors, we were offered chairs, of which there was a large choice, from elaborately carved and gilded hideosities to the simple Viennese bent-wood, cane bottomed variety, and we sat for some time, while there was a continual coming and going, with great formality, through a door on the right. Our turn arriving, we were ushered into a small square ante-chamber, where three bent-wood chairs were arranged in a formal row in front of two others. We were asked to make ourselves comfortable in the three chairs. A box of fresh Manila cigars of large size, ostentatiously wrapped in tin-foil, and with a specially large and highly ornamental band, was handed us to select from, and while we were lighting up, a small individual, in full evening black suit and flowing black tie, presented himself before us. Never having seen the gentleman before in civilian's dress, I did not for a moment recognize him, but was struck at once by the Chinese cast of his head and features. An instant later I saw, of course, it was Aguinaldo, and we all three sat down, after a handshake, and began our chat.

My companion did not delay to make his complaint and expressed his opinion quite as forcibly as when he was talking with the secretary. Aguinaldo listened attentively, but no trace of emotion disturbed the weary calm of his expression. At last he said, in scarcely audible tones:

"I will attend to this matter of the strikers!" and abruptly changed the topic by asking us if we did not wish to attend the opening of the Congress. Of course we were only too glad to be present under the auspices of the President himself, and the secretary was summoned and instructed to see that we were well placed in the assembly. In the course of the desultory conversation which followed, we tried hard to draw from him some kind of an opinion on subjects of public interest, but to every leading question he invariably replied:

"My people will decide," or, "I shall be obliged to refer this to my people in whose hands I am."

Therefore there was nothing said worthy of record.

He is not a very good Spanish scholar, and does not express himself in very fluent Castilian, even when he wishes to talk, and on this occasion he had evidently made up his mind to avoid committing himself to any statement which might be quoted later. Perhaps he had read an interview which appeared in a Hong-Kong paper, which described him as absolutely ignorant, not only of the geography of the East, but of the prominent political facts which every schoolboy is more or less familiar with. During the interview his manner was quite irreproachable, but he spoke in such a low tone and so indistinctly that we had considerable difficulty in understanding him. His personality on that occasion was decidedly unimpressive, and as far as I could judge, his mental characteristics are in no degree unusual. He undoubtedly has the acute cunning of the half-bred native, much of the astuteness of the Chinaman, with the extraordinary personal vanity and the light mental calibre of the Filipino. The interview took place, to be sure, under exceptional circumstances, and he may not, in his preoccupation, have done himself justice, but I never met him when he impressed me as anything more than a figurehead in the hands of active and more or less reliable advisers.

Many of those about him that day had evidently more mental capacity, were certainly better educated than he is, and easily his superior in the external qualities, at least, which distinguish leaders among men. Nothing that he did on the occasion of the opening of the congress, and nothing he has since done, has caused me to modify this opinion; but it has rather become more firmly fixed, and the impression has become, indeed, more convincing.

Up to the time of the definite organization of the revolutionary government, which did a great work in harmonizing many diverse and conflicting interests, and brought into line many obstreperous leaders, Aguinaldo's powers were mostly dominant over the lower class of the people of his own tribe the Tagalos. They had a superstitious veneration for him, which is not unusual in the Philippines whenever a man among the people comes to the front, for his eminence is generally atributed to superhuman powers, and he is supposed to possess a particularly effective *ang ting ang ting* or charm which protects him from harm and gives him a rank above his fellows.

Charms and amulets are commonly worn by the people. They sometimes consist of a piece of calico shaped like a chest protector on which are rudely drawn in ink crude representations of religious symbols, sometimes of a bit of paper with mystic words in magic circles, and oftener of a small object which is popularly believed to be a charm like the rabbit's foot among our southern negroes. Aguinaldo's followers frequently carry in their mouths, during a fight, a slip of parchment on which the leader's name is written and this fetich is supposed to turn aside the enemy's bullets. There are many stories told of his superhuman powers and of his absolute immunity from bodily injury at the hands of his antagonists.

After a half-hour's talk which the President did not seem anxious to have ended, we took our leave with almost as much ceremony as if we were retiring from the presence of royalty. This we did because we saw others go through a still more formal withdrawal and we were anxious to avoid wounding the susceptibilities of the natives.

At the large basilica of Barasoain we found a large number of the delegates already assembled, and the guards drawn up to receive the expected cortège of the President and his suite. The bald interior of the church was sparsely relieved by crossed palm-leaves and wreaths fastened to the columns which divide the nave from the aisles, and on the great bare spaces between the windows. In the middle of the nave were two bent-wood chairs; on either side and behind these, in the aisles, were seats and benches for spectators. To the left of the chancel a long table, draped with blue and red, was arranged for the secretaries, and opposite it were special seats for invited guests, and in the front one next to the chancel rail we were assigned our places. The chancel was hung with a great white drapery, rudely painted to represent ermine, and a broad border of red cloth with palm leaves and wreaths framed in this curtain. Crossed insurgent flags ornamented the pilasters on each side, and in the middle of the chancel, under the imitation ermine, was a long table draped with light blue and crimson, and behind this three large carved chairs. While we were waiting for the functionaries to arrive, we had an excellent opportunity of studying those who had come from all over the island to assist in the foundation of a republic—for this was their professed purpose. Every man was dressed in full black costume of more or less fashionable cut, according to his means or his tastes. Many of them wore full evening dress, some of them had silk hats of quaint shape and well-worn nap, others bowlers of the season of 1890, but all, to a man, were in black. It was a sweltering hot day, too, and they suffered for their adherence to the etiquette of the new Filipino government. But statesmen all do have to suffer in hot weather, if one may take as true the definition of the difference between a statesman and a politician which is that a statesman always wears a buttoned-up black frock-coat, and a politician a sack-coat or a cut-away, or any coat he likes. That difference came to my mind at once when I saw these statesmen fanning themselves vigorously with their hats, and just behind them the natives, politicians all of them, in cool, almost diaphanous, garments, with their shirts worn as the Russians and Chinese wear theirs. Such types as there were among these statesmen! Such queer-shaped heads, such a mixture of distinct racial characteristics in the features of many, such unmistakable lines of pure Indian breed in the profiles of others! All were dark skinned, had strong-growing black hair and sparse mustaches or beards. Scarcely a sign of the frost of age showed on the head of any delegate. Few among them would have escaped notice in a crowd, for they were exceptionally alert, keen, and intelligent in appearance, and, as a mass, much superior to the native as one sees him in ordinary life. I will not be sure, however, that the dress was not a little responsible for the impression they made on me. Possibly they would not have looked so distinguished if they had worn their shirts *à la Russe*.

At last, to the sound of the national march, the delegates moved in a body to the door and then back again, divided, and then Aguinaldo, looking very undersized and very insignificant, came marching down, bearing an ivory stick with gold head and gold cord and tassels. A group of tall, fine-looking generals and one or two dignitaries in black accompanied him, and half surrounded him as they walked along. Mounting the chancel steps, Aguinaldo took the middle seat behind the table, the Acting Secretary of the Interior took the place on his right, and a general occupied the carved chair on his left. Without any formal calling to order, the secretary rose and read the list of delegates, and sat down again. Then Aguinaldo stood up, and after the feeble *vivas* had ceased, took a paper from his pocket, and in a low voice, without gestures and without emphasis, and in the hesitating manner of a schoolboy, read his message in the Tagalo language. Only once was he interrupted by *vivas*, and that was when he alluded to the three great free nations—England, France and America—as worthy models for imitation. He next read a purported translation in Spanish with even more difficulty, and when he had finished there was quite a round of cheers, proposed and led by the veteran general Buencamino, for the President, the republic, the victorious army, and for the town of Malolos. Then Aguinaldo arose and declared the meeting adjourned until it should reassemble prepared to elect officers and to organize in the regular manner. The long-talked-of and ever-memorable function was over.

Aguinaldo's message has never to my knowledge, been printed in Tagalo, but any one slightly familiar with that language could readily understand that his sentiments were more fully declared than those which were handed us as his message printed in the Spanish language, or at least were differently expressed. General Merritt issued his proclamation in three languages. Many of the delegates at the congress were only moderately familiar with Spanish, and it is a common thing for the Filipino newspapers to print in both Tagalo and Spanish, but their reports of the congress contained the Spanish version only. I supposed at the time that I was the only foreign correspondent present, but later I discovered another, whose type did not readily mark him as a foreigner. He was the correspondent of the Japanese papers, the *Chingaishógioshimpó,* the *Jijishimpó,* and the *Taiwannichinichishinbun.*

The Spanish version of the massage reads in translation as follows:

"REPRESENTATIVES:—The work of the revolution being happily terminated and the conquest of our territory completed, the moment has arrived to declare that the mission of arms has been brilliantly accomplished by our heroic army and now a truce is declared in order to give place to councils which the country offers to the service of the government in order to assist in the unfolding of its programme of liberty and justice, the divine message written on the standards of the revolutionary party.

"A great and glorious task, an undertaking within the capacity of every class of patriots, is it for undisciplined troops to fight and to break lances in opposition to the injustice done to those whom they defend and protect. But this is not all.

"It remains for us, further, to solve the grave and supereminent problems of peace for those for whom our fatherland demanded from us the sacrifice of our blood and of our fortunes and now at the present time calls for a solemn document, expressive of the high aspirations of the country, accompanied by all the prestige and all the grandeur of the Filipino race, in order to salute with this the majesty of those nations which are united in accomplishing the high results of civilization and progress.

"To these great friendly nations, whose glorious liberty is sung by the muse of History was addressed the sacred invocation which accompanied our undertaking in its incredible acts of valor, to these nations the Filipino people now sends its cordial salutations of lasting alliance.

"At this opening of the temple of the laws, I know how the Filipino people, a people endowed with remarkable good sense, will assemble. Purged of its old faults, forgetting three centuries of oppression, it will open its heart to the noblest aspirations and its soul to the joys of freedom; proud of its own virtues without pity for its own weaknesses, here in the church of Barasoain, once the sanctuary of mystic rites, now the august and stately temple of the dogmas of our independence, here it is assembled in the name of peace, perhaps close at hand, to unite the suffrages of our thinkers and of our politicians, of our warlike defenders of our native soil and of our learned Tagalo psychologists, of our inspired artists and of the eminent personages of the bench, to write with their votes the immortal book of the Filipino constitution as the supreme expression of the national will.

"Illustrious spirits of Rizal, of López Jaena, of Hilario del Pilar! August shades of Burgos, Pelaez and Panganiban! Warlike geniuses of Aguinaldo and Tirona, of Natividad and Evangelista! Arise a moment from your unknown graves! See how history has passed by right of heredity from your hands to ours, see how it has been multiplied and increased to an immense size to infinity by the gigantic strength of our arms, and more than by arms, by the eternal, divine suggestion of liberty which burns like a holy flame in the Filipino soul. Neither God nor the fatherland grants us a triumph except on the condition that we share with you the laurels of our hazardous struggle.

"And you, representatives of popular sovereignty, turn your eyes to the lofty example of these illustrious patriots!

"Let this example and their revered memory, as well as the generous blood spilled on the battlefields, be a potent incentive to arouse in you a noble spirit of emulation to dictate with the great wisdom your high mandate demands, the laws which in this fortunate era of peace are destined to govern the political destinies of our country."

Besides inducing comparative harmony between the leaders of the insurgents, the formal establishment of a revolutionary government had the effect of gaining the support of many of the educated natives who had hitherto refrained from taking an active part in the movement and had neither contributed money nor had openly encouraged the insurrection. In the organization of the congress, Pedro A. Paterno was chosen president of the assembly, Benito Legarda, vice-president and Gregorio Araneta and Pablo Ocampo first and second secretaries. These names were the best guarantee that the newly established government was representative of the people of cultivation and education and wealth as well as of the lower classes who had initiated and carried on the revolt against the Spaniards. The President and Vice-President were influential and wealthy citizens of Manila and the latter had made a tour of the world with his whole family and had visited the United States during the period of the Chicago exposition. The secretaries were both well known members of the legal profession and by their influence was brought into the councils the most eminent man of the Tagalo race Cayetano Arellano whose conversion to the cause of the insurrection, though tardy, was of great moment. Arellano is a man universally esteemed for his uprightness of character and his sound judgment as well as for his culture and education and has been for years a professor of jurisprudence in the university of Santo Tomás and the attorney of the municipal government of Manila. In the early days of the trouble he retired to a secluded country house near the shore of the Laguna de Bay and, until the present, had steadily refused to countenance the insurrection in any way. It was therefore considered a triumph for the new government to secure the co-operation of this eminent citizen and he was chosen Minister of Foreign Affairs. I do not know whether he ever performed the functions of the office, if indeed there were any to perform. It never came in my way to meet this gentleman and, indeed, he was only seen once in Manila during my stay there, but I visited many of the leading Filipino residents of the town in their own houses and always found them very agreeable and well informed gentlemen. Not a single one of them professed to be in favor of Filipino independence, asserting that it would be absolutely impossible for any one tribe, however, powerful, to dominate with permanent authority a population composed of such a mixture of races, every one of which was jealous of the others. When men of superior mental calibre and high standing in the community like those of whom I speak came into the controlling body of the newly established government, holding these opinions, it promised well for the policy to be developed at Malolos and there was a hopeful prospect that the hysterical ambitions of misguided people might be controlled and brought within reasonable bounds by the sober advice and the calm judgment of the most eminent men of the Tagalo race. Subsequent events have proved that their influence was without permanent results.

When I left Manila on September 22, the congress was busy drawing up laws and preparing a scheme for the government of the country, and it was so fully preoccupied with this work that it might almost have been believed to be sincere in the desire for the state of peace which had been the text of the President's message. News of continued activity of the insurgent forces all over the island of Luzon and of extensive preparations for a campaign against the Spaniards in Panay and other adjacent islands proved, however, that the professed aspirations for the resumption of the arts of peace were only empty phrases and that it was a case of the lion and the lamb lying down together in contentment after the lamb was safe inside the lion.

It may possibly be understood from this detailed narrative of the incidents of the capture and the occupation of Manila and of the complicated and unpleasant relations which arose between our troops and the insurgents that the natives are what the French would call *difficile* and I must therefore explain that I have only given one side of the picture. Most of our men had never any dealings with semi-barbaric people and they were absolutely unable to comprehend their nature or to appreciate the motives of the Filipinos who were, from the American point of view, almost as far removed from the condition of civilized man as are the anthropoid apes. Personally, I never had any difficulties with the natives except those which naturally resulted from the state of tension which existed. The officers and the soldiers with whom I came in contact under ordinary circumstances were always courteous and friendly and the natives not bearing arms were as gentle and mild mannered as any other people of Malay stock. They have many and grave faults, but they have remarkable virtues as well. Since their faults are different from those to which we are accustomed they take a more prominent place in our estimation of their character and the temperament of this interesting race. They are said to be irregular in their habits of work and are shiftless and improvident. That is, of course, partly the result of climate and of long oppression, but it is really temperamental at the bottom. They are also commended for loyalty to those for whom they conceive an affection, for remarkable domestic virtues and for generous instincts of hospitality. They are extremely sensitive and nervous and have a strong sense of justice which, if once outraged breeds in their minds a spirit of vindictivness which almost amounts to a madness.

Although they manufacture and sell a crude and strong kind of spirits they are habitually temperate. It happened to me on one or two occasions, especially in the middle of September when our men had been paid off and there was no little drunkenness among them, to find among the natives a surprising ignorance of the effects of alcohol which, if I had not observed myself, I should certainly be loath to believe possible.

A curious incident occurred one afternoon when the men were spending their money freely, having exchanged their pay at the proportion of two to one for Mexican coin and the town was alive with Chinamen carrying sandal wood chests which were greatly esteemed by the soldiers. I was crossing Malate square on my way to the cable office, when a native came up and asked me to go to the assistance of one of our men who was suffering from sunstroke. I hurried off with him to an enclosure in front of a house on the street and, looking through the iron railings, saw a volunteer on top of a boundary wall between two gardens, swaying to and fro and evidently incapable of even sitting upright. He presently fell over into the garden, quite limp and disjointed, and lay there for a while, then staggered to his feet and reeled into the deserted house. I saw at once, of course, that it was a case of too much drink and explained it to the anxious natives who crowded around. But they would not believe it and insisted that it was the effect of the hot sun. A few minutes later, some soldiers of the man's own regiment came along and attempted to drag their comrade to his quarters. He broke away, rushed into native shops, overturning their store of fruits and smashing things generally like a cowboy on a spree in a Western town. Not once did the natives lose their temper or make a move to use force, but patiently endured the rough usage and tried to quiet the uproarious volunteer and to persuade him to go home. The last I saw of him he was struggling with the guard like a madman and as I went on my way the women were still pointing to their foreheads and saying with an expression of pity:

"Sun too hot, sun too hot!"

The love of music is universal among the natives and they learn to play any instrument with great facility. In some of the ordinary *nipa* huts I saw upright pianos and in nearly every one was hanging a guitar or a similar article of improved construction. Under one of these dwellings, built on the low ground near the palace, a native workman was always busy making excellent and highly finished mandolins, and after dark the sound of human voices accompanied by the tinkle of strings was heard on every side. Native melodies are rarely sung in the neighborhood of Manila, and the music is all distinctly Spanish in character or was, at least, until it was corrupted by the stale refrains of the once popular music-hall songs, "After the Ball Is Over" and "Ta-ra-ra Boom de Ay," which were speedily in great vogue everywhere.

We had little opportunity of studying the indigenous art of the Philippines, but the native, as might be expected from his temperament, has a natural inclination in the direction of art and many students of the Manila School of Fine Arts show a considerable degree of talent, particularly of an imitative order. A few small articles of native wood carving which are barbaric in design but precise and highly finished in execution are the only specimens of the unadulterated art of the country which I managed to find and those were sold me by a native in the insurgent trenches. There is less to be seen in the way of distinctive and characteristic manufactures in Manila than in any other colonial town in the East and the Chinese seem to be the only artisans who produce anything which is not imitated from Spanish or, at least, from European models.

CHAPTER XVIII

By the courtesy of Colonel Pope, the chief quartermaster, I was permitted to take passage on the transport *City of Rio de Janeiro* which was to sail on September 22. Depressing indeed was the contrast between the passengers who came aboard in the harbor and those who had landed at Cavité only a few weeks before in the full prime of health and exuberant spirits. The vessel had been selected as a temporary hospital ship, on account of her cleanliness and her spacious accommodations, to transport to San Francisco all the convalescent sick and wounded whom it was thought advisable to send home. Although there were only one hundred and forty-eight assigned to the ship, the embarkation went on for nearly two days. Slowly and painfully the hollow-eyed, emaciated and haggard soldiers crawled up the steep companion ladder and, once on the clean and shady deck, they took a long breath of the refreshing sea air and thanked God they were out of Manila. Limp and helpless men, ghastly spectacles of wretchedness and misery, were carried aboard on stretchers and carefully placed in bunks in the hospital prepared on the main deck amid-ship. Those who could get about were given berths in the cabin staterooms which were numerous enough to accommodate everybody. Almost every organization in the army of occupation was represented on the steamer and the list included eight commissioned officers.

The order for the immediate departure of the steamer had been issued on the 10th, but there had been many delays incident to the preparation for the voyage and much time was lost on account of the inexperience of the company commanders in making out the papers for their men according to the dictates of the Army Regulations. Dr. G. W. Daywalt of San Francisco, who was one of the party on the *Newport,* was chosen for his well-proved capabilities to have charge of the floating hospital and an efficient corps of assistants and nurses was detailed for the trip.

When the plan of sending home the convalescents had been first considered it was proposed to furnish them with the regular army ration. This would have been fatal to a large proportion of the sick, nearly half of whom were recovering from typhoid fever or from dysentery and more humane councils prevailed and, since it was discovered by some student of the Army Regulations that the rations for men in hospital could be commuted at sixty cents per diem, a contract was made with Captain Ward of the *City of Rio de Janeiro* to feed the patients for that sum. Remembering the experience of the invalided soldiers sent home from Cuba it is most satisfactory to be able to record the fact that this contract was carried out with liberality and that the convalescents had the very best diet and attention. They had their meals comfortably in the saloon and the officers of the ship did everything in their power to make the men contented and happy. Those who are accustomed to sea travel will appreciate what this means.

I copy a bill of fare of a day chosen at random to show what was provided:

Breakfast—Cornmeal mush, beefsteak, dry hash, hot rolls, boiled potatoes, bread and butter, coffee.

Dinner—Vegetable soup, roast beef and mashed potatoes, apricot and peach pies, bread and butter, tea, pickles, etc.

Supper—Irish stew, dry hash, baked potatoes, stewed prunes, bread and butter, tea, etc.

This part was satisfactory enough, but, on the other hand, the ship was sent away without a penny of money in the hands of the surgeon-in-charge to pay for anything at Hong-Kong or any other port, or for any incidental expenses on board ship or at landing. Anticipating the probable need of coffins, application was made for a reasonable number of these, but none could be allowed. The surgeon-in-chief in Manila, Dr. Lippincott, paid for certain necessities out of his own pocket and I fancy Dr. Daywalt's connection with the trip was not a profitable one. The Army Regulations and the cut and dried system which was not invented for the conditions prevailing in the Philippines did not recognize the possibility of an emergency and there seemed to be no way of providing for the expenses of burial of those who might die on the way home. At that time the Red Cross Society, which had a large and well provided branch in Manila was scandalously managed and nothing could be had from that source.

We were ready to sail at three o'clock in the afternoon and, just before the order was given to start the windlasses, a weary and haggard old man dressed in a ragged brown uniform toiled up the ladder and, as he stepped on the deck, was asked for his papers. He replied that the hospital steward had told him he would find them on the steamer. Search was made but they were not discovered and, although he was identified by one of the hospital corps as a patient who had received permission to go home, there was nothing to do but to follow the orders and refuse him passage, particularly as he had no authority to draw rations. No one who was present will ever forget the look of horror and distress which came into his lustreless eyes when the captain told him that he must go back, explaining that he was strictly ordered to take no one without his papers. It was the expression of a man who hears his death sentence pronounced and knows that he has been unjustly convicted. There was no resentment in his look, only utter hopelessness, despair and the weariness of long suffering. He leaned a moment against the rail and then, straightening up as well as he could, said in a low piteous tone: "For God's sake, gentlemen, let me go! If I am sent back I shall die. I belong to no regiment, I have no money and I am too ill to work as you see."

"Who are you, then?" demanded the captain with all the sternness he could command.

"I came out as one of the cooks of General ——— and worked hard day and night in the mud camp cutting wood, boiling water, getting meals in the pouring rain and always wet and tired. When we got into Manila the fever came on me and I was sent to the hospital where I have been ever since. You don't know what it is, gentlemen, to be alone as I am, with no officer to look out for me and no comrades. It means misery and it means homesickness! I was in a Massachusetts regiment in the rebellion and when this war broke out the old war fever got me so badly that I had to go. I thought I was as young as anybody else, but they wouldn't take me on account of my age. But I had to go. I could not see the fellows marching away and leaving me and so I finally got a place as a cook.

"But I am too old for the work. I found it out too late. Gentlemen, have pity on me! If you send me ashore you send me to my death! I am worn out. I am too old. I am homesick! I would crawl all the way to San Francisco if I could. I will work for you. I will shovel coal. I will clean the decks. I will wash the dishes. I will do anything if you will let me go. I am homesick! I am homesick! I am homesick!" and he broke down utterly.

The wretchedness of this poor waif on the turbulent sea of humanity was too much for us and we took the captain aside and agreed to be responsible for the man's keep if there was no other reason why he should not stay on board.

"I'll chip in myself, of course," said the captain, "but the officers must be certain of the identity of the fellow, that's all."

Then, turning to the man, he said, with a noticeable quaver in his voice:

"All right, these gentlemen agree to see you through and you may stay aboard," and as he walked quickly away to his chart room we saw him pass the back of his hand under the peak of his cap. The old man staggered below and we did not see him again for days for he stowed himself in some remote corner. Later on the stewards reported that he was better and was always at work cleaning the quarters.

It was a soft, hazy day and the outlines of the mountains were but faintly seen through the quivering air. We ran along the familiar shore, took a last look at the Luneta, the hospitable clubhouse, the stone fort, the white house at May-tubig, the bamboo thickets and the clustering houses at Ca-vité. Then, as we slowly passed the towering island of Corregidor, the domes and lofty buildings of Manila faded away into the vibrating distance, the great expanse of the China sea opened out before us and the western coast of Luzon stretched away in a grand succession of bold headlands until lost in the perspective. Fortunately the sea was quite motionless except for a slight ruffling of the surface caused by the gentlest of breezes. The cool sea air gave great comfort to the invalids who had so long breathed the atmosphere of a hospital ward. Stretched in reclining chairs or on cots the sick and wounded who were able to be on deck welcomed the change of scene, and improved rapidly from the first hour. Sad to say, there were among those in the hospital several whose vitality was so low that the flickering spark of life did not respond to the change of air and fresh comforts and two died before we reached Hong-Kong. A firing party was organized among the wounded men, services were read by one of the officers, and the haunting wail of the too familiar call blown on a captured Spanish bugle echoed over the sea while the steamer drifted slowly away from the little ring of troubled waters which alone broke the glassy surface now glorified by the reflection from the wonderful sunset sky. Thus many a chapter of an active life was ended on that dreary voyage.

THE END